ONCE THEY WERE ☟ W9-COL-456
AND THIEVES. NOW, THEY WERE
MEN AND WOMEN MAKING A STAND—
AT ADOBE WALLS

HANK TYREEN: He'd robbed, scouted, and hunted
buffalo for a living. Now, the man who had once risen to
the rank of major in the Confederate army faced a last
battle, against an overwhelming Indian attack.

BILL HICKOK: In Leavenworth, Kansas, he took on the
Masterson brothers and Hank Tyreen in a shooting
contest. For the next ten years, they would stand shoulder
to shoulder in a land exploding with war.

SILKY SOMMERS: She was the most prized whore on
the rough and tumble Kansas frontier. But she had found
a way out of the life and the promise of a future by a
good man's side—if they can get out of Adobe Walls
alive.

RACHEL STEWART: She came to the frontier as an
innocent, witnessed the horror of an Indian attack, and
survived captivity amongst the Cheyenne. She had
traveled a few thousand miles in a short lifetime, and had
one more journey left to go.

BEN SPICER: The buffalo skinner was a surgeon with a
knife and a warrior with a gun. He knew the country, the
herds, and the hostiles, and he knew the kind of fight that
lay ahead . . .

Adobe Walls

ADOBE WALLS

Robert Vaughan

St. Martin's Paperbacks

ADOBE WALLS

ISBN: 0-312-96737-3

Printed in the United States of America

St. Martin's Paperbacks edition / November 1998

St. Martin's Paperbacks are published by St. Martin's Press, 175 Fifth Avenue, New York, NY 10010.

10 9 8 7 6 5 4 3 2 1

Prologue

The sign that stretched across Belle Meade Street read "Meade, Kansas, Celebrates Our Nation's Independence Day, July 4th, 1904."

Hank Tyreen sat in the Prairie Star Bar, nursing a beer. His table afforded him an excellent view of the depot, and he saw the bunting-bedecked train when it arrived. A delegation of the leading citizens of Meade were at the depot to welcome Governor Willis Joshua Bailey.

Programs had been printed and passed out, advertising the events of the day. It would start off with a few remarks by the mayor, then the Pledge of Allegiance to the flag, as recited by Miss Plummer's third-grade class. That would be followed by a few "Patriotic Numbers," as played by the Meade County Band.

Governor Bailey's speech would be next. Getting Governor Bailey to come to the Fourth of July celebration in a town as small as Meade was quite an accomplishment, and the delegation had been full of self-congratulations when they told Hank of their coup.

The final entry on the program was "Recognition of Distinguished Guest." Hank thought that was a little redundant. If Governor Bailey had already spoken for an hour, where was the need to recognize him?

Hank saw a handsome, well-dressed man coming toward

the saloon. The man smiled, nodded, tipped his hat, or shook hands with nearly everyone he passed. He was Meade's representative in the State House, and being personable was part of his job. Then, he had always been personable, Hank thought. From the time he was old enough to talk, he was a charmer. He was also Hank's son.

Tom Tyreen opened the door and looked inside. When he saw his father he smiled.

"Mom said I'd find you here," he said.

Hank lifted his glass of beer. "Come join me."

Tom shook his head. "Can't," he said. "And you don't have time for another. Come on, Dad, the governor wants to meet you."

"Why does he want to meet me?" Hank asked. He finished his beer, then wiped his mouth with the back of his hand. "I didn't vote for the son of a bitch."

"Why wouldn't he want to meet you?" Tom asked. "After all, you're one of Meade County's leading citizens."

Grumbling his protest, Hank stood up and walked over to take his hat from the peg. As he did so, he saw his reflection in the mirror. His face was narrow and lined, the handlebar mustache he wore was white, as was his hair. He leaned closer to the mirror and studied the image.

"My God," he said under his breath. "I'm old. When did I get old?"

One

Hank Tyreen was tired. It wasn't just the tiredness of the long ride back to Mississippi from Appomattox, it was a bone-deep, butt-tired exhaustion from four years of war. As he rode south on the Natchez Trace, he put a little more weight in the stirrups and switched positions to get some relief from the saddle weariness.

Just ahead he saw a building. It was clear that at one time it had been an inn, but over the years it had been enlarged to accommodate a store, a barbershop, and even a couple of rooms out back for sleeping. A crudely lettered sign nailed to one of the porch supports read "Food, Drink, Goods. Beds ten cents, blankets five cents."

The result of the additions was a rambling, unpainted wooden structure that stretched and leaned and bulged and sagged until it looked as if the slightest puff of wind might blow it down.

Two men in blue uniforms were sitting on a bench out front. One of the men was big, with a bushy red beard. The sergeant's stripes he was wearing were the light blue color of infantry, though his tunic was so dirty that the chevrons barely showed. The other man was beardless and his tunic sleeve was bare, except for the ghost shadow of where stripes had once been. He was rail-thin and hard-looking. The two Union soldiers studied Hank as he dismounted.

What they saw was an average-size man of twenty-five who looked thirty-five. One could almost see in his blue eyes the death and horror he had witnessed over the last four years. The country was no longer at war, but it was obvious that Hank was not yet at peace.

Hank was wearing a gray jacket with a single gold star on his collar, denoting the rank of major in the Confederate Cavalry he had just served. Like hundreds of thousands of other men in gray, he was a forgotten soldier in the defeated army that had served the failed cause of a now defunct nation.

. The big Yankee scratched his beard while the other spat a stream of tobacco juice onto the dirt. Neither man spoke to Hank as he tied off his horse. A nondescript yellow dog was sleeping in the shade of the porch, so secure with his position and the surroundings that he didn't even open his eyes as Hank stepped around him to go inside.

The interior of the inn was a study of shadow and light. Some of the light came through the door, and some came through windows that were nearly opaque with dirt. Most of it, however, was in the form of gleaming dust motes that hung suspended in the still air, illuminated by the bars of sunbeams that stabbed through the cracks between the boards.

Hank heard a scratching noise coming from the back of the room, and when he looked toward the sound he saw a young woman on her hands and knees, using a pail of water and a stiff brush to scrub the floor. She glanced up at Hank and brushed a strand of pale brown hair back from her forehead. Her eyes were gray, and one of them tended to cross. When she smiled, she displayed the gap of a missing tooth.

"Mister, you lookin' for someone to warm your bed?" the woman asked hopefully.

"No, thanks," Hank answered.

Showing her disappointment, the woman went back to her scrubbing. The proprietor came out of one of the back rooms then, wiping his hands on the apron that, at one time, might have been white.

"What can I do you for?"

"Thought maybe I'd get a beer and somethin' to eat," Hank said.

"Got no beer. Got some whiskey, though. Beans, bacon, and biscuit's the only thing we got to eat. But the biscuits is real good. My girl, Mary Lou, made 'em." He nodded toward the woman on her hands and knees.

"It sounds real tasty. That'll do fine," Hank said. He took a table over in the corner of the room.

"Take the man his whiskey, Mary Lou," the proprietor ordered.

Mary Lou got up from the floor and took the glass of whiskey to Hank. She leaned over the table as she set the glass in front of him, affording him an eyeful of her ample breasts. She smiled another silent invitation, and Hank actually felt some sympathy for her. During the war, when any warm female body would be welcome company to a lonely soldier, Mary Lou probably did all right. But the dissipation of her profession, plus the missing tooth and misshapen nose, which Hank suspected were the results of a few violent encounters with drunken soldiers, had given her a face that would be hard-pressed to attract customers during normal times.

Hank smiled back at her but did nothing to encourage any further solicitation.

"Here you go," the proprietor said a few minutes later, putting the food on the table in front of him. "If you don't mind my askin', who was you with?"

"Dumont's Cavalry."

"I got a boy in the Fourth Mississippi Infantry." The proprietor nodded toward Mary Lou, who was once more scrubbing the floor. "He's her brother. We ain't heard nothin' from him for near 'bout six months now. His name is Tanner. Jimmy Tanner. You run across him, by any chance?"

"Sorry, I haven't," Hank replied as he took a spoonful of beans. "But there are hundreds, probably thousands still out on the roads, coming back home. If he was a long way off and afoot, it'll take him a while."

"Yes, sir, that's what we keep a-tellin' ourselves."

"Hey, you, Reb!" a gruff voice called.

Looking up from his meal, Hank saw that the big red-bearded Yankee sergeant and his skinny friend had stepped inside.

"Something I can do for you, friend?"

"I took a look at that horse you was ridin'. It's wearin' a U.S. brand. How'd you come by it?"

"I needed a horse, so I took it."

"Yeah, well, me an' my friend need a horse. Seein' as the one you're ridin' is U.S. government issue, why don't we just take yours? What would you say to that?"

"Go ahead."

The sergeant was puzzled by Hank's answer.

"What?"

"If you think you can take him the same way I took him, go ahead."

"How'd you take him?"

Hank stared coldly at the Yankee sergeant. "I killed the son of a bitch who was riding him."

"What? You mean you admit to stealin' him?"

"I didn't say anything about stealing him. I said I took him. There's a difference. At Saylor Creek I killed a Yankee captain. When the rest of the Yankees skedaddled, all the riderless horses left the field as well. All but this horse. It stayed with the man who had been riding him, and I admired him for that, so I took him as my own."

While he was talking, Hank, his action concealed by the table, had eased his pistol from his holster. Now he brought up his hand and cocked the pistol. It made a deadly-sounding click as the sear engaged the cylinder. "Now, if you fellas think you can take him the same way . . . try."

The bearded sergeant realized he had just been tricked. Hank now had the drop on him.

"No," the Yankee said, holding out his hands as if to

stop Hank. "No, we ain't got in mind nothin' like that. We was just curious, that's all."

"Shuck your pistols, lay 'em on the floor, then go sit at the table over there. Mr. Innkeeper, I want you to give both these boys a whiskey, on me."

"Yes, sir," the innkeeper replied.

Hank watched the Yankees pull their guns out of their holsters and lay them on the floor. He made a motion with his pistol, and they moved over to the table he had pointed out. The innkeeper brought them both a drink.

"The war's over, boys," Hank said. "We can keep on killing each other, or we can start trying to live together. Which will it be?"

"We got nothin' agin you personal, Reb," the sergeant said.

Hank put his pistol on the table in front of him, then lifted his glass toward them. "Then I'd say we've made a good beginning," he said, toasting them.

Home, for Hank Tyreen, was a farm just outside Tunica, Mississippi, a small town on the east bank of the Mississippi River just across from Arkansas. Though much was said about this being a war to protect the right to own slaves, the Tyreens had no slaves. All of the fieldwork had been done by John Tyreen and his two sons, Hank and Beauregard. Hank's mother, Amanda, did for her men by cooking, cleaning, sewing, and doctoring.

Early in the war Hank's younger brother was killed at Shiloh. Bo died in Hank's arms, smiling proudly because, though it had cost him his life, he had been the first to reach the enemy's position. Hank's mother died very soon after that, from "heartbreak," his father's letter had said.

In his letters of late, John Tyreen had told Hank of the crippling taxes that had been leveled against all the landowners. "I haven't been able to get a crop out for the last two years," Hank's father wrote. "And I don't have enough money to pay the taxes. I am the third generation to farm this land. I don't know what I would do if I couldn't pass it on to you."

Hank wanted to write back to his father, to tell him not to worry about it, that together they would work something out. But he didn't write because he knew he would get there before the letter did.

It was nearly dark by the time he turned up the road that led to the old homestead. Even from here he could see that the house needed a coat of paint, but the setting sun made the windows shine gold, and he thought he had never seen anything so beautiful.

Just ahead, to the right, was the small family burial plot. Tyreens had been buried there for one hundred years. His great-grandparents were there, and though they were gone before his time, he knew the story of Rufus and Ellen Tyreen, how they had come here from Virginia to carve a home out of the wilds of Mississippi. His grandparents were there, also. Seth Tyreen, his grandfather, used to take him fishing and claimed to know where every fish was in every pond, stream, and river within a radius of ten miles.

Hank's mother and brother were there, too, so Hank headed in that direction, intending to pay his respects before going on up to the house.

When he reached the little cemetery, he saw a fresh grave alongside those of his mother and brother.

"Pop!" Hank said, dismounting and hurrying through the gate to look down onto the markers. He felt a profound sense of sadness when he saw the name on the headstone.

JOHN WILBUR TYREEN
born
October 3, 1811
died
April 25, 1865

As Hank stood over the graves he realized that his entire family was here. His mother had been an only child, his father's sister had died a spinster and was buried in this same small plot. He had never felt so alone.

Sadly Hank rode to the barn. There was no livestock of any kind that he could see, not even a chicken. But he did manage to find some hay for his horse, and the watering trough was full.

Taking his saddlebags with him, he walked up to the house. Two one-by-eight planks were nailed into the door frame, making an "X" across the front door, effectively barring anyone from getting inside. There was a sign on the door.

KEEP OUT
PROPERTY CONDEMNED FOR
NONPAYMENT OF TAXES AND
SEIZED BY THE U.S. GOVERNMENT

With a shout of anger, Hank kicked at the boards until he broke them, then he pulled them out as the nails creaked in protest.

The house, as Hank knew it would be, was completely empty. The carpets, pictures, and furniture had been taken. Even the chandeliers had been removed. Using the boards and the sign as fuel, Hank started a fire in the living room fireplace, then lay down on the bare floor beside it and went to sleep.

The next morning, as Hank rode into town, smoke and flames climbed into the sky behind him. He had set fire to the house, barn, granary, even the privy. Maybe the government had taken over the farm, but he would be damned if he would let anyone else enjoy the fruit of the labor of four generations of Tyreens.

"Hank, my boy, welcome home," Gilmore Blanton said when Hank stopped off to see the man who had been the family lawyer for as long as he could remember.

"Hello, Mr. Blanton."

"Are you just getting into town? Or have you been out to the place yet?"

"I went out there last night."

Blanton shook his head sadly. "Then no doubt you saw your father's grave. I was hoping I would be able to see you first, to . . . prepare you for what you would find."

"Was Pop in bad health? If so, he never mentioned it in any of the letters he wrote."

"Actually, I thought he was doing very well, considering the fact that he lost both Amanda and Bo early in the war. I know he missed you terribly, but he was also very proud of you, and reported every promotion you got."

"Then if he was getting along so well, how did he die?"

"It happened the same week he was evicted from the farm. It was too much for him, Hank. His heart just gave out."

"You were our lawyer, Mr. Blanton. Was there nothing you could do?"

"I tried to negotiate a settlement, but they wouldn't hear of it. And I tried to secure a loan on the farm, but the taxes were higher than the loan value. In the end, the best I could do was get permission to bury your father in the family plot."

Hank sighed. "Well, I'm thankful for that."

Blanton got up from his desk and walked over to a chest. He opened it and took out a Bible and a paper-wrapped package.

"I was able to save this for you. It's the family Bible. I don't know how religious you are, but it will keep you in touch with who you are. There are entries as far back as the late seventeenth century."

"I thank you for that," Hank said. "That Bible meant a lot to Pop."

"And I got a couple of pairs of pants and a couple of shirts for you. I figured that when you got home, you might want something to wear besides that uniform."

"Yeah, thanks again. I'd just as soon not be wearing this uniform when I go see Lucinda."

Blanton cleared his throat and looked away.

"What is it?" Hank asked. "Has something happened to Lucinda?"

"Not exactly."

"What do you mean by 'not exactly'?"

"Lucinda is married, Hank."

Hank said nothing, but he put his hand in his pocket to feel the pocket watch. Just inside the watch case was a lock of Lucinda's hair. Four years ago, on the night before DuMont's Cavalry left for the war, Colonel DuMont had hosted a gigantic gala in the ballroom of Trailback Plantation. On that night Hank and Lucinda had walked through a garden scented with wisteria, verbena, and sweet shrub and sworn their undying love for each other.

Then, the war had been nothing but an exciting adventure. But Hank's brother was killed at Shiloh, Colonel DuMont was killed at Antietam, and attrition took a very heavy toll on the proud young regiment that had gathered at Trailback on that night.

Hank had been the last commander of the DuMont Cavalry, and at war's end, not one in ten of his men even knew who DuMont was or had ever heard of Trailback. Trailback was no more. The beautiful old house, which had been one of the finest examples of antebellum architecture in the state, was burned to the ground back in 1863, during the march on Vicksburg.

Blanton waited for a response from Hank, and when Hank said nothing, he supplied more information on Lucinda George.

"Lucinda married a man named Gerald Boyer. He came down here from Ohio . . . oh, that was three or four months ago, I reckon. He bought the old Patterson place and fixed the house back up really nice."

"The Pattersons sold their place?"

Blanton cleared his throat again. "Well, no, not exactly. Their place was seized for taxes, same as yours. Boyer bought it at public auction. But you can't really blame him for it, Hank, he didn't have anything to do with assessing the taxes—''

"He just took advantage of the situation," Hank interrupted.

"Yes, well, it's all on the up-and-up. And Boyer actually is a very decent sort of person."

"I met a lot of Yankees. They were all decent people," Hank said. "I probably killed a lot of decent people."

"Listen, Hank, you aren't going to cause any trouble, are you? They seem to be getting along very well. And, Lucinda's pregnant."

"Mr. Blanton, I haven't seen Lucinda in over three years. Whatever words we spoke to each other then are long over with. I wish her the best."

Blanton heaved a sigh of relief. "I'm really glad to hear that. Some of the folks around here were concerned with what you might do when you got back."

"Nobody needs to be worried about anything. I'll be moving on."

"Where will you go?"

Hank pointed in the general direction of the Mississippi River. "Who knows? Somewhere out there," he said.

"How are you fixed for money?"

"I have two dollars."

"Confederate?"

"Yankee."

Blanton pulled out some money. "Here are forty dollars more."

"No thanks," Hank said, waving off the offer. "Since I'm not going to be here, I don't know when I could pay you back."

"You don't have to pay me back. I took a milk cow from your farm before the government moved in to clean it out, so the money is rightfully yours. Unless you'd rather have the cow."

Hank chuckled, as thankful for the light moment as he was for the money.

"Well, if you put it like that, I reckon I will take the money."

Blanton gave Hank the money, then the two men shook hands. Hank took the Bible and his package and left Blanton's office.

As Hank rode down the main street of Tunica, he looked around at the town. It was no longer the town of his youth. There was an empty lot where the courthouse once stood. Dunnigan's General Store was now Bloom's Mercantile. The feed store, apothecary, and hardware store also had new names, names he had never heard before.

The streets were crowded with soldiers in blue uniforms, for Tunica was a debarkation point for Union soldiers taking the riverboats back north. The Yankees crowded the saloons and filled the streets with their loud talk and frequent laughter.

There were also some men in tattered gray, defeat and despair evident in their faces. He recognized a few of them. He saw Billy Wright sitting in the sun, an empty trouser leg where his right limb should have been. Billy and Hank had once been a team, of sorts. Billy was one of the fastest runners in the state. Hank was one of the best rifle shots, and the two often performed at the various county fairs. They not only won the prize money, but often wound up taking home additional winnings from wagers they had placed on each other.

Now, Hank and Billy made eye contact. Although the two men had been friends in happier days, now neither had it in him to speak. Instead Hank nodded, Billy nodded back, and Hank rode on.

Hank managed to catch the ferry just before it left the Mississippi side. Without so much as a glance at the place he was leaving behind, he walked to the front of the boat, where he stared across the river and into the trees.

Two

For a while Hank wandered around, always ready to go to the next town to "see the elephant." Although he was never totally dissatisfied with where he was, or with what he was doing, neither was he ready to settle down.

A store clerk's daughter in Stone County, Missouri, thought he might be looking for love, and she made herself available, but it didn't work out. A circuit-riding preacher told him he was looking for his soul . . . and Hank agreed, at least insofar as he knew that his was a lost soul.

In his quest, he killed alligators in Louisiana, picked cotton in Arkansas, rode shotgun guard in Texas, and tended bar in Missouri.

In the spring of 1868 Hank found himself back in northwestern Arkansas. The Ozark Mountains rose ahead of him, the green hills coming up from the earth like islands rising from the sea. Hank found the Ozarks a pleasant place to be. The dappled shade of oak, hickory, pine, cedar, sassafras, maple, and black gum trees kept him out of the sun's glare.

When he made camp that evening, a squirrel scampered out onto a fallen log, chattering nosily as it raced about trying to find and unearth some long-ago buried nugget. Hank shot him for supper. He hated having to do it, but he was growing tired of beans without meat.

He skinned, cleaned, and spitted the squirrel, then cooked

it over an open fire. He watched it brown as his stomach growled with hunger. The squirrel was barely cooked before he took it off the skewer and began to eat it ravenously, not even waiting for it to cool. When all the meat was gone he broke open the bones and sucked out the marrow.

After his meal he allowed himself a smoke, filling his pipe only one-fourth of the way to conserve his tobacco. The song of the whippoorwill put him to sleep.

At dawn the next day the notches of the eastern hills were touched with the dove gray of early morning. Shortly thereafter a golden fire spread over the mountaintops, then filled the sky with light and color, waking all the creatures below.

Hank rolled out of his blanket and began digging through his saddlebag of possibles for coffee and tobacco. He had been very conservative in his use of tobacco, so he had enough for a morning smoke, but he had no coffee.

Without coffee, Hank made do with a tea made from boiled sassafras roots and sweetened with wild honey. He would have enjoyed a biscuit with his tea, but he had no flour. He had no beans, either, and was nearly out of salt. The bacon had been used up a long time ago.

Hank poured a very careful measure of tobacco into his pipe, then lit it with a burning stick from the fire. After that he found a mossy rock protruding from the side of a hollow and went over to sit down. It was as comfortable as a chair made of leather and oak, and he sat there, smoking his pipe and contemplating his next move.

It was clear that he was going to have to go into town to replenish his supplies. He had not talked to another human being in nearly a month, but, strangely, it wasn't something he was particularly looking forward to doing. Although he had not been a man of solitary habit in his youth, over the past couple of years he had come to treasure his time alone. It was as if he were making up for the war, when thousands of men were crowded together for no other reason than to kill or be killed.

He emptied his billfold and turned his pocket out onto

the rock to count his money. Six dollars. That would be enough to provision himself one more time, but after that, what?

The answer was obvious. He was going to have to find some work.

Lebanon was a town of some importance in northwest Arkansas. Boardwalks ran the length of the town on either side of the street. At the end of each block, planks were laid across the road to allow pedestrians to cross to the other side without having to walk in the dirt or mud. Mounted, Hank waited patiently at one of them while he watched a woman cross, holding her skirt above her ankles, daintily, to keep the hem from soiling. Then his horse stepped across the plank and headed toward the livery at the far end of the street.

A young black man took his horse from him and, talking soothingly to it, led it into the barn. An old man got up from the barrel he had been sitting on and walked, with a limp, over to Hank.

"Cost you a quarter a night," he said, nodding toward the horse. He pulled out a red handkerchief, blew his nose, then stuffed the handkerchief back into his pocket.

"That include feeding him?"

"Hay only. Oats'll cost you five cents extra."

Hank gave him a silver dollar.

"Just take out for one night," Hank said. "If I need to leave him in tomorrow, I'll be back."

"If you ain't paid for another night by four o'clock tomorrow afternoon, he'll be turned out," the old man warned.

"Fair enough."

"Oats?"

"Hay will be good enough."

The old man looked at the silver dollar, then held it up to his mouth and bit it. Convinced it was good, he gave Hank his change in the form of six pie-shaped pieces of silver cut from a dollar.

"Here you go. Six bits."

"Know of any work around here?" Hank asked.

"Ron Dumey is slaughterin' hogs. He'll be puttin' on some extra hands, but only for the slaughterin'. It ain't nothin' permanent."

"Where will I find him?"

"Just go north of town two miles, tomorrow mornin' 'bout sunup. You won't have no trouble findin' him. Hell, you'll smell it. You ever slaughtered pigs before?"

"I was raised on a farm."

"Then I don't need to tell you it ain't pretty work."

Hank spent four bits for his supper that night. He felt a little guilty doing it, because fifty cents would have bought a week's supply of beans. But he enjoyed the meal of pork steak, gravy, biscuits, and fried potatoes so much that he figured it was worth it.

After his supper he went into a bar, where he allowed himself exactly two beers. A couple of the bar girls sidled over toward him. One was fairly young and prettier than average for someone in this business. He put his hand in his pocket and almost pulled out the money it would take to visit her, but at the last moment he changed his mind. He shook his head slightly, and with a small smile of disappointment, the girl moved on.

Hank spent the night with his horse, sleeping in the straw that covered the floor. He hadn't made any arrangement to sleep here, but most of the time the stable owners didn't mind. Some would charge an extra quarter, and Hank was ready to pay that if need be. But when he woke up just before dawn the next day, he had still not been challenged, so he saddled his horse and rode north, looking for Dumey's place.

Dumey's farm was bustling with activity. The pigs were squealing with such intensity that Hank could almost believe they were aware of their mortality. There were two big kettles of boiling water in which the just-slaughtered pigs were dipped, then scraped to rid their hide of hair. After that the hogs were skinned and gutted. The skins went into kettles to be rendered down to lard, and the entrails were saved for sausage and chitterlings.

The work was hard, hot, and smelly, and when Hank finished that evening, he wasn't sure he wanted to come back the next morning. He said as much to a couple of the other workers he had met during the day.

"Hell, I don't think any of us would come back the next day if we could draw out what he owes us," Lonnie Stone said. "That's why the son of a bitch ain't goin' to pay any of us till the end of the month."

Lonnie was a smaller than average, bandy-legged man with a narrow face and a hooked nose. He was unremarkable in every way, except for his eyes. His eyes flashed with humor, as if their bright blue color hid some hilarious joke.

"Wait, I told him when I signed on this morning that I only intended to work for a week," Hank said.

Zeb Franklin laughed. "You only goin' to work a week, huh? And you think ol' Dumey's goin' to pay you?"

"That was my understanding," Hank said.

"Hell, that stingy Dutchman ain't goin' to pay no one till after the last squeak of the last hog. And then he'll only pay them that's still here. Them that quits in the middle will like as not get nothin' a'tall."

At thirty-five Zeb was the oldest of the three men. He was tall and gangly, with dark hair and a full beard. One of his front teeth was missing. Lonnie had been teasing him about it during the day because two weeks earlier Zeb had pulled and sold a gold tooth in order to finance a drinking spree.

The workday was over, and the three men were sitting under a tree, eating cracklings, the one benefit of their employment.

"I'll be damned if I'm going to stay here for an entire month," Hank said, spitting out a rind that was too tough to chew.

"What are you goin' to do?" Lonnie asked.

"I don't know," Hank answered. "But I didn't go

through four years of war to wind up killing pigs. Especially somebody else's pigs."

Lonnie laughed. "Back when I was with Quantrill, we killed other people's pigs all the time. But we ate 'em whenever we killed 'em."

"You was with Quantrill?" Zeb asked.

"Yeah. What about you?"

"I was with ol' Jeff Thompson," Zeb replied. "Where was you, Hank?"

"Back east," Hank answered without going into detail.

"Sometimes I wish the war was still goin' on," Zeb said.

"What do you mean?" Lonnie asked.

"I know it might sound funny to folks to hear me say that. But I tell you the truth, when I was with Thompson I never was hungry, and I never was without enough money to buy myself a new shirt, or shoes, or somethin' to drink. But for the last three years I ain't done nothin' but work like a dog, and I ain't goin' to have a pot to piss in or two coppers to rub together till that goddamn Dutchman takes a mind to pay us."

"Yeah, I know what you mean," Lonnie said. "You know what I keep thinkin' about? I keep thinkin' about that tax money the bank'll be shippin' back to Fayetteville tomorrow mornin'. Hell, if ol' Quantrill or Bloody Bill Anderson had ever got wind of somethin' like that, we'd meet those folks on the road and relieve them of their burden."

"You say there's tax money being shipped tomorrow?" Hank asked.

"Five thousand dollars, from what I hear," Lonnie said. "The damn Yankees has been collectin' it for six months. Now they're sendin' it back to the district headquarters in Fayetteville. No tellin' what will happen to it then. Like as not it'll line a few Yankee pockets."

"It could wind up in some Yankees' pockets," Hank said. He picked up a particularly meaty crackling and examined it for a moment, then stuck it in his mouth. "Or it could wind up in ours," he added. He smiled at the surprised expressions on Lonnie's and Zeb's faces.

"What . . . what do you have in mind?" Lonnie asked.

Now Zeb grinned broadly. "Sounds to me like he's got in mind robbin' the tax man."

"That's exactly what I've got in mind."

"I don't know," Lonnie said. "What with them shippin' that much money, they're goin' to have guards, you gotta know that."

"I'm sure they will have guards. They had guards when you were with Quantrill, didn't they?"

"Well, yeah, but things was different then."

"The only difference is a matter of timing," Hank said. "If we had done this then, it would have been an act of war and you wouldn't be nervous about it. But doin' it now makes it robbery, and that's got you jittery."

"No, the robbin' part don't bother me none. But if we was doin' this in the war, it would all be planned out. I mean, we had officers to do our plannin' for us."

Hank laughed. "Well then, if that's all that's bothering you, there's no problem."

"What do you mean?"

"I'll be damned," Zeb said. "I think I know what he means." He pointed to Hank. "I been studyin' on where it was that I seen you before, and now I know. It was at Shiloh. You was a lieutenant with DuMont's Cavalry, wasn't you?"

"Yes."

"You mean, you was an officer?" Lonnie asked.

"Yes."

"Whatever happened to ol' Dumont?" Zeb asked.

"He was killed at Antietam."

"Who took command of the regiment, once DuMont was gone?"

"I did," Hank said.

"You took over? As a lieutenant?"

"I was a major by then."

Zeb laughed out loud, then slapped his hand against his knee. "Lonnie, don't you be worryin' none 'bout havin' somebody plan this here little fracas tomorrow. I reckon the *major* here can handle it for us all right.''

Lonnie had not spoken since learning that Hank was not only an officer, but an officer who had once commanded an entire cavalry regiment. He continued to stare at Hank.

"I didn't ever know no real officers, leastwise not one to talk to," Lonnie finally said. "And especially not one as high as a major."

Hank smiled at him. "What about it, Lonnie? Do you want some of that tax money?"

"Yes, sir!" Lonnie said. "You damned right I want some of it!"

Three

With the promise of a share of the money, Hank, Zeb, and Lonnie were able to recruit three more men to join their little band. That left Ron Dumey's hog-slaughtering operation a total of six men short. When the old farmer turned out his hired hands the next morning for another day of pig slaughtering, only three remained to answer the call.

Ten miles from Dumey's farm, on the pike that led to Fayetteville, Hank and his men were waiting under a cluster of trees. It was raining, and the road was covered with water and flushed with black mud.

The five men with Hank were veterans of the recent war and as such took orders easily and efficiently. This could have been any unit commanded by Hank during the war. The only difference was, these men weren't in uniform, though even if they had been, no one would have been able to tell. They were all wearing oil slickers and wide-brimmed hats, pulled low to keep out the rain.

Zeb stood in his stirrups, scratched his crotch, then settled back again. He looked over toward Hank.

"Major Tyreen, if you ask me, them Yankees ain't goin' to be comin' out in this kind of weather," he said.

Hank took off his hat and poured water from the brim, then put it back on. He reached down and patted his horse soothingly.

"They'll come," he said. "They'll be wanting to move that tax money out as soon as they can."

Hank had sent Lonnie about half a mile down the curve in the road, to be on the lookout. Now Lonnie came riding back.

"Major, they're comin'," he said. "I seen 'em."

"Good."

"Maybe not so good."

"Why not?"

"That ain't an ordinary guard they're ridin' with. They got military outriders. Eight of 'em, four ridin' in front and four ridin' in the back."

"Hold on, here," one of the others said, his tone of voice showing his obvious anxiety. "Nobody said nothin' 'bout no soldiers. If I had known there was goin' to be soldiers, I wouldn't have come."

"Did you expect them to hang the money out on a hook for us?" Hank asked. "If the soldiers scare you, you can ride out of here now."

"Hell, *I* ain't a-goin' nowhere," one of the other men said. "I fought the Yankees for damn near nothin' before. At least this time I'll be gettin' something out of it. And it sure as hell beats slaughterin' pigs."

The man who had lodged the protest looked at the others, then realized he was alone in his fears. He nodded. "I ain't a-goin' nowhere, either," he said. "I was just commentin', that's all."

"Good, I'm glad you're all still with me," Hank said. "Now, all we have to do is stick to our plan and we'll all come out of this all right." He called toward someone back in the edge of the trees. "Poindexter, you got that tree notched?"

"Yes, sir, she's all ready, Major. All it'll take is about two whacks and it'll drop right across the road, clean as a whistle."

"What about behind 'em, Major?" Lonnie asked.

"Don't worry about that. They can't get the coach turned around on this road. The tree will keep them from going forward, and we'll keep them from going back."

"Hell, if you ask me, we ought to just shoot the sons of bitches. They're all Yankees anyhow," a man named Morris growled.

"We'll do it my way, Morris," Hank replied. "Now, all of you, get into position."

The men melted back into the woods and waited as the coach and its escort detail came up the road. From the shouts and whistles, Hank knew that the driver was having to work the team exceptionally hard to pull the heavy coach through the thick mud. A moment later they came around the curve.

With an eye trained by four years of military ambushes, Hank looked at how the detail was deployed. Four of the soldiers were riding in front of the stagecoach, and four more soldiers were riding behind. The officer in charge was riding between the four lead soldiers and the coach. In addition to the military detail, the coach driver and the guard were also armed.

By now the rain was falling so hard that visibility was limited to a few hundred feet, and for the moment that was decidedly to Hank's advantage. His men were hidden in the trees, completely out of sight, whereas the soldiers and the stagecoach were on the road, in plain view.

Hank held up his hand, preparatory to giving the signal, when unexpectedly the detail stopped. The officer in charge rode to the front of the detail, stopped, then looked down the road.

"Well," Hank said under his breath. "You're smarter than I thought you were, Yankee. You know this is a good place for an ambush, don't you?"

The officer in charge sent two of his soldiers down the road ahead of them, and Hank turned in his saddle to make certain his men were well concealed. He motioned for Poindexter, who was standing by his notched tree, to get out of sight. At his signal, Poindexter slipped back into the woods, and Hank was reassured by the fact that he couldn't see him, even though he knew where to look.

If the soldiers who rode ahead had been more observant,

the officer in charge might have been forewarned. There were some freshly cut wood chips floating on the water in the road, put there from the notching of the tree. Unfortunately for the escort detail, the point riders didn't notice them. Even the notch itself could have been seen if they had looked, the fresh cut bright against the dark trunk of the tree. But they didn't look. They were interested only in keeping their collars turned up and their hat brims turned down to keep out as much of the cold spring rain as possible. They saw no need to be doing what they were doing, and they had ridden here only to humor their commander.

The soldiers weren't thinking of any possible danger facing them. They were thinking of the dry barracks they would find when this trip was over. They rode at a quick trot through the narrow, muddiest part of the road, then they turned their horses and went back, reporting to the commander that all was well.

The officer in charge, a lieutenant, sat on his horse for a long moment, as if contemplating the report. For a moment Hank had an idea that the Yankee lieutenant didn't believe his men and was going to check out the road for himself.

"You've got a hunch, don't you, Yankee?" Hank murmured. "Yeah, I know what you're feeling. I've felt it myself, many times."

Finally the Yankee lieutenant gave the order to proceed.

With a sigh of relief, Hank pulled up his kerchief, covering the bottom half of his face. This was a signal for others to do the same so that all would be effectively masked. He waved once, and Poindexter returned to his position by the tree. Hank stood by, watching the coach and its escort come ahead, waiting until the detail was committed.

At the appropriate time Hank brought his hand down. There were two sharp reports as the ax took the final two bites from the towering cypress tree. With groans, creaks, and loud snapping noises, the tree started down, then fell across the muddy road with the crashing thunder of an artillery barrage. At the same time that the tree hit the road

in front of the coach, Hank's men moved out onto the road
behind them and fired several shots into the air.

"You're surrounded!" Hank shouted, urging his horse
onto the road from the trees right alongside. He leveled his
pistol at the soldiers. "Throw down your guns and put up
your hands."

"Road agents!" one of the soldiers said, and he threw
down his rifle. The other soldiers, perhaps taking their cue
from him, threw down their weapons as well. Only the Yankee lieutenant refused the order. He brought his pistol up
from beneath his poncho and pointed it at Hank, then pulled
the trigger. Hank saw the cylinder turn and heard the hammer click, but the cartridge misfired.

Hank aimed at the officer. "Drop your gun, Lieutenant!
Drop it now! Don't make me kill you!"

The lieutenant lowered his pistol, then let it drop into the
mud. When Hank looked menacingly at the driver and shotgun guard, they threw down their weapons as well.

"Now, I want all you boys to get down off your horses,"
Hank ordered.

Grumbling, the men got down. As soon as they did, Lonnie and Zeb started collecting the horses.

"You're stealing our horses?" asked the Yankee lieutenant.

"We're not stealing them, we're just denying you the use
of them," Hank explained. "We're going to take 'em with
us for a mile or so, then we'll let 'em go. Like as not, they'll
wind up back in your own stable. Driver, throw down the
money box."

The driver threw down the box. Using a pry bar, Lonnie
pulled the hasp loose, then opened the lid. His effort was
rewarded by the sight of several stacks of greenbacks.

"You're making a big mistake, mister," the lieutenant
said. "That money belongs to the United States government."

"Is that a fact?" Hank asked sarcastically. "Well, before
it belonged to the government, it belonged to the people. So
I'm taking it back."

"I see. You're taking it back for the people, are you?"

Hank chuckled. "Sure, why not? We're people, aren't we?"

The other robbers laughed at Hank's joke.

At that moment, Hank saw the end of a pistol poke out from the passenger window. He fired at the stagecoach, his bullet hitting the steel tire on the left rear wheel of the coach. The rim shaved the bullet into tiny shards, none of which were big enough to cause serious injury, but all of which sprayed the interior of the coach with painful pellets.

"Get out of the coach, now," Hank ordered. "The next shot will kill somebody."

The coach door opened and a man stepped down onto the ground. He appeared to be injured. He was an overweight man, wearing a dark suit and a white shirt. The front of his shirt was peppered with red from the half dozen tiny pricks made by the shredded bullet. It was he who had been holding the pistol.

"I'll have you know that I am a federal agent for the revenue service," the overweight man blustered. "You will never get away with this. I intend to see to it personally."

"You do that," Hank said.

By now Lonnie and Zeb had loaded all the money into two big sacks. They tied the necks of the sacks together, then handed them to Hank, who laid them across his saddle in such a way as to allow one bag to hang down on each side of the horse.

"Lieutenant, would you and your boys happen to be wearing those nice warm Yankee longjohns, right now?" Hank asked.

"Why do you ask?" the lieutenant replied.

"I just don't want you catching a fever when I leave you here, that's all. Shuck out of them clothes. All of you."

"Now, just a damn minute, mister," one of the soldiers, a sergeant, said. "I ain't doin' nothin' of the kind."

"You heard the major, Blue-belly," one of Hank's men said, laughing. He made a signal with his carbine. "Get out of them."

"Major, huh?" the lieutenant questioned. He looked at Hank and the men with him, all of whom were still wearing masks. "Thanks for that piece of information. It should make it easier for me to hunt you down."

"You do that," Hank said, angered that their operation had been compromised by the small piece of information that he had once been a major. "In the meantime, get undressed."

Grumbling and protesting, the soldiers began to undress. A few moments later all of them, including the lieutenant, were standing in the mud in their longjohns. This was in accordance with the plan, since Hank believed that a lack of clothing and horses would preclude any chase. The two men he had assigned to pick up the uniforms now did so.

"You two, unhitch the team," Hank said to the driver.

"What's the reason for that?" the driver asked.

"No reason," Hank replied. "I just want to keep you folks busy for a few minutes after we're gone, that's all. It'll take you that long to get back into harness. By then we'll be gone."

When everything was done, Hank gave the order to move out.

The revenue agent, whose name was Adolphus Pringle, opened his shirt. The wounds were little more than superficial scratches inflicted by tiny shards of the shaved bullet. The shards brought blood, even though they barely penetrated the skin.

Pringle's fear turned to anger, and he took it out on the young lieutenant who was in charge of the escort detail.

"Lieutenant Murchison," Pringle said, "I hold you totally responsible for this outrage, sir. You were charged with the mission of protecting me, and the money, and you failed."

"Mr. Pringle, you aren't being fair," the coach driver protested. "Lieutenant Murchison did everything he could do. He tried to face them down, and his gun misfired. For that, he was nearly shot."

"Nearly shot? My dear sir, I *was* shot," Pringle said.

"It's a fine state of affairs when I, the civilian, am injured, while none of the soldiers are asked to shed as much as one drop of blood."

"Let me see your wounds," Lieutenant Murchison offered, starting toward the rotund man.

"No!" Pringle said, holding out his hands to stop the young officer. "My wounds will keep until we see a real doctor. I'll not let you butcher me with any of your so-called field medicine."

"Very well, Mr. Pringle," Murchison said. Lieutenant Joe Murchison looked over at the driver. "How much farther is it to Fayetteville?"

"About ten miles, I reckon," the driver replied.

"You go ahead as soon as you get your team back into harness. In the meantime, my men and I will get under way."

"Get under way? Well, how are we goin' to do that, Lieutenant? We ain't got no mounts," one of the soldiers said.

"We'll march," Joe said.

"March? You mean walk? Cap'n, you aimin' to walk us all the way into town?"

"You heard the driver. It's only ten miles. That's just a short stroll to the infantry."

"But we ain't infantry, Cap'n. We're cavalry," one of the others protested.

"Oh, you're cavalry, are you?" Joe teased. "Then tell me, trooper, where is your horse?"

The others laughed at Joe's remark.

"The only horse you're goin' to be ridin', Johnson, is shank's mare," someone else said, and that, too, brought laughter.

"Let's go, men," Joe said, and in marching order, they began sloshing through the mud toward Fayetteville.

A few minutes later the coach passed them, the driver having reconnected the team. As it passed, Pringle leaned out the window.

"Believe me, Lieutenant, your commanding officer will

hear of your incompetence," he shouted, shaking his fist at Joe. At that moment the front wheel of the coach fell off into a mud-filled pothole, and as it did so, it splashed muddy water onto Pringle's face, in his hair, and on his suit jacket.

"Driver!" Pringle sputtered. "You are an imbecile!"

The soldiers laughed heartily as the coach continued its slipping, sliding transit down the road.

They made a strange sight when they came into town a couple of hours later, covered with mud and marching in formation as if on parade drill, though dressed only in their longjohns.

The citizens of Fayetteville, many of them still sympathetic to the failed Confederacy, got great enjoyment out of seeing the soldiers coming into town in such a condition. They stood in front of their houses and in the doors of the stores and saloons, and they laughed and hooted at Joe and his men.

"What kind of company have you got there, Lieutenant?" someone shouted. "Is that the new uniform they got you Yankee boys wearin' now?"

"You remember the Zouaves, don't you?" another asked. "Well, this is like the Zouaves, only they call this the Underwear Brigade."

"No, no! This is the Pantaloon Dragoons!"

The comments were met with more laughter, and one of Joe's men, unable to bear the ridicule, burst out, "You wait till I—"

"You're in formation, soldier. No talking," Joe hissed sharply.

Looking neither left nor right and fuming silently under the cruel and ceaseless ribbing, the men marched, in parade, up Central Avenue to the railroad depot, where the revenue agent, Adolphus Pringle, was waiting, along with Joe's commanding officer, Captain John Hamilton. Joe brought his detail to a halt and saluted his CO.

"I expect you had better come inside, Lieutenant Murchison," Hamilton said, and Joe dismissed his men, then

followed Hamilton and Pringle into the station house, where
Hamilton had made his temporary headquarters.

Someone gave Joe a blanket, and Hamilton poured him a
cup of coffee. Joe accepted both with thanks, then sat down
when Hamilton indicated that he should do so.

"Mr. Pringle tells me that you were ambushed on the
road."

"Yes, sir," Joe answered. "They dropped a tree across
the road in front of us, then moved up from the rear."

"Then his soldiers threw down their guns like the Rebels
at Appomattox," Pringle said. "I was the only one with
enough gumption to attempt to fight them off, and for that
I was wounded."

"Wounded, Mr. Pringle? I've seen worse cuts shaving,"
Hamilton scoffed. He turned his attention back to Joe. "Do
you have any idea who it was?"

"They were all masked, but as we are only on temporary
assignment here, I doubt I would have recognized any of
them anyway," Joe said. "I suspect it was a group of former
Confederate soldiers, though. They called their leader 'Major,' and they were well disciplined and well organized."

"Which is more than can be said for your soldiers, Lieutenant," Pringle said.

"Mr. Pringle," Hamilton started, but Joe held up his
hand.

"No, Pringle is right, sir," Joe said. "My men offered
no resistance. I take full responsibility for that."

"Yet the driver tells me that you did try to resist, but
your pistol misfired."

Joe laughed. "Yes, I did do that, but it was in a moment
of anger. I'm fortunate the leader of the outlaws kept a cool
head."

"Joe, my boy, I worry about you," Hamilton said with
a chuckle.

"Why are you worrying about him? Don't forget, I was
the only one they shot at. Fortunately they missed."

"They didn't miss, Mr. Pringle," Joe said.

"What do you mean, they didn't miss?"

"If they had wanted to kill you, they would have. He shot at the wheel as a warning. I don't think they really wanted to hurt anyone. They just wanted the money."

"How much money was in the shipment?" Hamilton asked.

"Four thousand eight hundred dollars," Pringle said. "A sizable amount of money, gone forever now, due to the incompetence of the army."

"I'm sure you will redouble your efforts to bleed the widows and orphans," Hamilton said dryly. "Surely you haven't squeezed every possible cent out of them yet."

"You disapprove?"

"Under the circumstances, I think the taxation is a little harsh," Hamilton said.

"May I remind you, Captain, that the money I raise helps to pay your salary, and the salary of all government employees?"

"Yourself included, I'm sure," Hamilton replied.

"Myself included," Pringle agreed. He managed a sarcastic smile. "We are all, you might say, feeding from the same trough."

Half an hour later Joe had just washed off the mud and put on a clean uniform when Captain Hamilton knocked on the door. He had a bottle and two glasses with him.

"I thought you could use this," Hamilton said, pulling the cork.

"Thank you, sir. You don't know how much I could use it. I appreciate your coming by," Joe said.

"I have something else I think you will appreciate," Hamilton said. "In fact, I'm sure you will."

Joe looked at Hamilton questioningly as the captain poured the liquor.

"We've just received telegraphed orders. Tomorrow morning we tell Arkansas good-bye. We are to return to Fort Hays, Kansas."

Joe smiled broadly. "That's wonderful news, sir. I'll

drink to that.'' He held out his glass toward Hamilton's.

Hamilton held up his glass as well. ''And to our comrades at Fiddler's Green,'' he said.

''Fiddler's Green,'' Joe replied.

Four

"Whoowee! There's near 'bout eight hunnert dollars here!" Zeb said when he counted his share of the divided money. "Lord, I ain't never had that much money at one time in my whole life. Hell, iffen you was to put together all the money I ever had in my whole life, I don't think it would be this much."

"This was like takin' candy from a baby," Lonnie said happily. "So, when do we do it again?"

Hank was by his horse, stuffing his share of the money into his saddlebag. He looked up when Lonnie asked his question.

"Did you ask when we were going to do this again?" Hank asked.

"Sure," Lonnie replied. "I mean, this come off real good."

"I'm with Lonnie," one of the others said. "I don't see no reason to quit now."

"What exactly did you have in mind, Carl?" Hank asked.

"Well, hell, I don't know," Carl replied. "I'm the first one to say that I ain't very smart when it comes to plannin' this sort of thing. You're the boss, we'll do what you say."

"If we're going to do what I say, then I say we aren't going to do it anymore," Hank said.

"Don't do it no more?" Carl replied in a disbelieving

voice. "Why, man, this is the golden goose. You mean you're goin' to just turn your back on it?"

"That's what I mean."

"But it was so easy," Lonnie said.

"We were lucky, Lonnie," Hank said. "It went easy because nobody really expected us. But believe me, the word is out now. Next time they send out a tax shipment, they will be more alert to a possible holdup."

"Well, hell, we won't do no more tax shipments. We'll find something else to rob."

"Like what? A stagecoach? A train? A bank? A store?" Hank asked.

"Somethin' like that, yeah."

Hank shook his head. "Stealing tax money from the federal government is one thing. In my mind, they stole it themselves. But stealing from private folks is something else again, and I don't want any part of it."

"What if we decide to go on without you?" Johnson asked.

Hank tightened the cover flap on his saddlebag, then mounted his horse. He looked down at the men he had just led.

"Then I wish you luck," he said, touching the brim of his hat as he rode out of camp.

"Well, I'll be damned," one of the other men said. "Would you look at that? He rode out on us."

"What are you bitchin' about, Carl?" Hank heard Zeb ask. "He got us all eight hunnert dollars apiece, didn't he? Did you ever reckon you'd have eight hunnert dollars?"

"No, I reckon not," Carl replied.

Hank didn't look back.

Hank had not been in northwest Arkansas for long and so had made very few acquaintances. Because of that, he didn't believe that any of the soldiers or any of the passengers on the stage could have recognized him, especially as he had worn a mask. But he could not overlook the fact that there were five others with him when he pulled the job . . . five men who were from this part of the country. And Hank was fairly certain that if they all stayed around long enough, especially if they tried another robbery, they were going to get caught. If one of the others got caught, it would inevitably lead to him. That left him with only one alternative, and that was to leave the state.

Hank rode north into Missouri, but as he had already spent some time in Missouri, he felt it might be well to put even more distance between himself and the site of his robbery. So he continued to ride north and then west until he reached the Missouri River. There, he went over into Kansas.

He still had most of his money when he rode into town at Leavenworth, Kansas. There, he stabled his horse, bought oats instead of hay, had a big meal at the restaurant, then went into the first saloon he came to.

The Crystal Palace was considerably nicer and more plush than any saloon Hank had been in before now. A sign behind the bar invited customers to "Ask our mixologist to make you a Whiskey Punch." The bartender, or mixologist, wore a brocaded vest with a sparkling solitaire diamond holding his white tie in place. A watch with a massive gold chain was worn across his chest, while women's garters held up his sleeves. The barkeep had a waxed handlebar mustache and hair parted in the middle, festooned into spit curls, and well oiled with a pomade. He was, in fact, quite a dandy, as befitting a representative of an establishment as posh as the Crystal Palace.

Hank bought a whiskey, was pleasantly surprised to see how smooth it was, then turned his back to the bar to survey the room. Half a dozen bar girls were moving from table to table, laughing, joking, and flirting with the men. Like everything else about this establishment, the girls were first class. They were all pretty, and none of them had the hard-worn look so common among most girls of their trade.

One of them, a dark-haired girl with flashing brown eyes, saw him looking at her. Smiling prettily, she came over to talk to him.

"Don't think I've seen you in here before," she said.

"Haven't been here before," Hank answered. "Can I buy you a drink?"

"Thank you. What's your name?"

"Hank." Hank didn't give his last name. He was pretty sure that nobody had connected his name with the robbery down in Arkansas, but he figured it wouldn't hurt to be cautious.

"I'm Silky," she said.

Hank fingered her hair. "It certainly is."

The girl laughed, a low, throaty laugh. "No, not my hair, silly," she said. "Silky is my name. Silky Sommers."

"I'll be damned. Don't know as I've ever heard of a name like that."

"So," Silky said, thrusting one hip out provocatively as she sipped her drink, "are you new in town?"

"Just arrived," Hank said. "Uh, miss, I don't mean to be too forward or anything, but I was wonderin' if we couldn't, maybe, cut to the chase here?"

"Cut to the chase? What do you mean?"

Do you have a room in the back of this place? Or maybe a crib somewhere that we could go to?"

Silky smiled. "You don't believe in beating around the bush, do you? All right, I suppose we could go for a short time."

Hank shook his head. "No, ma'am," he said. "I don't want it to be for a short time. I mean, do you have a place we could go to for all night? I don't have a hotel room yet, and I thought perhaps I could kill two birds with one stone, so to speak."

Again the girl laughed. "Oh, heavens, I don't know if I want to be killed with a stone. Besides, you could get ten hotel rooms for what it would cost to spend the night with me."

"I've got enough money for ten hotel rooms," Hank said easily.

"Do you now?" Silky looked at the clock. "All right,"

she said. "But the all-night arrangement doesn't start until eleven o'clock. Be back here then."

"Be back here? There's no place to be back from. I'm not going anywhere."

"All right, but you do understand that I'll be busy between now and eleven, don't you?" Silky asked. "I can't spend that much time with you."

"Yes, ma'am. I know how it works," Hank said. "I'll just find some way to occupy my time."

Silky finished her drink, then with a final smile moved on. Shortly after she left, a man got up from a table where a card game was in progress. One of the other players, seeing Hank watching them, held out his hand toward the empty chair.

"Want to join us, mister, for a few friendly hands of poker?"

"Thanks," Hank answered, pulling out the chair with a scrape of the legs against the hardwood floor. "Don't mind if I do."

The man who had invited him was very well dressed, in a suit, tie, and vest. He was medium height, with a round, clean-shaven face and a short haircut under a small-rimmed, round-crowned hat. Another man who was at the table was also well dressed, perhaps even a bit more elegantly, for his vest was silk and he wore a cravat with a diamond stick pin. His hat was black, with a wide rim and a low, flat crown. The hatband was of silver and turquoise. He had a handlebar mustache and wore his hair in long, curling locks. The hair and mustache were strawberry blond.

"The name's Masterson," said the man who invited Hank into the game. "Bat Masterson. This is my brother Ed, that's Glen Matthews, and the handsome figure there is James Butler Hickok . . . though folks call him Wild Bill."

"Wild Bill?" Hank replied.

Hickok laughed. "Some eastern newspaperman dreamed up that moniker," he said. "It seems to have stuck with me."

"My name is Hank." He paused for a moment, then,

because he knew everyone else's last name, figured it would be even more suspicious of him not to say his own. "Tyreen," he concluded. "Hank Tyreen."

"Where are you from, Hank?" Bat asked.

"Mississippi."

"Fight in the war?"

"Yes," Hank said. He looked around the table. "Is that a problem with anyone? I thought the war was over."

Masterson laughed. "The war is over, and whichever side you were on is no problem to anyone here."

Hank chuckled. "Sorry," he said. "I've run into a few who are still fighting it. I just want to put it behind me."

The cards were dealt, and there was no further talk of the war. Hank won a little money, not very much, but as he was just killing time until eleven o'clock anyway, he was thankful he wasn't losing. He glanced up at the clock several times until Hickok, with a little laugh, made a comment about it.

"Mr. Tyreen, no matter how many times you look up at that clock, eleven o'clock isn't going to come around any sooner."

The others around the table laughed.

Somewhat embarrassed, Hank laughed, too. "How did you know I was waiting for eleven o'clock?"

"Hell, mister, everyone in the saloon knows," Masterson answered, and again the men around the table laughed. "We saw you talking to Silky."

"Oh."

"Silky is a nice girl," Masterson said. "You'll like her."

"I know she's my favorite," Hickok said.

"Hell, she's the favorite of anyone who can afford her price," Ed said. There was more laughter.

Hank wished now that he hadn't made the arrangement with Silky. It wasn't so much that she had been with other men . . . or even with all the other men. What bothered him was the public way in which a business that he thought should be private was being conducted.

"Damn, the cards aren't running well for me tonight,"

Hickok said with a grumble as he lost another hand. It was Hickok's steady losing that kept Hank a little ahead of the game. As it so happened, Hickok's money was being spread around rather evenly so that no one person was winning heavily.

"If this keeps up, I'm going to have to go back to work pretty soon," Hickok said as a new hand was dealt.

"What sort of work do you do, Mr. Hickok?" Hank asked. He was interested in what type of employment would provide enough money to allow a man to dress as expensively and play cards as recklessly as Hickok was doing.

"I've done all sorts of work, Mr. Tyreen," Hickok replied. "I've scouted for the U.S. Army, I've sheriffed, and I've gambled. But none of it pays like buffing."

"Buffing?" Hank replied, unfamiliar with the term.

"Buffalo hunting," Bat Masterson explained. "Wild Bill is a buffalo hunter. So are my brother and I."

"What do you do with a buffalo once you kill it?"

"You are aware, are you not, that right now, even as we speak, railroads are being built all across the West?" Ed Masterson asked.

"I know that there is a railroad that's being built to the Pacific."

"Yes, but that isn't the only one. They are building railroads from all over to connect to the Union Pacific. And the men working on those railroads must be fed, so the railroads need meat."

"I see. So you sell the meat to them."

Ed Masterson chuckled. "We do, but you still aren't seeing the whole picture," he said. "Supplying meat to the railroads is just a part of it. The smallest part of it, as it turns out. The real money comes from buffalo hides."

"That's right," Bat agreed. "The railroad pays us for the meat, but they don't care what happens to the hides. We sell the hides for six dollars apiece."

"Last time out, I brought in over three hundred pelts," Hickok said. "That was for no more than four weeks' work."

"Three hundred pelts . . . times six dollars? Why, that's . . ."

"A lot of money," Hickok said, laughing. "Plus what the railroad paid me for the meat."

Hank shook his head. "There has to be a catch here," he said.

"No catch."

"If there's that kind of money to be made from hunting buffalo, why isn't everyone doing it?"

"You think buffing is easy, do you?" Ed Masterson asked.

"I don't know, I've never done it," Hank admitted. "But how hard can it be? They're pretty big targets. They can't be all that hard to hit."

"Hard to hit," Bat repeated, laughing. "Mr. Tyreen, you are a funny man."

"Let me tell you what buffing is like," Hickok said. "You are either too cold or too hot. You are too wet or you are about to die of thirst. You go for days, weeks at a time, without seeing another human being except for the skinners and cutters you've hired."

"And believe me, friend," Bat added, "when I tell you that the kind of person who will cut and skin buffalo is not the kind of person you want to engage in any long, philosophical conversations."

"Well, I've been hot, cold, wet, and thirsty before," Hank said. He chuckled. "And I'm not that much of a philosopher anyway, so not having anyone to talk to wouldn't be that much of a bother to me."

"That isn't the all of it," Ed added. "They call it buffalo hunting, and hunting is the right word. That's big, wide-open country out there, and a herd of buffalo has a lot of area to get lost in."

"And when you do find the herd, like as not the Indians will have found it as well," Hickok said. "You see, they think every buffalo in the world belongs to them . . . like it's their own private herd. And if they find the buffalo at the same time you do, then you'll be lucky enough to get out of there with your own hide . . . let alone any from a buffalo.''

"Oh, and don't forget the stink," Bat said.

"The stink?"

"When the hides are cut off and the meat is trimmed out for the railroad, the carcasses that are left smell to high heaven. And that stink sticks to you," Ed said.

"That's why we put on all this sweet-smelling tonic as soon as we can get to a barbershop," Hickok said.

Bat laughed. "Bill, you're such a dandy you'd wear that sweet-smelling stuff anyway," he said. "You just use the buffalo stink as an excuse."

Hank was so intrigued by the idea of buffalo hunting, or "buffing," as the others called it, that he began asking all sorts of questions. What kind of gun would he need? What about ammunition? Did he need to load his own? What about wagons, cutters, and skinners? Where did you sell your skins, and how did you make arrangements with the railroad to get a contract to furnish meat?

"It's a pretty expensive operation to get started," Hickok explained. "It'll cost you at least five hundred dollars for a couple of wagons, teams, rifle, ammunition, and supplies. Do you have that much money?"

Hank thought for a moment before he answered. He didn't really know these people that well. There was no need for them to know how much money he had. In fact, if they knew, their first and most logical question would be, how did a drifter, such as he obviously was, come by the money?

"I can get it," he answered.

"I know where you can get a hundred of it," Bat said. "If you're good enough."

"Good enough at what?"

"Shooting," Bat explained. "There's going to be a marksmanship contest tomorrow. The winner will get one hundred dollars."

"You don't say? What does it cost to enter?"

"Five dollars," Bat said. "The bartender can put you

down." He nodded across the table. "Ed, Bill, and I are already in."

"All right, I'll enter," Hank said.

Bat smiled. "I was hoping you'd say that. Now, would you care to make a little side wager of, say, . . . ten dollars?"

"Against who?"

"It's a pot, actually. There are three of us in it now. Whoever scores the highest of us three will win the pot."

"Yes, I'd like to get into it, if there are no objections."

"Objections? My dear fellow, I would never object to having another sheep to shear," Hickok said.

"Honey, it's eleven o'clock," a woman's voice said.

"You have enough money for all this, Mr. Tyreen?" Hickok asked. "Five dollars to enter the contest, ten dollars to enter the pool, and five dollars for Silky?"

Hank raked in the pile of coins and paper money in front of him. He held up a five-dollar bill and smiled. "Well, here's the five dollars for Silky, thanks to you, Mr. Hickok," he said.

"Ouch," Hickok teased. "It's bad enough I have to lose at cards, it's even worse when I know I'm financing another man's pleasure."

Again the table laughed as Hank followed Silky through the back door of the saloon and down the alleyway for a short distance. At the end of the alley he saw a very small house, or crib, as it was called. The house consisted of one room only, and though it was a very utilitarian structure, built for one purpose, he saw that Silky had managed to give it some personality. There was a flower bed in front of the house, and colorful gingham curtains hung in the windows.

"Pretty flowers," Hank commented.

"Thanks," Silky said, obviously pleased by his comment. She reached down to pick off a couple of dead leaves, stems, and flowers. "I really need to get out here and do some work on them."

Inside the little crib, Silky lit a candle. Then she poured

some water from a pitcher into a basin and, taking the water with her, stepped around behind a screen.

Hank could hear the splash of water as she began her ablutions. He looked at the bed. It was made, though somewhat crookedly. He had been so involved with the card game that he hadn't noticed whether or not Silky had left the saloon before. Had she brought a man in here since they spoke earlier?

The thought was a little disconcerting, but he put it behind him. After all, entertaining men was what she did, and whether she just now brought one in here, or whether she entertained him last night, it was all the same. Why should it matter to him?

Actually, it didn't matter to him, so he put it out of his mind.

When Silky stepped out from behind the screen a moment later, he was surprised to see that she was totally nude. And though he knew that most whores promised much more than they were able to deliver, in this case he was not disappointed. Silky was all she promised and more. She was slender, except for the flare of her hips and the gentle rise of her relatively small but well-formed breasts. Somehow, without her clothes, she looked younger than he had thought. For a moment he wondered just how old she really was.

He didn't allow himself to speculate on her age. After all, she was a prostitute, and prostitutes were without history; therefore they were without age.

"Honey, you don't even have your clothes off yet," Silky said, her voice indicating that she was puzzled by that fact.

"What's the hurry?" Hank replied. "We have all night, don't we?"

Silky laughed. "Yes, we do," she agreed. "It's just that most men are so . . ." She stopped in midsentence. It was as if she were embarrassed to continue the statement about "most" men. "But that's all right," she said. "You're different."

"Does it bother you that I am different?"

''No. I like it.''

Hank sat on the edge of the bed. ''Will you help me take off my boots?'' He held out his left leg.

Smiling at him, Silky swung a long, naked limb over his leg, pivoting as she did, so that she wound up facing away from him. Hank found the image of her bare behind intensely erotic, as she struggled with his boot.

As soon as his boots were off, Hank removed his clothes. Silky turned back to watch him with eyes that managed to be both smoky and amused. As soon as he was naked she leaned into him, pressing her bare breasts against his chest, grinding her pelvis against his, pushing him down onto the bed as she did so.

They lay on the bed, exploring each other's bodies with their hands until, finally, Hank climbed on top. For the next few minutes there was only the sound of heavy breathing, a few groans of pleasure, and the symphony of creaking bedsprings.

Afterward, they separated and lay together, their skin a glowing golden color in the soft light of the single candle.

Silky saw a long scar of puffy purple flesh on Hank's left thigh. She put her finger on it and traced it, gently, for its entire length.

''Where did you get this?''

''At Lookout Mountain.''

''Where's that?''

''In Tennessee.''

''Did you get into a fight there?''

Hank chuckled. ''You might say that,'' he said.

''What about?''

''Some friends and I were on top of the hill, and some other people wanted us off.''

Silky laughed. ''You mean like the children's game of 'King of the Mountain'?''

''Sort of like that.''

''You played very rough.''

''Yes.''

Suddenly the smile left Silky's face. "Wait a minute, you're . . . you're talking about the war, aren't you? That was a battle in the war."

"Yes."

"I'd almost forgotten about the war."

Hank thought of the Yankee captain whose slashing saber had struck his leg with fire just before Hank had shot him. "Yeah, I'd almost forgotten it, too," he said.

Hank laid his head back on the pillow. He had spent last night on the ground, and he hadn't gotten a hotel room for tonight because he'd reasoned that he could have a woman, and a bed, with the same expenditure. Now he intended to take advantage of it, and he closed his eyes.

"Do you really want to sleep? Or would you like to do it again?" Silky asked. As she talked, her hand was busy reawakening Hank's interest.

Hank opened his eyes again and smiled up at her. "Well, if you're going to put it that way, I can always sleep later," he said.

The entire town was turned out the next day for the shooting contest. Hank was reminded of one of the county fairs back in Mississippi. The ladies manned booths selling everything from canned peaches to baked goods to quilts. A traveling medicine wagon had set up operation at the far end of the street, and the barker was doing a brisk business.

The most important event of the day, however, was the big shooting contest, and after two hours of participation, the field had been narrowed down to four people: Bat Masterson, his brother Ed Masterson, Wild Bill Hickok, and Hank Tyreen. For several minutes, as bets were made and covered, the four shooters matched each other, shot for shot, with no apparent separation between them.

Rarely had such shooting been seen anywhere, and as word spread, the ladies and then even the medicine show barker closed down their own operations so they could witness the magnificent marksmanship that was on display here.

Finally the judges conferred, then decided to move the

target farther away. They did that, and the four men stayed neck and neck until they were shooting from three hundred yards. At the three-hundred-yard mark, Ed Masterson fell out of the contest, one of his bullets striking three-quarters of the way in and one-quarter of the way out of the bull's-eye.

There were no other dropouts until the four-hundred-yard range, when Bat dropped out. Now, only Hickok and Hank remained. The target was moved to five hundred yards.

"Hey, we're out of targets," one of the judges said.

"Light a candle," Hank suggested. "We'll use that as the target."

A candle was lit, and Hickok fired first. The flame flickered at the pass of the bullet but did not go out.

"Hit," one of the judges said.

"No, he missed it," Hank said.

"I hit it," Hickok insisted. "Didn't you see the flame flicker?"

"That was from the wind of the passing bullet. You didn't hit it. If you had, the candle would have gone out."

Hickok laughed. "There is no way you are going to snuff a candle from five hundred yards. Not without hitting the candle itself."

"I can do it," Hank said matter-of-factly.

Hickok pulled out a long thin cigar and lit it. "You can do it?"

"Yes."

"How sure are you?"

"How sure do you want me to be?"

"We can end the match with this shot," Hickok said. "If you snuff the candle, you win. If you don't, I win. Neither of us will need to shoot again."

"Come on, Bill, I know he's new," Bat said. "But you don't really expect him to take a sucker bet like that, do you?"

"Depends on how sure he is about his shooting," Hickok said. "What do you say, Mr. Tyreen? Are we on?"

"Call me Hank," Hank said. He stared at the target at

the far end of the street. He nodded. "All right, we're on."

A buzz of excitement passed through the crowd as news of the arrangement moved quickly from mouth to mouth. The contest was to end, right here and right now, on one all-or-nothing shot.

All the contestants were using the same rifle to ensure fairness. That rifle, a forty-five-caliber Whitworth, was furnished by the marksmanship committee. The Whitworth was a long, heavy, octagon-shaped barrel of the type favored by Berdan's Sharpshooters during the late war. It was especially designed for accuracy.

Hank inserted a brass tube down the barrel, then poured in the powder. He then tapped a paper wad down to seal in the powder. Next he used a bullet starter, a pistonlike arrangement that helped to seat the bullet, which was slightly larger than the diameter of the lands but not quite as large as the diameter of the grooves. The end of the piston was shaped to fit the nose of the bullet. With a smart blow from the palm of his hand, Hank drove the bullet down into the barrel, engaging it in the rifling. He then used a ramrod to push the bullet down until it was properly seated.

With the loading ritual completed, Hank picked up a little dirt from the street and dropped it, watching the drift of the dust. Next he rubbed a little dust on the site bead at the end of the rifle barrel. Then, using the sling to help him hold the rifle steady, he aimed at the tiny, flickering flame five hundred yards away.

"Now, don't get nervous," Hickok said just as Hank started to aim. A few laughed. Hank smiled, looked, then aimed again. He took a deep breath, let half of it out, and slowly began to squeeze the trigger.

The rifle boomed and rocked back against his shoulder. A great billow of gunsmoke obscured his vision of the target for a moment, but he didn't have to see it. The reaction of the crowd told him what had happened, as they cheered and applauded his shot. When the smoke drifted away he saw that the candle had been extinguished.

"Hank, let me be the first to congratulate you," Hickok

said with an extended hand and a genuine smile. "Never thought I would meet the man who could outshoot me, but you damn sure took my measure. Would you like to try it with pistols?"

Hank smiled back. "Thanks, Wild Bill, but I think I'll quit while I'm ahead."

Five

In November Black Kettle moved his village to a camp on the banks of the Washita, in the northwestern part of Indian territory. It would be a good place for the Cheyenne to spend the winter, Black Kettle thought, for there was water, fish, and plenty of game. Also, he had been told by General Hazen that if he kept his people here, well south of the Arkansas River, they would be safe from the soldiers.

That was of some concern to Black Kettle, because a few of the younger braves were riding up into Kansas, where they were raiding farms and isolated houses, stealing what they could, and sometimes killing indiscriminately.

Black Kettle was more of a medicine man than a warrior chief. In fact, if he had his way, the Cheyenne would think only of the hunt and never of war. But even hunting was difficult for the Cheyenne now, for they had been told by the soldiers that they could not go north of the Arkansas River to hunt, even when the buffalo came.

His people were dispirited. Without the buffalo, there was little to eat. They had been promised a ration of beef by the Indian agent, but the promised beef had not materialized. Even if it had, it was a poor substitute for the buffalo. Black Kettle did not care much for beef, and he knew that his people felt as he did.

But Black Kettle had no wish to see his village subjected

to the kind of murderous attack he and his wife had lived through at White Antelope's village at Sand Creek, so he counseled obedience to the white man's law.

Sand Creek proved, however, that even obedience to the white man's law would not always protect you. There, Colonel Chivington and his Colorado militia had murdered men, women, and children, even as the terrified Indians were gathering around a tepee flying the American flag.

White Antelope, head of the Sand Creek village, Black Kettle's very good friend, and an old man of seventy-one, believed that the soldiers did not understand that his people were a peaceful band, so he had raised the American flag over his tepee to show loyalty. Then, carrying a white flag of surrender, he started walking toward Colonel Chivington. Despite his effort to surrender, he was shot down. Sometimes Black Kettle believed he could still hear the old chief singing the Cheyenne death song as he lay dying.

> *There is not a thing that lives forever*
> *Except the earth and the mountains.*

Black Kettle realized then that if he stayed, he would be killed, despite the protection of the American flag and the flag of surrender. He grabbed his wife by the hand, and they darted down a ravine, miraculously escaping Chivington's band.

Black Kettle was the leader of his village, and he was determined not to let them be attacked again. If the soldiers demanded that he keep his village south of the Arkansas, then that was what he would do. And if the young warriors wanted to make trouble north of the Arkansas, or up in Kansas, they would have to deal with the soldiers themselves, because he would not make counsel on their behalf.

Black Kettle came out into the village circle to sit near the fire as the sun set. The village circle was a good sitting place, and many from the village would gather around the fire's warmth at night and talk of the events of the day. Sometimes they would tell stories, and tonight, Black Kettle was in just such a mood. Besides, he thought, a good story would lift their spirits so that they would not think of the hunger gnawing at their bellies.

"Listen," Black Kettle said, "and I will tell you the story of a warrior named Cheyenne."

Those who were around him, the men of the council, the warriors, and those who would be warriors, drew closer to hear his words. The women and children grew quiet, not only because it was forbidden to make noise while stories were being told around the campfires, but also because they knew it would be a good story, and it filled them with excitement to hear it.

"A warrior named Cheyenne?" one of the younger listeners said. "I know that the people are called Cheyenne, but I did not know that there was a warrior with that name."

Black Kettle looked at his young questioner as if cautioning him to be quiet and listen, for only by listening could all his questions be answered.

"Once there was a young man," Black Kettle began. He held up his finger and wagged it slowly back and forth. "He was not Kiowa, he was not Arapaho, he was not Comanche, and he was not Cheyenne."

"What was he, Grandfather?" one of the children asked. Black Kettle was not the young questioner's biological grandfather, but he was the spiritual grandfather of them all.

"He was before," Black Kettle said. "He was in the time of the beginning, before the winter count, when he could speak with the animals, and the spirits of the earth, fire, wind, and water."

"He could speak to animals?" one of the listeners asked.

"Yes. But the young man did not know this was unusual because he had always been able to do so, and it seemed a natural thing for him. Then, one day as he stood watching an eagle fly, he thought that perhaps he would try to fly, too, so he leaped into the air and he beat his arms like the wings of the eagle, but he could not fly and he fell to the ground . . . *ker-whump*."

Black Kettle made the *kerwhump* sound in such a way as to amuse the children, and they all laughed.

" 'Foolish one, you cannot fly,' the eagle taunted, and he soared through the air and laughed at the young man.

"Then the young man saw a coyote running swiftly, so swiftly across the plains, and he ran after the coyote, thinking to catch him, but he couldn't. 'Foolish one, did you think you could run as swiftly as I?' the coyote mocked.

"Then the young man saw a bear. The bear smelled honey in a comb, which was high in a tree, and the bear, with his great strength, pushed the tree over so he could have the honey. The young man was very impressed with the bear's great strength, so he, too, tried to push over a tree. But he could not. The bear, who was enjoying his honey, saw the young man, and he teased the young man and called him a weakling and told him he had no business trying to push over a mighty tree in the first place."

Black Kettle shook his head sadly and clucked his tongue.

"What did the young man do next, Grandfather?"

"Oh, the young man felt very bad," Black Kettle said. "He tore out his hair, and he gashed his face with rocks, and he cried out in anger and in despair. 'I cannot fly like the eagle,' the young man said. 'I cannot run as swiftly as the coyote, nor do I have the strength of the bear. Why am I on earth if I cannot do any of these things?'

"Suddenly, the young man heard a strange-sounding voice, carried on the wind. 'Go to the mountain,' the voice called."

Black Kettle made his voice wail in a terrible sound, and the smaller children were frightened. Some cried, and others clutched the hands of their mothers. The older children were frightened, too, but they welcomed the fright because it made them feel brave to listen to the story without betraying their own fear.

"The young man climbed the mountain," Black Kettle continued. "And as he climbed it, the voice in the wind continued to speak to him. 'You are a worm,' the voice in the wind said. 'You are a blade of grass. You are an ant, a mote of dust. You are nothing. You cannot fly, you cannot run swiftly, you have no strength. Climb to the top of the mountain.'

" 'Why should I climb to the top of the mountain?' the young man asked.

" 'You will know why when you get there,' the voice in the wind answered.

"The young man began to do as he was instructed, but he did so with a heavy heart. He believed that the voice was instructing him to climb to the mountain so he could jump off and kill himself. He was frightened and sad, but he felt that he must do what the voice told him to do."

"And did he climb to the top of the mountain and jump off, Grandfather?"

Black Kettle held up a finger, as if to caution the young questioner against impatience, then he went on with his story. "As the young man climbed, a strange thing happened. The sun beat down upon him, and it made him very hot. As he grew hot, he began to sweat. When he sweat, all the poisonous thoughts passed from his body. He was no longer frightened, or confused, or ashamed. Only reason remained in his body, and with reason, the young man could think quite clearly. It is true, he thought, he could not fly like an eagle, but an eagle could not use his wings as hands. It is true, he could not run as swiftly as a coyote, but a coyote could not walk upright. It is true, he did not have the strength of the bear, but the bear could not make poems and music, or dance to the rhythm of the drums. When the young man reached the top of the mountain, he thought of all this, and he spread his arms wide and looked out over the valley, far below.

" 'Why don't you jump?' a woman's voice asked, and when the young man looked around there he saw Ptesan-win."

"Buffalo Cow Woman!" one of the children said, for Ptesanwin was the most sacred of all the legends of the Kiowa. "What did the young man say to her?"

" 'No,' the young man said. 'I will not jump. I am not a

worm, I am not a blade of grass, I am not an ant or a mote of dust. I am a man! I am sorry if that displeases you, Buffalo Cow Woman, but I know now that I am a man.' "

"Was Buffalo Cow Woman angry?" the impatient youth asked.

Again Black Kettle held up a finger, calling for quiet.

" 'You have not displeased me,' Ptesanwin said. 'Listen to what I say. Do you see that your period of trial is over? Now you have the sacred wisdom, and from this day forth you will be the master over all the animals and over all the things of nature. You shall have a name, and your name shall be called Cheyenne, and your people shall be many, and they will be mighty hunters, and dancers, and drummers, and singers.'

" 'But wait,' the young man called. 'Wait, I have questions to ask. There are many things I do not know. How will I learn what is needed to know to be worthy of the fine name you have given me?'

" 'I have given you not only a name, but the gift of wisdom. It is for you to acquire the way to use it.'

" 'But how shall I do that?'

" 'As you climbed the mountain you were puzzled,' Ptesanwin said. 'But you labored as you climbed, and as you labored, you began to sweat. As you sweat, you gained wisdom. Now, I tell you, when you wish to attain wisdom, you need only to build a sweat lodge and you will sweat out the poisonous thoughts so that only reason remains.'

"And that is why, even today, wise men use the sweat lodge," Black Kettle interjected into his story. Then he continued.

"The young man left the mountain and returned to the valley below. When he returned, he discovered that all the animals had been struck dumb as their punishment for mocking Cheyenne. The animals could no longer speak to him. They could not speak to each other, and every animal had to go for all time after that, unable even to speak to their own kind."

"Is that why men can speak to each other, but animals

cannot speak?'' one of Black Kettle's listeners questioned.

"Yes," Black Kettle said. "For it was intended that men would rule over animals."

"What happened to Cheyenne after that?" another child asked.

"Cheyenne took a wife and had many children, and the children took wives and had many children. I am the child of one of those children, just as you are the children of my children. And thus we are all named for the one who was called Cheyenne."

After Black Kettle finished his story there were others who told stories as well. If the story was to be a tale of bravery in battle, the one who spoke would walk over to the lodge pole and strike it with his coup stick, then everyone would know that he was going to tell a story of an enemy killed in battle. In such stories the enemy warriors were always brave and skilled, because that made the warrior's own exploits all the greater.

Not all stories were of enemies killed in battle. Some were of hunting exploits, and some told of things that had happened in the time of their father's father's father that had been handed down through the generations to be preserved as part of their history.

One of those who spoke little, but of whom many tales were told, was Stone Eagle. A short time earlier, Stone Eagle, who wanted revenge for the massacre at Sand Creek, had lead the chiefs Red Cloud, Dull Knife, Old-Man-Afraid-of-His-Horses, and over one thousand warriors in a war party against the soldiers.

They reached the hills overlooking a bridge across the Cimarron. On the opposite side of the river was a small military stockade, stagecoach station, and telegraph office. The stockade was manned by about one hundred soldiers, and when Stone Eagle tried a frontal attack against the soldiers, he was driven back by cannon fire and by the long-range fire of the soldiers' rifles. As the soldiers were protected by the heavy timbers of the stockade, Stone Eagle was unable to dislodge them, even though he had superior numbers.

Stone Eagle tried a few ploys. He sent ten warriors down toward them to act as decoys, but they were unable to draw out the soldiers. The next morning he sent twenty, and this time the soldiers came out as far as the bridge but would come no farther.

Stone Eagle, Red Cloud, Dull Knife, and Old-Man-Afraid-of-His-Horses held a council during the second night, trying to decide what to do. Dull Knife wanted to take some warriors down in the middle of the night and try to set fire to the stockade, but Stone Eagle insisted that only cowards fought at night. They finally decided that they would try another frontal assault the next day, massing all their numbers.

The next morning, though, before they could launch their attack, they were surprised to see an entire platoon of cavalrymen ride out of the fort, cross the bridge, then head westward at a trot. The soldiers had come out of the fort to provide an escort for an approaching wagon train.

Elated at their good fortune, Stone Eagle mounted all his warriors, and they swarmed down on the wagons and the escorting soldiers.

The soldiers reached the wagons, then, in a classic formation, circled the wagons, and dug in. The soldiers fought bravely, and Stone Eagle's own brother was killed in the first few minutes of fighting. Angered and grieving, Stone Eagle led the Cheyenne into ever-decreasing circles around the wagons, lashing their ponies to make them go faster and faster. Stone Eagle was wearing his medicine bonnet and carrying his sacred shield, so he knew that no bullets would strike him.

As the circle tightened closer to the wagons, the soldiers continued their firing until, finally, all the soldiers were out of ammunition. When the soldiers stopped firing, the Cheyenne charged straight for the wagons and killed all the soldiers. They were very disappointed by what they found in the wagons, though. They had hoped for weapons and ammunition, but there was nothing in the wagons but bedding and mess chests.

When Stone Eagle returned, he told the others in the council that the white men had been taught a lesson and would now obey the treaty they had signed. Stone Eagle believed the whites would no longer come into the no-man's-land that lay south of the Cimarron and north of the Arkansas.

But Stone Eagle's thesis was about to be disproved, for even as the Cheyenne shared stories around the campfire, a small train of six wagons was making up in Larned, Kansas. One of the members of the wagon train party, nineteen-year-old Rachel Stewart, accompanied her mother and Mrs. Wilkerson into the general store. A tiny bell attached to the door announced their entry, and the store owner, a pleasant-looking man wearing a white apron, came toward them, smiling.

"Well, ladies, what can I do for you?" he asked.

"Quite a bit, I hope," Mrs. Stewart answered, taking out a list. "We are six families, and we need provisions to last us for at least six months."

"My, my," the store clerk said, looking at the long list. "You do have quite an order here. Where are you going that you will have to have a six months' supply?"

"Down into the southwestern part of the state," Mrs. Stewart said. "There is land to be had for free there."

The store clerk looked up. "You are with the wagon train that's making up, aren't you?"

"Yes."

"You folks be careful," he said. "I know there's free land down in the Southwest, but the reason so much of it's available is that most folks are afraid to go south of the Cimarron."

"But we have been told that there are no Indians north of the Arkansas."

"No, ma'am, there aren't supposed to be any. But now an' again . . . well, you folks just be careful, that's all."

"I'm sure my husband and the other men will be able to protect us, should any Indians get adventurous," Mrs. Stewart said. "If you would, please, start filling our order. I imagine it's going to take some time to get the entire order together and loaded onto the wagons, and my husband does want to get away as soon as possible. He figures it will take us two weeks to reach our destination, and we want to be there in time to build some shelter before the snow flies."

"Yes, ma'am, I don't blame you for that. We're a good month to six weeks away from our first snow, but the early snows can be quite brutal," the store clerk said. "I'll get right on it."

"Sir?" Rachel said, speaking for the first time. She held up a notebook and a five-cent piece. "I'm taking this notebook with me. Here is the money."

"Do you need pencils?"

"No, thank you," Rachel replied. "I have a supply of pencils."

Leaving her mother and Mrs. Wilkerson in the store to see to the order, Rachel took her notebook outside. Then, finding a place to sit and wait as the wagons were loaded, she began her journal.

THE STEWART FAMILY ODYSSEY
by
Rachel Stewart
6TH OF OCTOBER, 1868

Our train trip from Springfield, Illinois, was quite fascinating. We crossed the great Mississippi River at St. Louis, then came right across the middle of the state of Missouri, often running parallel with the Missouri River. Although St. Louis is quite a large metropolitan area, once you leave the city you find yourself in a magnificent wilderness of trees and hills, too numerous to count.

We were able to travel by train until we reached a place called Fort Larned, Kansas. Here, we were told we would be giving up our comfortable accommodations on the train, so that we may continue the journey in wagons.

I am not looking forward to travel by wagon, but Papa says that in days of old, everyone traveled in this way. And I guess what was good enough for our ancestors will be good enough for us. We have lots of blankets and buffalo robes, so even if it turns very cold before we reach our destination, we should be warm and cozy.

The wagon train had been on the trail for the better part of a week. Although the nights were cool, the days were still warm, and some days, such as this one, were actually hot. As the steel-rimmed wheels rolled across the hard-packed earth, they picked up dirt, causing a rooster tail of dust to stream out behind them. The wood of the wagons was bleached white, and under the sun it gave off a familiar smell. Rachel sat in the sun on the dried seat of the wagon, reading over the latest entry in her journal.

THE STEWART FAMILY ODYSSEY
On the Trail
14TH OF OCTOBER, 1868

Our days begin approximately one hour before dawn. Nearly all are sleeping at this time, and the wagons have been drawn into a circle, for this has proven to be the most convenient method of encampment. We are awakened by whistles and shouts from those who have been standing the last hours of the night watch. Within seconds after being awakened, men and women begin emerging from their night quarters, on board the wagons in some cases, under them in others. It is hard to leave the warmth of our blankets and buffalo robes, but no one is the laggard, for we know we must be to our new homes before winter hits in all its fury.

For those who are tending the cattle that accompany us, the first job is to move the livestock from their night corral, which is inside the circle of wagons. Also included within this herd are the many milk cows that provide us with milk, butter, and cheese. They must be milked, and that is the responsibility of the children.

I help the other women prepare the breakfast meal, which is eaten between the hours of six and seven. During that time, too, the teams are connected to the wagons, the tents are struck, and all is made ready to get under way. We begin our day's journey at the stroke of seven o'clock, when Papa lets out a mighty roar of: "Move 'em out!"

Papa alternates who shall lead and who shall ride at the rear, so that one is not always required to "eat the alkali dust" of the others. And although Papa was voted as wagon master, he takes a turn with the others in bringing up the rear. Today, it is our turn.

Some ride in the wagons, some walk alongside. Papa and Mr. Gibson ride on horseback. We move at a steady pace until noon. At noon we stop for a meal. The teams are cut loose from the wagons to allow them to graze, but they are not unyoked, thus making it easier to get under way again when the meal is over.

By evening, humans and animals are tired. We have been on the move since before dawn, and as the sun is sinking slowly before us, we look for a suitable place to spend the night. Each night we set out guards to watch for Indians, but, though we were cautioned about the savages before we left Larned, we have, so far, seen not so much as one Indian.

Suddenly there was a creaking, snapping sound, and the wagon lurched so badly that Rachel was nearly tossed out. She looked up from her notebook, startled.

"Oh!" she gasped. "What was that?"

"Whoa, horses," Mrs. Stewart called, pulling back on the reins. The team stopped and the wagon sat there, listing sharply to the right.

"Mama, what is it?" Rachel asked. "What is wrong?"

"I think we've broken an axle," Mrs. Stewart said grimly. "Will! Will Stewart!" she called.

The wagons in front of them, unaware that they had stopped, continued on at their same dogged pace and were slowly but surely pulling away.

"They are leaving us," Rachel said.

"Will!" Mrs. Stewart called again, and Rachel added her own voice so that her father, who was on horseback near the first wagon, heard them and looked around.

"Matt!" Will called. "Matt, stop the train!"

Matt Gibson held up his hand, and the wagons stopped. Matt and Will turned then and rode back to the wagon.

"Oh, damn," Will said as he saw the broken axle. "I was afraid of this."

"You were afraid of it?" Matt asked. "You mean you knew of the possibility of breaking an axle, but you came without changing it?"

"I saw that the axle was cracked before we left Larned," Will said. "But I didn't want to spend the money for a new axle. I was hoping it would hold."

"So what are we going to do now?"

"Well, I did pick up a spare axle. It's used, and is cracked nearly as badly as this one was. But at least it isn't completely broken. And if it will last as long as this one did, we will be there before we have any more trouble."

"How long will it take to change it?" Matt asked.

"About half a day," Will said.

Matt took off his hat and ran his hand through his hair, as if in thought. "All right," he said. "We'll hold up here a while."

Jumping Wolf, an ambitious Cheyenne subchief, gave the reins of his pony to another, then climbed to the top of the hill. He knew the warrior's secret of lying down behind the crest of the hill so that he couldn't be seen against the sky-line, so he lay on his stomach, then sneaked up to the top and peered over. There, on the valley floor below him, he saw the six wagons. It was obvious that the whites had no idea they were in danger. It would be easy to count coups against them.

Jumping Wolf smiled, then slithered back down the hill into the ravine, where the others were waiting.

"Did you see them?"

"Yes," Jumping Wolf answered.

"When do we attack?"

"Now," Jumping Wolf replied. He pointed down the ravine. "We will follow the ravine around the side of the hill. We will be upon them before they suspect our presence."

"Can you move that rock, Sarah?" Will asked. His voice was strained because he and Matt were struggling at the end of a long pole. The pole had ben placed under the front part of the wagon, and they had used it like a lever to lift the wagon. Now they were waiting for Sarah to slide a rock under the good part of the axle so they could let the wagon down onto the rock and still have the front of the wagon elevated. That way they could pull off the damaged part and replace it.

"There," Sarah said from beneath the wagon. She was in some danger at this point, because if Will or Matt lost his grip, or if the pole should slip, the wagon would fall on her. "I think I've got it now."

"Slide out from under there now," Will said, and his voice almost cracked under the strain.

Sarah rolled over, then crawled out, and with a mighty sigh of relief, Will and Matt set the wagon down on the rock.

"Whew," Matt said, wiping the sweat from his forehead. "I'm glad that part is over."

"You and me both," Will said. He got down and crawled under the wagon to begin pulling away the broken axle.

Sarah moved closer to watch him. "Do you think—"

Matt held up his hand to stop her. "Listen," he said.

"What is it?" Sarah asked. "I didn't hear anything."

"Listen," Matt said again.

All three were quiet for a moment, with only the sound of the ever-present prairie wind moaning its mournful wail. Then they all heard what Matt had heard, the distant thunder of pounding hooves.

"Get out from under there, Will," Matt said. "We've got company comin', and I don't think it's anyone we want."

The battle was short and violent. Jumping Wolf had nearly twice as many warriors as the total number of people in the small wagon train. Within a short time after the initial attack, the wagons were in flames and men and women were falling, mortally wounded. Rachel's parents were both killed, but she, miraculously, was still untouched. She hid behind a clump of rocks and watched as the Indians galloped, whooping and shouting, through the remains of the wagon train.

Jumping Wolf leaped over the rocks and in and out of gulleys, shouting with joy as he pursued the fight. The men and even the women of the wagon train fired at him, but it was as if he were impervious to their bullets. He leaped upon a burning wagon and looked at his handiwork, chortling in glee as the last white defender was put to the lance. Now that all the men, women, and children of the wagon train were dead, he would go to each of them and touch them with his coup stick. That was because as the leader of this war party, he could count coup not only on those he had killed personally, but on all who were killed. He began singing a victory song.

From her position behind the rock, Rachel saw that one little girl, about five years old, was still alive. The little girl's name was Sue, and Sue got up and started to run.

One of the Indians saw her running and started after her. Leaning down from the side of his horse, he brandished a war club right above Sue's head.

"No, don't! Leave her alone!" Rachel shouted. She jumped up from the rock and started toward the little girl, but the Indian reached her first and smashed her head with one crushing blow of his club.

The little girl fell, then lay on the ground, deathly still and quiet, with her eyes wide open.

"Oh, Sue, no!" Rachel ran to the little girl and cradled her in her arms.

"Child dead," a voice said.

Rachel looked up to see about a dozen Indians around her.

"What are you going to do now?" Rachel asked. Perhaps it was shock, the shock of the attack, of seeing her family killed, and of seeing the little girl clubbed down so senselessly. Whatever it was, it took away all her own fear, so that she asked the question not as a person in hysterics, but almost as a person disinterested in the answer. If they told her they intended to kill her now, at this very moment, it would have meant nothing to her.

The Indians looked at each other in surprise. Never had they heard such a calm-sounding voice from one who was about to die. The fact that it was a woman's voice made it all the more shocking to them. They began speaking to each other in their native language so Rachel could not understand what they were saying.

"She is a woman with powerful medicine. See, how she does not fear to die."

"She fears death," Jumping Wolf said.

"She shows no fear."

"She will show fear of me," Jumping Wolf said. *"When I raise my coup stick to strike her, you will see fear in her eyes."*

"No, I think not. I think Hawk Heart Woman is without fear in her eyes."

"Hawk Heart Woman? You have named her?"

Jumping Wolf did not like the way the conversation was going. He had led the battle, and he had won a great victory. But now this woman, who was his enemy, was being called

Hawk Heart Woman by the warriors. Hawk Heart Woman was a name of respect. If she kept the name of respect, it would take away some of the glory of his victory. He could not let her keep the name. He must shame the name away from her.

"Her medicine is not strong enough to overcome the fear of dying," Jumping Wolf said. *"This I will prove to you. I will raise my war club over her head. If she shows fear, I will kill her. If she shows no fear, I will let her live."*

"She will show no fear," one of the warriors said.

Jumping Wolf raised his war club, and he let out a menacing, bloodcurdling yell.

Rachel was resigned to dying now, and the strange, almost numbing calmness that had come over her before was still present. She was staring into the abyss, and she didn't flinch.

"Show fear, woman," Jumping Wolf said in English. "Show fear, for I am about to kill you!"

The brief instant Jumping Wolf held the war club over her head might have been the only moment remaining between Rachel and eternity. It was a fleeting moment in the lives of those standing there, watching, but it was a lifetime to Rachel, and she was composed to live the rest of her life in dignity.

"Show fear!" Jumping Wolf shouted, and with that shout, Rachel realized that, ironically, the final victory was to be hers. She smiled at the thought.

"Ayiee," one of the warriors said in his own language. *"Look at Hawk Heart Woman, how she smiles in the teeth of death! Surely she has the greatest medicine."*

Jumping Wolf, frustrated by the turn of events, drew his war club back in anger and started to bring it crashing down on Rachel's head, despite his promise to let her live if she showed no fear. But the warrior nearest him grabbed it and wrenched it from his hand.

"No, Jumping Wolf," the warrior said. *"She has bested you. Would you go back on your word now? The woman will live."*

"Arrrghhh!" Jumping Wolf shouted in anger and frustration. Now, not only had his enemy been given a name of respect, but she had bested him and made a fool of him.

"Come," said the one who had taken Jumping Wolf's war club from him. *"Follow me back to the village. We will take Hawk Heart Woman before the council. Perhaps we can learn something of her strong medicine."*

A couple of the Indians took Rachel gently and led her to a horse, then helped her to mount. She realized then that, for some reason, she was going to be allowed to live. What she did not realize was that her action had caused Jumping Wolf to lose command of his war party. And she did not realize what a mortal enemy she had just made.

Six

It was midway through the second day of the patrol, and the column Lieutenant Joseph Murchison was leading was on the beaten trail, moving slowly but steadily. The plains stretched out before them in motionless waves, one after another. As each wave was crested, another was exposed and, beyond that, another still.

The march was a symphony of sound: jangling equipment, squeaking leather, and the dull thud of hoofbeats. Those same hoofbeats stirred up grasshoppers to whir ahead of them in awkward flight. Underneath, the dusty grass gave up a pungent but not unpleasant smell. Murchison took out his watch. Noticing that it was time for another break, he held up his hand.

"Sergeant Quinlin, give the men and horses a short blow," he ordered.

"Yes, sir," Quinlin replied, and he passed the order on to the men, then dismounted.

The soldiers dismounted as well. Some of them stretched out on the ground for a moment, while others walked around to stretch out the kinks of saddle weariness.

Murchison climbed the adjacent hill to scan the horizon. He saw only dusty rocks, shimmering dry grass, and more ranges of hills. He started to drop the glasses when he noticed one outcropping of rock that looked slightly different from the others. He examined it more closely.

"Sergeant Quinlin," he called, "would you come here, please?"

Quinlin ran up the hill so that he was puffing quite audibly by the time he reached his commander. "What is it, sir? What do you see?"

"Have you made this journey before, Sergeant?"

"Yes, sir, several times."

"Then it may be nothing." He handed his field glasses to Quinlin. "But if I'm not mistaken, those are burned-out wagons. Were they here the last time you were here?"

"No, sir, they weren't," Quinlin said. "Nor have they been reported, for if they had been, they would be on the field map in the headquarters."

"That's right, they would be, wouldn't they?" the lieutenant said. Every item of any significance was annotated on the field map—a farmhouse, an abandoned way station, even something as minuscule as a broken wagon wheel.

"Well, we'd better make a note of it so we can—" His words were interrupted by Quinlin.

"Oh, sweet Jesus!" Quinlin exclaimed. He was still looking through the glasses. "Sweet, sweet Jesus!"

"What is it, Quinlin? What do you see?" Joe asked.

Quinlin returned the field glasses. "Bodies, sir. A lot of bodies."

"Let's get the men mounted," Murchison said.

Sergeant Quinlin ran back down the hill. "Mount up, men! We've seen something ahead!"

"What is it, Sergeant?" someone asked, and half a dozen others repeated the question.

"It's something the lieutenant wants to investigate," Quinlin replied without saying anything more. "Now, would you be for getting mounted, please? Or is it a engraved invitation you'll be wantin'?"

Joe reached his own horse, then swung into the saddle, wondering what they would find when they reached the wagon. Would the bodies be swollen and purple? Would they be hacked to pieces? Had the women been abused before they were killed?

"Forward at a trot, Sergeant," Joe ordered.

The column broke into a trot at Sergeant Quinlin's command. Sabers, canteens, mess kits, and rifles jangled under the irregular rhythm of the trotting horses, and dust boiled up behind them. Joe held the trot until they were within one hundred yards of the burned-out wagon.

"At a gallop!" he called, and he stood in his stirrups and drew his saber, pointing it forward. The saber was drawn not as a weapon, but as a signaling device, for a drawn saber meant that carbines should be pulled from the saddle scabbards and held at the ready.

Every nerve in Murchison's body was tingling as the group of soldiers swooped down on the wagon. He was alert to every blade of grass, every rock and stone, every hill and gully. When they reached the last wagon, Joe held up his hand, calling the men to a halt.

"Line of skirmishers, front and rear!" he ordered, and two squads of horse soldiers moved into position.

Lt. Murchison swung down from his horse, and Sergeant Quinlin started to dismount as well.

"No, Sergeant," said Murchison, holding up his hand. "I think one of us should be ready to assume mounted command."

"Very good, sir," Quinlin replied, taking the reins of his commander's horse.

Joe Murchison walked toward two clumps on the ground. As he approached, he could hear the buzzing of flies. He gasped when he got there. It was a man and a woman, lying side by side in the grass. Both bodies were penetrated by several arrows. The woman was still clothed, but the man was stripped naked, and the top of his head was cut away. Brains were spilled onto the ground.

"Sergeant, assign a burial detail," Joe ordered as he walked back to the horses.

"Yes, sir," Quinlin said. He called for half a dozen men, who, moved by morbid curiosity, didn't even protest the order as they took shovels and began to dig the graves.

"Sergeant!" one of the men called. "We found something!"

Sergeant Quinlin went over to see what it was. When he returned a moment later, he was carrying a small, leather-bound notebook.

Lt. Murchison stood there with his hands on his hips, looking out over the killing ground. Had they been able to put up a fight? Was the army not doing all it could do to protect such people?

"You might want to take a look at this, sir," he said. "It appears that one of them was keeping a diary."

Joe Murchison opened the book and read aloud from the front page:

"THE STEWART FAMILY ODYSSEY
by
Rachel Stewart
6TH OF OCTOBER, 1868

"Our train trip from Springfield, Illinois, was quite fascinating. We crossed the great Mississippi River at St. Louis, then came right across the middle of the state of Missouri, often running parallel with the Missouri River. Although St. Louis is quite a large metropolitan area, once you leave the city you find yourself in a magnificent wilderness of trees and hills, too numerous to count."

Joe looked up. "It goes on that way," he said. "I really don't want to read any more of it."

"I don't blame you, sir. 'Tis a painful thing, to be sure. Did the lass happen to make a note of the date of her last entry?" Quinlin asked.

The lieutenant looked down at the journal again. "October fourteenth."

"'Twas only yesterday," Quinlin said sadly.

''If we had been here twenty-four hours earlier, these people would be alive today,'' Joe noted.

''Perhaps, Lieutenant, but we had no way of knowing they were out here. Sure'n they hadn't asked for army escort.''

''I know,'' Joe said. ''But it doesn't make this any easier to accept.'' He took in the field of bodies and burned-out wagons with a sweep of his arm.

''The poor lass,'' Quinlin said, shaking his head.

Murchison sighed, then closed the book. ''Trumpeter, sound to horse. We'll be getting under way again.''

When Lieutenant Murchison and his patrol returned to Fort Hays with word that a wagon train had been attacked and every man, woman, and child had been killed, Custer swore to find and punish those who were responsible. He sent Captain Hamilton and a company of the 7th Cavalry into the field in pursuit of renegades. Joe was glad that Custer had sent Hamilton's company out, because he was a platoon leader in Hamilton's company, and he wanted to be a part of any punitive expedition that would take revenge for the atrocity he had found.

Hamilton's orders from Brevet General George Armstrong Custer were short and to the point.

''Find the Indians who are conducting these depravities and punish them.''

Hank Tyreen was two weeks into his first buffalo hunt. So far it was not going well. He had hired a cutter and skinner, bailing them both out of jail, where they had spent the previous sixty days serving a sentence for drunk and disorderly conduct. They also owed money to the saloonkeeper for damage they had caused during the drunken brawl that had gotten them thrown into jail in the first place. Hank paid that as well.

He did all that because he felt that since he had no experience as a buffalo hunter, he ought to at least have experienced helpers along, and Arnie and Deekus were the only experienced skinner and cutter not already engaged.

Unfortunately for Hank, the two reprobates he had hired were of little help. Whatever knowledge they might once have possessed had been long ago destroyed by their alcoholism. By the third day out, both of them were drunk, and they managed to stay drunk. This, despite the fact that Hank conducted what he thought was a thorough search of the supplies, throwing away every bottle of whiskey he could find. Somehow the two men managed to keep a generous supply hidden from him, and the problem was exacerbated by the fact that the whiskey they were drinking was the cheapest that could be bought. The rotgut was a powerful and foul-tasting substance that didn't just intoxicate the drinker . . . it numbed him.

In a stupor, the two drunks drove the wagon in a halting, jerking fashion across the plains, fighting among themselves when they were sober enough to carry on a conversation. In the meantime, Hank would ride out at a forty-five-degree angle to the right front of their direction of travel . . . describe a large arc around the front, then return to the wagon from the left front in a forty-five-degree angle coming back toward them. It was a sweeping, searching method he had devised during the war, when he would send out scouts to locate the enemy. It worked then, and he had no doubt that it would work now, even though he was looking for buffalo rather than Yankee soldiers. And just as Hank was recalling having used this same tactic in the past to find soldiers, he found just that: soldiers. He stumbled across a cavalry platoon.

"Who in blazes are you?" the lieutenant in charge of the patrol asked, surprised to find a white man wandering around alone.

Hank started to answer the question, but he paused in midsentence. Incredibly, he suddenly realized that this was the same lieutenant who had been in command of the escort detail he had robbed down in Arkansas. It seemed impossible, but he was certain of it.

"Speak up, mister," the lieutenant said when he saw the

expression on Hank's face. "I asked you a question. Who are you, and what are you doing south of the Arkansas River?"

Hank breathed a sigh of relief. It appeared that the lieutenant did not recognize him as the leader of the men who had robbed him.

"I'm sorry, Lieutenant," Hank said. "I'm just a little surprised to see the army out here, that's all."

"*You're* surprised to see *us*?" the lieutenant replied. "What do you think we are, finding you out here where you've no business being?"

"No one said anything to me about not going south of the Arkansas River. Why shouldn't I be here?"

"Well, if you aren't particularly partial to your scalp, no reason at all, I don't guess," the lieutenant said. "What are you, a buffalo hunter?"

Hank smiled. "Yes, well, right now I am more of a hunter than a finder, I'm afraid. This is my first time out, and I have yet to see a buffalo."

"It's probably just as well you haven't, for if you had, surely the Indians would have seen you. You still haven't told me your name."

"I'm sorry. My name is Tyreen. Hank Tyreen." Hank watched the lieutenant's face carefully, but there was no reaction. The lieutenant had either forgotten or had never heard Hank's name in conjunction with the robbery.

"I'm Lieutenant Joe Murchison of Captain Hamilton's troop of the Seventh Cavalry. We are on a two-week scout, out of Fort Hays. Do you have a camp near here, Mr. Tyreen?"

"Yes, about two miles back. My cutter and skinner are there."

"If you don't mind, we'll ride back to your camp with you and round them up. I want you men back on the other side of the river."

"All right," Hank said. "I sure don't have any ambition of running into an Indian war party."

As the patrol started back in the direction of Hank's camp,

Joe turned command over to his sergeant, then moved out of line to ride alongside Hank.

"Mr. Tyreen, I have the strangest sensation that we have met before," Murchison said. Hank looked sideways at him. He knew that the young lieutenant was trying to piece together where they had met, and if he studied it long enough and hard enough, he was likely to come up with it. Hank decided to give him some confusing hints.

"It could be that we have met before," Hank suggested. "I just came up from Texas. Were you down there?" In fact, Hank had not been in Texas for over a year, but he was purposely giving the young officer misinformation.

Joe shook his head. "No, I'm afraid not. I've never been to Texas."

"Well, then maybe we ran across each other during the war," Hank said. "But if that is where we met, my bet is that we were on opposite sides. I was a soldier of the Confederacy, a private in Cobb's Legion." He called himself a private to counter the fact that one of his men had called him "Major" during the robbery.

Again the lieutenant shook his head. "I was too late for the war," he said. "I graduated from West Point the year after the war ended."

"You were lucky," Hank said, and this time he meant what he said. "No man should have to go through what we went through."

"I'm sure that's true, though you can understand that as a professional soldier, I wish I had been able to experience it."

Suddenly Hank stood in his stirrups and looked ahead.

"What is it?"

"I see smoke ahead, Lieutenant," Hank said. He pointed. "And it's coming from just about where my wagons should be."

"At a gallop!" Murchison ordered, and the patrol rode at full speed toward the smoke.

*   *   *

Arnie and Deekus were both dead. Both had been scalped and their bodies filled with arrows. The two wagons were burning, and the teams that had drawn the wagons were gone.

"Are these your men?" Joe asked.

Hank nodded. "Yes, they are. Why so many arrows, do you suppose?" he asked. "Surely it didn't take this many to kill them?"

"The arrows are shot by all the members of the war party, one at a time, so that they could also claim coup against their enemies," Sergeant Quinlin explained.

"Some enemies they were," Hank snorted. "Two old drunks who never hurt anyone but themselves."

"Mr. Tyreen, I think perhaps you should come with us," Joe suggested. "It would be safer for you."

"Thanks, I will," Hank said.

Rachel did not know why she had not been killed. She mounted the horse they brought for her and went with the Indians back to their village, riding hard to keep up with them. The only way she could do it was to block her mind to all thought, merely taking one moment after another to see what would happen next.

When they reached the Indian camp, Rachel saw all the women and the children of the village. They were gathered along the banks of the stream, staring at her with eyes open wide in curiosity and wonder. She vowed to herself that she would show them no more fear than she had shown the one who had raised his war club to her. She might be killed, but she would not die for their pleasure. Of that she was certain.

The Indian who had threatened her with the war club now came up to her and, gruffly, pulled her down from the horse. He and another Indian led her past the crowd and into a tepee, where they pushed her roughly to the ground. Then they spread out her arms and legs and tied them with rawhide thongs to stakes that had been driven into the ground.

One of the Indians left, and the one who stayed behind

was the one who had threatened her before. Rachel knew that he spoke English.

"What is going to happen to me?" she asked.

"You are going to die," Jumping Wolf answered.

"Why must I die?" Rachel asked. "I mean you no harm."

"Do you fear death?" Jumping Wolf asked.

The shock that had allowed Rachel to take her fate so calmly before was now wearing off. Had they killed her immediately, she would have borne up under it. But she had been kept alive, and now she was embracing life with an appetite she hadn't known she possessed.

She wondered how best to preserve her life now. Should she plead for it? Or should she show disdain?

Another Indian stepped into the tepee before Rachel could answer. He was a much older man, and there seemed about him an aura of dignity and authority.

"What is your name?" the older Indian asked.

"My name is Rachel."

"Now your name shall be Hawk Heart Woman."

The other Indian, the one who had wanted to kill her, snorted and said something in disgust, then left the tepee.

"Jumping Wolf does not approve of your name."

"Jumping Wolf? Is that the one who wants to kill me?"

"Yes, but he cannot kill you now, because your medicine is too strong. That is why you have been named Hawk Heart Woman."

"Hawk Heart Woman," Rachel said. "Yes, that is a good name. What is your name?"

"My name is Black Kettle."

"Are you a chief, Black Kettle?"

"Yes," Black Kettle said.

"Then you can tell me why I am a prisoner."

"You are a prisoner because you were not killed. Would you prefer death?"

"I would prefer to be free," she said. "You are a chief. Your people must do what you say. Order them to set me free."

Black Kettle shook his head. "I am a chief only as long as my people listen to me. If I tell them something and they do not want to listen, I will no longer be chief."

"But why would you want to keep me prisoner? I am of no value to anyone."

"I will speak for you at the council," Black Kettle said. "Perhaps they will listen to me."

At that moment there was a commotion outside the tepee as someone began shouting. Black Kettle moved to the door flap and opened it to have a look. A moment later he came back in.

"What is it?" Rachel asked. "What's going on?"

"Soldiers come," Black Kettle said.

"Soldiers are here, now?" Thank God, Rachel thought to herself, maybe they will rescue me.

Black Kettle shook his head. "The soldiers are not in the village, but they have come into our land."

Jumping Wolf, who was now trying to win back the respect he had lost when Hawk Heart Woman bested him, was riding back and forth through the village, exhorting others to follow him for the attack on the soldiers.

"Come, if you are brave and would defend our sacred ground against the invasion of the whites! Come, join me if you are a warrior . . . stay behind if you are a woman or a child!"

Jumping Wolf's defiant challenge did just what he wanted it to do. It goaded others, those who would not have normally come, into joining the war party, simply because to stay home now would be considered cowardly.

Even Stone Eagle, the mightiest warrior of them all, came from his tepee to hear the challenge.

"Ho, Stone Eagle!" Jumping Wolf said, pointing at him. "The soldiers have come into our land. Will you lead us?"

"Yes! We want Stone Eagle!" White Horse shouted, and the others joined in.

Neither Jumping Wolf nor White Horse was jealous of Stone Eagle's popularity, and Jumping Wolf would gladly relinquish his own leadership if Stone Eagle agreed to come.

All knew of Stone Eagle's great success in battle, and it was better to be a follower in a victorious battle than to be the leader in a battle that failed.

"I will come," Stone Eagle said.

The others cheered loudly, but Stone Eagle held up his hand.

"Before I can come, however, I must purify myself."

"Purify yourself?" Jumping Wolf asked. "How have you been defiled?"

"My medicine comes from never allowing anything metal to touch the food I eat," Stone Eagle explained. "This morning I ate some bread. Only after I ate it did I learn that an iron fork was used in cooking it."

"That is bad," Jumping Wolf agreed. "Very well, Stone Eagle, purify yourself. When you have regained your medicine, come join us. I will lead the warriors until you arrive."

Stone Eagle held up his hand and nodded and, by his nod, let the others know that Jumping Wolf's leadership of them had his approval. If it wasn't quite as good as having him lead them, it was at least a war party that was being conducted with his approval and authority.

Within less than ten minutes after being called out, more than five hundred Indians were ready to go, all in war paint and feathers and carrying their best rifles, bows, and lances. When the war party left the camp amid whoops and shouts, there was not one villager whose heart did not swell with pride at such magnificent warriors.

The village was quiet after the warriors rode away. Rachel lay on the ground, listening to the laughter of children at some game and the chatter of women at work. Except for the fact that she could not understand what they were saying, it seemed remarkably like a quiet afternoon in any small town.

The rawhide bindings were beginning to restrict the blood circulation to her hands, and she opened and closed her fingers several times, as if by that action she could pump the blood through. She pulled at them a couple of times, hoping to free herself, but each time she pulled, the bindings got tighter.

The flap of the tepee opened and someone came in. Because of the way she was lying, she couldn't see at first, but she could feel whoever it was standing there, looking down at her.

"Please," she said. "If you are going to stand there and look at me, come around where I can see you."

To her surprise she heard the person moving then, and when she saw him, she gasped. He was much bigger than any Indian she had ever seen. He had broad shoulders and strong chest muscles. He was, she had to admit even under these circumstances, a very handsome man.

"You are Hawk Heart Woman?" the man asked in English.

"My name is Rachel Stewart," she answered.

"You should be proud of the name the people have given you. They do not give away such fine names for no reason."

"I am proud of the name," Rachel said. She didn't want to antagonize them any more, and she feared that a sense of ingratitude with regard to her name would do just that.

The tall Indian squatted beside her, then he took his knife from its buckskin scabbard and cut the rawhide thongs.

"Oh, thank you," Rachel said gratefully. "Thank you very much."

"Do not try to run away," he said.

Rachel sat up and worked the thongs off her wrists and ankles, then began to rub them lightly. "I won't," she promised. "To tell the truth, I don't think I could run even if I tried. All the blood has been cut off."

The Indian continued to stare at her.

"What is your name?" Rachel asked.

"I am called Stone Eagle."

"Stone Eagle. It is a nice name." Again, she was merely making what she hoped would pass for pleasant conversation.

Stone Eagle looked a little surprised. "You do not know of me? You have not heard my name?"

"No," Rachel said. "Should I have? I'm sorry. I'm new to this country. My parents and I . . ." Suddenly she thought of her mother and father lying dead out on the prairie along with the Gibsons, the Wilkersons, and the other three families who made up the little party of travelers. Tears came to her eyes.

"Your mother and father were killed?"

"Yes."

Stone Eagle spat on the ground. "Jumping Wolf would make a name for himself by killing women and children."

"Jumping Wolf? Is he the one who brought me here?"

"Yes."

"He is an evil man," Rachel said. "I know he may be your friend. But he is an evil man."

"Jumping Wolf is not my friend."

"Where is he?" Rachel wasn't all that certain about her status. Since Jumping Wolf had captured her, did he consider her his property? And if so, and he came in now to discover Stone Eagle here, would they fight? The idea of the two Indians fighting over her, possibly to the death, frightened her. Surely the winner of such a battle would want to claim rights she did not want to give.

"Now he leads a war party. He believes that his victory over the women and children of the wagons has made him a warrior chief. But when he fights against the soldiers, I think it will not be so easy for him."

"Before, when I heard all the shouting, then the horses, was that a war party against the soldiers?"

"Yes," Stone Eagle answered. He stood again and looked down at her. Maybe it was her perspective—she was still sitting on the ground—but she wasn't sure if she had ever seen a white man as tall as Stone Eagle. He had to be at least six feet six inches tall. "I will tell woman to bring food," he said.

"Thank you."

Stone Eagle left. Rachel waited for a while, then stepped

outside the tepee and looked around. The village was arranged in a series of circles around a center circle. Women, children, and old men were sitting, talking, walking, working, or playing. There were very few young men in sight, and she decided that nearly every man of fighting age must have ridden out with the war party she had heard leave earlier.

Some distance away, she saw Stone Eagle. Stone Eagle was on his knees with his arms spread out beside him. He was looking right into the sun. She had never seen anyone do anything quite like that, and she stared at him in curiosity.

"Stone Eagle is purifying himself," said an Indian girl, coming up to stand beside her.

"Purifying himself? What do you mean?"

"His medicine was broken because he violated one of his laws. Now, before he can fight again, he must purify himself." The girl was exceptionally articulate.

"And staring into the sun will do that?"

"He is letting the sun look into his heart, to see that it is true. When the sun is satisfied that he harbors no evil, he will be pure and his medicine will be returned to him."

Rachel studied the girl. She looked to be around sixteen. "Who are you?" Rachel asked.

"I am called Running Deer. Here is food for you, and a robe to keep you warm. Stone Eagle asked that I bring these things to you."

"Thank you." Rachel looked at the food, some sort of meat and a type of bread. The bread was hot, and when she picked it up and smelled it, it smelled very good. She took a taste. "Uhmm, this is good," she said.

"It is what the whites call Indian fry bread," Running Deer said. "I think you will like it."

"Oh, I do like it. It is delicious," Rachel said. She realized then that she was much hungrier than she'd thought. "Running Deer, your English is very good."

"I went to the white man's school," Running Deer said. "I attended through the tenth grade. I know English, geography, history, and math. I can diagram sentences, name all the presidents, tell you what crops are grown along the Nile River in Egypt, and compute the area of a circle. But what good is all that for a young girl who lives in an Indian village such as this?'' She took in the village with a wave of her hand.

"I would think you would be pleased to have knowledge for knowledge's sake,'' Rachel said. She eyed a piece of meat.

"It is rabbit,'' Running Deer said.

"I beg your pardon?''

"The meat is rabbit. Don't worry, it is good.''

"Thanks.'' Rachel took a piece of meat, and as she began eating, she looked once more at Stone Eagle. Now he was painting his face, the bottom half yellow, the top half black. His nose was red. "Why is he painting himself like that?'' she asked. "Is that part of the purification as well?''

Running Deer looked over at him, then gasped.

"What is it?''

"Stone Eagle has put on his death face.''

"His death face?''

"He is going after the others, to do battle with the soldiers. He knows he will not come back.''

Seven

Lieutenant Joe Murchison was riding at the head of the patrol, bent low over his mount's neck. The horse's mane and tail were streaming out, its nostrils flared wide as it worked the powerful muscles in its shoulders and haunches. Hank was riding just behind, urging his animal to the fastest possible pace.

The little group of men hit the shallow river in full stride, and sand and silver bubbles flew up in a sheet of spray, sustained by the churning action of the horses' hooves until huge drops began falling back like rain. Joe led the men toward an island in the middle of the river.

"Bugler! Sound the dismount!" Joe shouted as they reached the island.

Raising the instrument to his lips, the bugler played his call, and the galloping column brought their steeds to a halt. In a few cases the halting action was so abrupt that the horses slipped onto their hindquarter haunches in response to the desperate demands their riders made of them.

Lieutenant Murchison leaped from his horse and hurried over to report to Captain Hamilton.

"Sir, there's a large Indian war party on our tail," he said.

"How many?"

"Too many to fight off, Captain!" said one of the soldiers who had been with Joe.

"Better get ready," Hamilton said. "We'll be making our stand here."

"Captain, we can't stay here! We got to skedaddle!" the frightened soldier said.

"First Sergeant!" Hamilton shouted.

"Yes, sir?"

"Shoot any man who tries to run."

"Yes, sir!" replied the first sergeant.

"Quinlin, who are our best marksmen?"

"That'd be me and Corporals McDonald and O'Braugh, sir," Sergeant Quinlin answered.

Hamilton pointed to the neck of the island, which faced the western bank of the river, the direction from which the patrol had just come.

"See if the three of you can squirm down through the tall grass. Take a position as near to the point as you can get, and do as much damage as you can when the Indians start across the water."

"Don't you be worryin' none, Captain. We'll have the heathens floatin' facedown in the river like so many logs. Mickey, Galen, with me!" Quinlin shouted.

"The rest of you men," Hamilton ordered, "dig your-selves in."

"We were ridin' light for the scout, Captain. We left our spades behind," said one of Murchison's men.

"Then use your mess kits, your knives, your fingernails," Hamilton replied. "I don't care how you do it, just do it! We've got about two minutes to get ready for them!"

As the men got on their knees and began digging desperately, Hamilton remained erect, walking back and forth calmly, holding his pistol by his side.

"Now, men, Quinlin, McDonald, and O'Braugh will engage first!" Hamilton shouted his instructions. "But don't be spooked into shooting when you hear them. I want you to hold your fire until I give the word. Hold it until the last possible moment. Then make your shots count!"

"Where do you want me, Captain?" Hank asked.

Hamilton looked at him, then looked at Joe. "You brought him in, Lieutenant. He belongs to you."

"Very good, sir, I'll look after him," Joe replied. He pointed to the buffalo gun Hank was carrying. "You any good with that thing?"

"I haven't used it on a buffalo yet," Hank admitted. "But I'm pretty good with a rifle."

"Good. Take up a position, but don't fire until you are sure you have a good shot."

"Right," Hank said. He looked around for a moment, then saw a large tree that had fallen. He found a position behind it that not only provided cover, but also gave him a place to rest the rifle when he was aiming it.

"Trooper Flynn!" Hamilton called.

"Yo, sir!"

"Are you riding Prince Barney?"

"Aye, sir, I am," Flynn replied.

"Get back to Custer. Tell him where we are. Tell him to send help immediately. We'll hold them off here for as long as we can. If he comes up fast enough, some of us may still be alive."

"Yes, sir," Flynn replied. "Horse holder! Bring up Prince Barney!"

"What's so special about Prince Barney?" Hank asked Joe.

"Prince Barney is the fastest horse in the regiment," Joe explained. "And Flynn is the best rider."

With the cavalry dismounted, every fourth trooper became a horse holder, and one of them now brought Flynn's horse to him. Quickly Flynn put his foot into the stirrup, then swung into the saddle.

"Go with God, lad!" shouted one of the sergeants, slapping Prince Barney on the rump. The other troopers cheered and called out words of encouragement to Flynn as he hit the water on the east side of the island. Hank watched horse and rider gallop away until they crested the embankment, then he turned back to await the Indians.

"I hear them!" one of the soldiers said nervously. His announcement wasn't necessary, however, for by then everyone could hear them. Above the drumming of the hoofbeats came the cries of the warriors themselves, who were yipping and barking and screaming at the top of their lungs.

The Indians crested the bluff just before the river; then, without a pause, they rushed down the hill toward the water, their horses sounding like thunder.

"Remember, men! Hold your fire!" Hamilton shouted. "Hold your fire until I give you the word!"

The Indians stopped just at the water's edge, then, holding their rifles over their heads, began shouting guttural challenges to the soldiers who were dug in on the island.

"Hu ihpeya wicayapo!"

"Huka!"

"Huka hey!"

"Get ready, men," Hamilton said.

The Indians rushed into the water, riding hard across the fifty-yard-wide shallows, whooping, hollering, and gesturing with rifles and lances. Then three warriors pulled ahead of the others, and when they were halfway across the water, Hank heard three distinct shots from the point of the island. The three warriors in front went down.

The remaining Indians crossed the river, then started up the sandy point.

"Fire!" Hamilton shouted.

The troop fired a volley that took out a significant part of the middle of the attacking Indians. Hank fired in concert with the others and saw the Indian he hit go down. Such was the striking power of the heavy bullet he was firing, though, that the Indian didn't merely go down, he was knocked backward from his horse as if someone had taken him off with a club.

The soldiers' devastating volley was effective, for the warriors who survived swerved to the right and left, riding by, rather than over, the soldiers' positions.

The Indians regrouped on the east bank of the river; then

they turned and rode back in a second charge. They were met with another volley as crushing as the first had been. Again, a significant number of the Indians in the middle of the charge went down.

The Cheyenne pulled back to the west bank of the river to regroup, watched anxiously by the men on the island. By now the river was strewn with dead Indians. There were at least fifty or sixty of them, lying facedown in the shallow water as the current parted around them.

"First Sergeant!" Hamilton called. "Get a count of our casualties!"

"Four killed, sir, and six wounded. Lieutenant Becker's wound is the worst."

Even as the first sergeant gave his report, Hank saw that Captain Hamilton was wounded as well, for his right thigh was red with blood.

"How badly wounded are you, Fred?" Hamilton called over to his second in command.

"I fear it is my death wound, Captain," Becker replied. He collapsed, and Lieutenant Murchison hurried over to him.

"Hang on, Fred," Joe said. "We're going to get out of here. We'll be tossing down a drink in a few days, telling tall tales about this fight."

Becker smiled wanly. "My next drink will be at Fiddler's Green," he said. "I'll see you there, Joe." He took a couple of racking breaths.

"Doc! Doc!" Joe called anxiously.

"Ain't no sense in callin' the surgeon, Lieutenant," the first sergeant said laconically. He spat out a wad of tobacco. "He's dead. He was one of the first ones to get it."

"Lieutenant Murchison," Hamilton said, "you are now second in command, sir. Make certain everyone has enough ammunition. If necessary, redistribute the ammunition from those who are dead or too badly wounded to fight."

"Yes, sir," Joe answered, and he left to go about his assignment, stopping at every position to talk to the defending soldiers, one man at a time.

Hank had bought a pair of binoculars to help him hunt for buffalo, and now he raised them to look across the water. He saw one Indian who was much bigger than the rest, riding back and forth in front of the others. The big Indian had painted the top half of his face black from just below the eyes up. His nose was red, and the bottom half of his face was yellow. He was holding a rifle over his head and shouting.

"Captain, somebody seems to be stirring them up," Hank said.

Captain Hamilton was also wearing binoculars on a strap around his neck, and now he raised them to take a look.

"It's Stone Eagle," Hamilton said.

"Cap'n, you sure it's Stone Eagle?" asked the first sergeant.

"Bigger'n hell and twice as ugly," Hamilton said. He handed his binoculars to the first sergeant. "See for yourself."

"Who is Stone Eagle?" Hank asked.

"He's the meanest and the smartest warrior they've got," Hamilton said. He looked again at Hank's rifle. It was a Sharps, fifty-caliber, with a barrel much longer than that of any of the other rifles on the island. The bullet it fired was also much bigger and heavier than the bullets used by the Henry repeaters of the soldiers.

"Mr. Tyreen," Hamilton said. He nodded toward the rifle. "I'm going to give you an important job to do."

"All right," Hank replied.

"Next time those heathens come at us, I want you to make a special effort to shoot that big son of a bitch. Take your time, get a good shot. But you need to kill him."

"All right," Hank answered.

"Cap'n," the first sergeant said, lowering the binoculars, "looks like they're fixin' to come at us again."

"All right, men! Get ready! They're comin' back!" Hamilton shouted.

Murchison came running back then, having physically checked all the other positions.

"The ammunition is redistributed, Captain," he said crisply.

"Take a position, Lieutenant," Hamilton said. "And keep your head down. I can't afford to lose any more officers."

Unlike the Whitworth Hank had used for the marksmanship contest, the Sharps was a breach-loading weapon, taking a one-piece cartridge. Hank slid the three-inch-long bullet into the breach, then got down behind the fallen tree and rested the barrel on the log. He thumbed back the hammer, then sighted down the long barrel.

With the big Indian in the lead, the Cheyenne started another attack.

The Indians came again, their horses leaping over the bodies of the warriors and horses who had fallen before. Hank waited for a good shot, but the big Indian was smart. Bending low, he managed to keep most of the horse between himself and Hank, so that Hank couldn't get a clear shot. Hank fired once but missed. Quickly he reloaded, then looked for another opportunity.

Stone Eagle must've sensed one of the three sharpshooters Captain Hamilton had sent down to the point of the island, because he suddenly sat upright on his horse and looked in that direction. When he did so, it gave Hank the opening he was looking for, and he squeezed the trigger. His bullet hit Stone Eagle just above the right ear, then exited through the top of his head. Hank saw the brain, blood, and bone detritus erupt from the top of Stone Eagle's head. The big Indian dropped his rifle as he pitched back off his horse.

When they saw their leader go down, the other Indians milled about for a moment, uncertain as to what they should do. One or two started forward, but it wasn't a concerted charge, and like Stone Eagle before them, they were shot down.

By now more than a hundred Indians lay dead on both banks of the river, in the water, and on the sandy beaches of the island. But the Indians had extracted their toll as well, for the number of wounded troopers had increased to thirteen including Captain Hamilton, and there were now six killed, including Lieutenant Becker.

The Indians did not make another charge against the island. Instead they crossed over in considerable numbers, both upstream and down, so they could occupy positions in the surrounding bluffs on both sides of the river. In this way they were able to keep Captain Hamilton and his troop effectively trapped on the island. Hank knew that their survival depended upon whether or not Trooper Flynn managed to get through to carry word of their plight back to Custer. If Flynn made it, Custer would no doubt be able to effect a rescue by nightfall. But if Flynn didn't make it, if he had been caught and killed by the Indians, it would be only a matter of time until every man on the island would suffer the same fate.

There was sporadic firing throughout the rest of the day as the soldiers on the island and the Indians on the bluffs continued to exchange shots. After sunset that evening, Hank counted more than two dozen campfires scattered about on both sides of the river. He and the others on the island listened as the warriors banged their drums and shook their rattles and bells. They could also hear the others singing their death songs and war chants.

As the soldiers looked anxiously out into the night, their subdued conversation echoed down the line:

"Did Flynn get through?"

"Sure he got through. He was on the fastest horse in the regiment, and in the entire U.S. Cavalry, too, I'm thinkin'."

"But he had a long way to go, and Prince Barney was tired. And there were a lot of Indians out today."

"Don't you be worryin' none about Flynn. You ever see that boy ride? Why, he can get more out of a jackass than most men can from a Thoroughbred."

"Yeah? Well, where's Custer? He shoulda been here by now."

"He'll be here."

*   *   *

"Do you have any food with you, Mr. Tyreen?" Joe Murchison asked.

"Why don't you call me Hank?"

"All right, Hank. Do you have any food with you?"

Hank shook his head. "No. All my supplies were in the wagon that was burned."

"'I figured as much. You can have Fred's ration. He won't be needing it." He handed a little leather haversack to Hank.

"Thanks." Opening it, Hank saw some dry beans, jerky, and hardtack. He pulled out a piece of jerky and took a bite. "Were you and Becker pretty close friends?"

"I was as close to him as anyone, I suppose. He was a little older than I am, and he fought in the war. I learned a lot from him."

"What about Hamilton?" Hank asked as he chewed on the jerky. "Was he in the war, too?"

"He sure was. He was a brevet brigadier general."

"A brigadier general? Well, what do you know," Hank said.

From somewhere out in the dark there came a long, bloodcurdling yell. Hank had never heard anything quite like it, and he jumped. "What in the hell was that?" he asked.

Joe chuckled. "You've not fought many Indians, have you, Hank?"

"I've never fought any Indians at all before today," Hank answered.

"Well, that's just something they like to do at night. As a matter of fact, they'll be doing it all night long. I don't think it means anything, really. They just do it to keep their enemies unnerved."

"Yeah, well, if they're wantin' to keep me unnerved, they're doin' a pretty good job of it," Hank confessed.

Joe laughed. "Don't let it get to you. That's just what they want."

"I'll try not to," Hank said.

"Lieutenant," Hamilton called, "would you come here, please?"

Joe hurried over to answer his wounded commander's summons. Though he wasn't called, Hank went as well.

"I want you to cut this bullet out of my thigh," Hamilton said, looking up at the two men as they arrived.

Joe looked at the ugly jagged wound, then blanched. "Captain, I'm not very good at that sort of thing," he said. "That wound is awfully close to a main artery. If the knife slipped and I cut it, you could bleed to death."

"I'd rather bleed to death than die of gangrene," Hamilton said. "Which is exactly what I'm going to do if I don't get that son of a bitch out of there."

"Please, Captain, see if you can find someone else, someone better with his hands than I am." Joe held his hands out in front of him. "I'm all thumbs. I can't even darn socks."

"Anyone?" Hamilton called. "Is there anyone here who will come cut this bullet out of me? Come on, boys! Haven't you ever wanted to carve around on your commanding officer?" he asked, trying to make a joke out of it.

No one volunteered.

"Son of a bitch!" he swore. "Son of a bitch! I can't believe that none of you are willing to help."

"General Johnston," Hank said.

Both Lieutenant Murchison and Captain Hamilton looked at him. "I beg your pardon?" Hamilton said.

"I was just thinking of General Albert Sidney Johnston," Hank said. "He was wounded at Shiloh, a leg wound, not much different from your own. He tried to get someone to help him, but everyone was afraid they would only make it worse, so no one did."

"What happened to him?" asked one of the nearby enlisted men.

"I'll tell you what happened to him," Hamilton said. "He died."

"He died?"

"He bled to death," Hank said.

"Mr. Tyreen, unless I miss my guess, you are telling that story from firsthand knowledge," Hamilton said.

"I was there, yes, sir."

"Wearing gray?"

"Yes, sir."

"I was there as well."

Hank sighed. "I'll take the bullet out for you."

"Bless you, sir."

"I don't suppose you have any laudanum?"

"Not a drop."

"Whiskey?"

Hamilton shook his head. "If we did have, I wouldn't drink any of it. I intend to keep a clear head for as long as I can."

"I'll need some to pour on the wound," Hank said.

"If you're needin' a wee bit o' the creature, lad, you might be for tryin' this," said one of the sergeants, handing Hank his canteen.

"Sergeant O'Connor, you have whiskey in that canteen?" Hamilton asked accusingly.

"Aye, Cap'n, but 'tis only a wee drop . . . for emergencies such as this, you understand," O'Connor said. He held up his hand. "Myself, I never touch the stuff."

O'Connor, who was one of the biggest tipplers in the troop, drew a laugh from the others at his declaration of innocence, and even Hamilton joined in. The humor was a welcome respite under the circumstances.

"Well I'm glad you've come so prepared," Hamilton said.

Hank poured some whiskey over the wound, washing away the blood and exposing the ugly black hole where the bullet had entered the flesh.

"Does anyone have a razor? A really good, sharp razor?"

"I have one in my saddlebags," Hamilton said. "Joe, would you get it?"

"Yes, sir," Joe replied, hurrying over to Hamilton's saddlebags. He returned a moment later with a bone-handled straight razor, which he gave to Hank.

Hank thumbed open the blade, tested its sharpness with his thumb, then poured whiskey over its edge.

"Nice razor," he said as he prepared to make the incision.

"My father gave it to me as a gift when I entered the Point. It keeps a very fine edge."

Hank picked up a good-size stick and handed it to Captain Hamilton.

"What's that for?" Hamilton asked.

"Bite down on it," Hank said.

"Oh. Yeah," Hamilton said. He put the stick in his mouth and waited.

"Joe, First Sergeant, hold open the wound," Hank said, showing what he wanted them to do.

The two men put their hands on each side of the wound, then began stretching it open. One of the others held a burning brand aloft so Hank could see what he was doing. Carefully he carved away the flesh until he'd located the bullet. Then, using the curved thumb hook that opened the blade, he got beneath the bullet and pried it out.

"Uhn," Hamilton grunted as he spat out the stick. "That wasn't all that bad."

"This is going to be worse, I'm afraid," Hank said.

"What?" Hamilton asked anxiously.

"First Sergeant, open up about three bullets and pour the gunpowder onto the wound."

"What are you going to do?" Joe asked.

"Cauterize the wound," Hank said. "We've got to get it closed or he still might get gangrene."

The first sergeant did as he was directed, and a moment later Hank ignited the little pile of gunpowder. It made a big flash and Hamilton cried out, then bit the cry off. There was the smell of burnt powder and seared flesh.

"Are you all right, Captain?" Hank asked.

"Yes," Hamilton replied in a strained voice. "Yes, thank you, Mr. Tyreen."

Hank nodded, then walked over to sit under a tree. He took out his pipe, filled it with tobacco, then lit it and was puffing contentedly when Joe came over to join him. He was carrying two tin cups, and he handed one to Hank.

"I prevailed upon Sergeant O'Connor for 'a bit o' the creature,' as he calls it," Joe said.

Laughing, Hank thanked him and took the proffered cup.

"Why did you tell me you were a private?" Joe asked.

"I beg your pardon?"

"Earlier, you said you were a private in the Confederate Army. You weren't a private."

"What makes you think that?"

"The way you've handled yourself here. And the easy way you gave orders to the first sergeant, even to me. You were an officer, weren't you?"

"Well, maybe I was."

"Why didn't you say so?"

"I wasn't sure how it would be accepted," Hank said. "Here I am, on an island with a lot of soldiers, and most soldiers don't like officers anyway, let alone an officer that wore gray."

"You'd be surprised at how many of these men wore gray," Joe said. "What was your rank?"

Hank started to tell him, then again recalled the scene on the road when he robbed the coach Lieutenant Murchison was guarding. One of his men had called him "Major," and Joe had picked up on it.

"Well, you know how the Confederate Army worked, don't you, Joe? We were all colonels," he said with a laugh.

★ ★ ★

Eight

When midnight came and there was still no Custer, even the most optimistic of the troopers began to lose hope. Hamilton was still conscious, but he was unable to move around much, so Joe and Hank went around checking on all the men as they improved their defensive positions, digging deeper and more effective rifle pits.

Hank congratulated one group on the job they had done during the day just passed, building up their confidence for the day to come.

"Listen to the heathens singin' over there," O'Connor said, squirting out a stream of tobacco juice. "Sure'n they'll be back tomorra, I expect, thick as they was today."

Hank smiled. "I'm sure you are right," he said. "But when they do come, we'll trade them thirty Indians for one trooper, just like we did today. Another day like today and they'll turn tail and run. Then, Custer or no Custer, we can just leave this place and go home."

While Hank was seeing to the men in their defensive positions, Joe was checking on the wounded. There was still a lot of fight left in most of them, but a couple of the more grievously wounded were barely clinging to life.

"How are the men?" Joe asked.

"Their spirits are good," Hank replied. "I told them to

pair off in sleeping partners, so one could sleep while the other stays awake.''

"Probably a good idea," Joe replied. "But Lo doesn't attack much at night."

"Lo?"

Joe chuckled. "It's a name we have for the Indians," he explained. "It comes from a poem, 'Lo, the Noble Red-skin.' "

Hank laughed as well. "Leave it to the cavalry to make a joke of it," he said. He filled his pipe again and offered some tobacco to Joe, who declined. "Joe, there was something Becker said just before he died that puzzled me."

"What was that?"

"Something about Fiddler's Green?"

Joe laughed. "You mean the Confederate Cavalry didn't know about Fiddler's Green?"

"We weren't regulars," Hank replied.

Joe nodded. "That may be true, but by God, you fellas could fight."

"I thought you weren't in the war."

"I wasn't. But I studied tactics at West Point, and nearly every example of the classic use of cavalry tactics was a Southern unit."

"Fiddler's Green?" Hank asked.

"It's the hereafter for the cavalryman," Joe explained. "Every officer and man who has ever heard 'Boots and Saddles' blown will wind up in Fiddler's Green after he dies. It's a spot halfway between heaven and hell. It's a glen, under some shade trees, alongside a meandering creek. We're all going to meet there, spend a few centuries drinking, singing, and spinning yarns. Then we're going to mount up and ride into heaven, kicking the devil in the ass if he tries to take any of our boys to the wrong place."

Hank laughed. "Sounds fine to me."

"It's an old cavalryman's myth, I admit," Joe said. "But you'd be surprised at the comfort the men take from such a thought. And if there is a hereafter like we're taught . . . who is to say that cavalrymen couldn't gather in a place they call Fiddler's Green if they want to?''

''I wouldn't want to be the one to try to stop them,'' Hank said. He smiled. ''I've run up against the U.S. Cavalry a few times before.''

From both sides of the river the incessant drumming and singing continued until after two in the morning. Finally the fearsome cacophony stopped, the last fire winked out, and for the last few hours before dawn all was quiet save for the gentle lapping of the river and the soft sigh of wind in the trees.

During the night, unobserved and unheard by the soldiers defending the island, the Indians moved out into the river and up and down the banks, to recover their dead. Even those Indians who had been killed at the edge of the island itself were recovered, so that when Captain Hamilton's company awoke the next morning, they had no visible sign of the havoc thay had wreaked against the Indians in the previous day's battle.

The Indians did not attack the next day, though they let it be known that they were still there. Sometimes they did this by long-range sniping. None of the bullets fired by the Indians found their mark. Occasionally, though, a dozen or so Indians would launch arrows in a high, parabolic arc, and they would come zipping down from above, silent and unexpected. Two soldiers were wounded in this way, and one horse was killed.

Sometimes one or two warriors, perhaps in a show of personal bravery, would ride, whooping and shouting, toward the island. Most of the time they would come only as far as midstream, where they would stop, shout what were undoubtedly insults, then turn and gallop back to the safety of their own lines.

The first couple to try it were shot at, without success. Captain Hamilton, realizing that the Indians were just showing off, ordered his men not to fire at the individual rushes anymore. He didn't know how much longer they would have to hold out, and ammunition, though not yet in critically short supply, was also not renewable.

Ironically, when the soldiers stopped firing, the individual Indian rushes also stopped. Without the danger, there was also no personal glory and thus no incentive for any of the Indians to do it.

As dusk approached on the second night, Hank heard music . . . not Indian singing, but martial music. It was the regimental band playing "Garryowen."

Captain Hamilton, who had been sleeping fitfully nearby, was awakened by the music, and he sat up. He listened for a moment, then a broad smile spread across his face.

"Listen, men! Listen!" he shouted joyfully. " 'Tis our own song, 'Garryowen'! The regiment is here!"

Very soon after the opening bars of music came the crash of gunfire. Then, bursting out of the dusk's blue shadows, came the 7th Cavalry regiment, more than six hundred strong, yelling at the top of their voices and firing carbines and revolvers. The Indians were caught by surprise, and those who weren't killed in the initial engagement made a mad dash into the surrounding hills.

Hank saw a buckskin-clad officer crossing the river in front of the troops, his big horse kicking up spray as it came toward the island.

"Is that Custer?" Hank asked.

"That is General Custer," Joe replied, smiling happily. "He does make a grand entrance, doesn't he?"

"Benteen!" Custer shouted to one of his officers. "Chase them down! Kill as many as you can."

"Yes, sir!"

As the regiment swept on by, led by the officer Custer had called Benteen, Custer dismounted in front of Joe and Hank.

"Where is Captain Hamilton?" Custer asked.

"I'm here, General," Hamilton answered, hobbling out to see him, supporting himself with a large staff someone had cut for him.

"Good for you, Captain, you are still alive," Custer said. "What is your report?"

"Thirteen wounded and eight dead. All present and accounted for, sir," Hamilton said, rendering a hand salute.

Custer returned the salute. "You did an excellent job here, Captain, holding off forces far superior in numbers to your own."

"General, our doctor was killed, and some of our men require immediate aid," Hamilton said.

"Surgeon! See to the wounded!" Custer ordered.

"Yes, sir!" replied the regimental surgeon, although he had already started about his task.

"Did Trooper Flynn get through to you, General?" Hamilton asked.

"Yes, he did. Good man, your Flynn," Custer replied.

"Yes, sir, he is. He saved our lives, that's for certain." Hamilton chuckled. "No angels' chorus could have sounded sweeter than our own regimental band playing 'Garryowen' when you arrived. O'Connor?" he shouted.

"Aye, sir?" the sergeant answered.

"If you've a bit o' the creature left," he said, imitating O'Connor's Irish brogue, "I'll be havin' a drop now."

"Aye, sir, I've some left, and 'tis proud I would be to be sharin' it with you."

Back in the Indian village, Rachel was awakened by loud cries and wails. She had never heard such a sound, and, frightened, she moved to the flap of the tepee and lifted it to look out toward the circle. She could see men on horses and men on foot, moving back and forth, backlit by the several campfires that were burning brightly.

For a moment she had no idea what they were doing, then she realized they were carrying something.

Bodies! They were carrying bodies and putting them down in the light of the fire. As each new body was put down, there would be another wailing outburst. The wailing was crying, and Rachel didn't need to understand the language to know that they were crying for their dead.

In addition to the dead, there were several who were badly wounded, and they were helped off the travois and supported as they shuffled slowly, painfully, into the tepees, where their women began tending to them.

One body lay apart from the others. Stone Eagle's giant frame lay near one of the fires. Oddly, no women were crying over his body, though several walked over to it and stood, silently, for a moment or two, looking down at it.

The activity awakened the entire village, and Rachel saw Running Deer. She walked out to stand by the young Indian girl.

"The soldiers fought well," Running Deer said. "They killed many of our warriors."

"I see that Stone Eagle was one of them," Rachel said.

"Yes. He was a great warrior, but his magic was broken."

"I don't understand," Rachel said. "He knew his magic was broken before he left. He painted on what you said was his death face. That means he knew he was going to die, but he went anyway."

"Yes."

"Why?"

"Because he was a warrior."

Rachel started to ask about Jumping Wolf, hoping against hope that he would be one of the dead. Before she could ask the question, however, she saw him, standing in the shadows just outside a golden bubble of light cast from one of the campfires. Two men were standing with him, and he was nodding as they were talking.

"This was Jumping Wolf's war party," Rachel said. "Perhaps he will be disgraced now."

Running Deer shook her head. "No. When Stone Eagle arrived, he became their leader. It is he who bears the disgrace of the defeat, not Jumping Wolf."

When Hank left the island they were now calling Becker's Island, he rode all the way to Fort Hays, Kansas, with the men of the 7th Cavalry. Shortly after he reached Fort Hays, he was put on the payroll of the U.S. Army as a scout. He had been recommended for the job by Lieutenant Murchison, the recommendation heartily seconded by Captain Hamilton and endorsed by Lieutenant Colonel Custer.

As Joe explained to Hank, Custer's endorsement was all that was actually needed. General Nelson Miles was the post commandant, and Colonel Smith was the commanding officer of the 7th Cavalry, but the 7th's tactical commander, the officer who went into the field with the soldiers, was Lieutenant Colonel George A. Custer.

"And Custer is the one who actually makes all the decisions," Joe said. "The other two, General Miles and Colonel Smith, go along with anything Custer says."

Being an army scout was not exactly what Hank had in mind for himself, but it couldn't have come at a better time. He had spent nearly all his money in outfitting his buffalo-hunting expedition. And what he hadn't spent on supplies, he had spent on fines and damages to get Arnie and Deekus out of jail. When the Indians burned his outfit, it left Hank broke.

"One hundred dollars a month and found," Joe said. "That's more than any of the EM are getting."

"One hundred dollars a month is fine," Hank replied. At this rate he figured that within six months, maybe less if the cards ran well for him, he would have enough money to re-outfit himself for buffalo hunting again. And this time he would have come by the money honestly.

Deep inside, a part of him thought that losing all his money from the first outfit was divine retribution. He had stolen that money. Nothing good could have come of it. Anything he accomplished now would be of more value . . . at least to himself.

As a scout for the 7th Cavalry, Hank Tyreen had all the privileges of an officer. This enabled him to take quarters in the bachelor officers' quarters, or BOQ.

Most of the other scouts declined the offer, preferring to take a room in Hays City, there to be closer to the saloons and whores. But Hank was trying to save money, and if that meant living in the BOQ for free, then he would do so. He was also authorized to take his meals in the officers' mess.

The officers' mess was a new experience for Hank. Although he had been an officer in the Confederate Army for the duration of the war, never had the situation presented itself to allow the niceties of an officers' mess. The officers, like the men, took their food when and where they could find it.

Captain Tom Custer, General Custer's younger brother, was a bachelor and thus took most of his meals in the mess. Tom was totally dedicated to his brother and was a courageous officer in the field, but like so many officers who served in the army, he tended to have a problem with alcohol.

Tom Custer had won two Medals of Honor during the war. He had also been appointed a brevet colonel during that time, so that when someone spoke of "Colonel" Custer, Hank had to listen closely to know which Custer they were talking about.

The Union Army had given temporary, or "brevet," ranks to many of its officers during the war. After the war most of the brevet officers returned to their permanent rank. Their authority and responsibility was commensurate with their permanent rank, though socially it was correct to refer to them by their brevet rank. Thus, Lieutenant Colonel George Custer was sometimes called Colonel and sometimes called General. Captain Tom Custer was sometimes called Captain and sometimes called Colonel. It could get very confusing at the dinner table.

"Mr. Tyreen," said Joe Murchison, "you are sharing the dinner table tonight with a most distinguished individual."

"Oh?" Hank said, looking at the other diners. "Well, looking at this august crew, I would say I am in distinguished company, period."

Captain Hamilton, who was still recovering from his wound, laughed. "Tactfully put, sir, tactfully put."

Joe laughed as well. "That's true, I would never slight

any of these gentlemen. But the officer to whom I refer is Captain Tom Custer. His brother may be the tactical commander of the Seventh Cavalry, and it is General Custer who garners the headlines, but General Custer never won the Medal of Honor. Captain Custer, on the other hand, is one of only two men to have won the medal twice during the late war. He captured a Rebel battle flag at Namozine Church and a second flag at Saylor Creek.''

"Here, here," Captain Hamilton said. He lifted his glass. "Gentlemen, I propose a toast to the hero of our mess."

The others lifted their glasses as well.

"Tell us about it, Tom," suggested Major Elliot.

"There isn't much to tell, really," Tom demurred. "I was young, and my blood was up. On April second, 1865, at Namozine Church, I made a dash into the Confederate lines, grabbed their battle flag, then beat it back to my own lines. Then, four days later, on the sixth, I did the same thing at Saylor Creek."

"You are too modest, Captain," Hank said. "At Saylor Creek, what you did was leap your horse over the breastworks, then dash through the lines and grab the flag away from the startled flag bearer. For this you were shot, and with blood streaming down your face, and while bullets were whizzing past you, you made it back to your own lines with the flag firmly grasped in your hand."

The others at the table looked at Hank in curiosity.

"You have read of my deed, sir?" Tom Custer asked in surprise.

Hank smiled. "No, sir. Until this moment, I never knew who that brave officer was."

Tom nodded. "Then you were there?"

"I was."

"And you witnessed this deed?" Joe asked.

"I did." Hank looked across the table toward Tom Custer. "Captain Custer, I am the one who shot you."

Tom put his hand up to the scar on his face. "I'll be damned," he said.

"I've often wondered if the brave fool I shot that day lived or died."

At the word "fool," several around the table gasped, but Tom held up his hand to quiet them. "No," he said, smiling. "I *was* a fool to do what I did."

"And very brave," Hank added. "How did you survive the wound?"

"The bullet smashed my right cheek, then passed out behind my ear. Had it been one-eighth of an inch to the left, it would have penetrated my brain, killing me instantly." As Tom described the wound, he raised his hand to his cheek and, using his finger, traced the path of the bullet for them.

"As I sit here today, sir, I can truly say that I am glad my aim was off by one-eighth of an inch. And I hope you hold me no malice."

"Malice? On the contrary, sir!" Custer replied. "It is not often one gets the opportunity to meet an enemy with whom one had direct personal contact, and greet that enemy as a friend."

"Here, here," Hamilton said, and as Custer held out his hand across the table to shake hands with Hank, everyone in the mess applauded.

"And now, gentlemen, another toast," Major Elliot proposed. "To our absent comrades at Fiddler's Green."

"To absent comrades," the others answered as one, and all the glasses were raised in salute, including that of Hank Tyreen, former major in the Confederate Cavalry.

Back in the Indian village, Running Deer proved to be a very valuable friend and ally to the white woman the Indians called Hawk Heart Woman. Running Deer brought several things to Rachel, such as knives, cooking kettles, water jugs, eating bowls, and spoons, to allow her to set up housekeeping. This was particularly important to Rachel, as thus far she had been totally dependent upon the generosity of others for every meal. And though she still had no way of obtaining her own food, at least now she had a way of preparing it.

She also learned that she need not worry about obtaining her own food, for the men of the village, when returning from a hunt, would always leave a portion of their game with her. At first Rachel thought they were singling her out, but Running Deer explained that all women who lived alone were treated the same way.

"If a woman has no man to do for her, all the men of the village adopt her as a grandmother, aunt, or little sister," Running Deer said. "That is why they have brought you game, berries, corn, and flour."

"What a wonderful thing to do," Rachel replied.

It wasn't only cooking utensils Rachel needed. Within a week she felt a need to change clothes, for the dress she was wearing was the same one she'd had on when she was captured. None of her clothes had survived the burning of the wagons, though, so she feared she was stuck with the situation.

Again Running Deer came to the rescue by bringing her a couple of dresses made from deerskin. They were wonderfully soft and prettily decorated with porcupine quills and bright blue beads. There was nothing to wear under the dresses, and at first she was keenly aware of that fact. But she knew that none of the Indian women were wearing underwear, either, and after a couple of days she stopped thinking about it.

Running Deer helped Rachel make a soft bed of stretched skin and fragrant grasses, and as they worked together, they began to develop a genuine friendship.

"Did you live with the white man when you were going to school?" Rachel asked as she and Running Deer worked on the bed.

"No," Running Deer replied. "I went to the mission school in Tahlequah."

"Then you've never been out among the whites?"

"No."

"Do you wish you had?"

"I like living here, with the people," Running Deer replied. Rachel knew now that when the Cheyenne used the words "the people," they were talking about themselves. "But there are things I would like to see."

"What would you like to see?"

"I have read that in the tall buildings of the big cities, there are little rooms that you can step into, and those rooms will rise, taking you to the top of the building."

For a moment Rachel had to think of what Running Deer was saying, then she laughed out loud. "You mean elevators," she said. "Yes, the tall buildings in the big cities do have elevators."

"And in these same cities you can turn a valve and have light, for the gas is piped in."

"Yes, and in some buildings, water is piped in as well," Rachel answered.

"Have you seen these things?"

"Yes, when I visited my aunt and uncle in Chicago."

"I am puzzled," Running Deer said.

"What has you puzzled?"

"With so many wonderful things for the white man to see and enjoy, why must he come to our land?"

"I can tell you why I came," Rachel replied. "Or, at least, I can tell you why my parents came. It was for free farmland."

"The land was free because it was taken from our people," Running Deer said.

For the first time since leaving Illinois, Rachel began to think about things from the Indians' point of view. She still could not forgive them for the savage murder of her family and friends. But she was beginning to see that they did have a side in the dispute.

Two days later a white man arrived in the village. There was a lot of commotion over his sudden appearance, but it was quickly obvious to Rachel that his presence was welcome. At first she didn't realize that he *was* a white man, for in the buckskins he looked more Indian than white. But he had long hair and a beard, something she had not seen on an Indian, and the hair was red.

"Oh, sir, you are white!" she said when she approached him.

The man, who looked to be in his late sixties or early seventies, stroked his beard as he looked at her. "You must be the one they are calling Hawk Heart Woman."

"Yes," Rachel said. "You have heard of me?"

The man chuckled. "You are the talk of all the Indians around here. They say you made a fool out of Jumping Wolf."

"I . . . I didn't intend to," Rachel said. "It just happened that way."

"Don't apologize, miss," the man said. "Among the Indians, apology is a sign of weakness. And the only thing that's keeping you alive right now . . . or from warming some warrior's robes . . . is your medicine . . . your strength. Do you understand what I'm saying?"

"I think so."

"See that you remember it. It is the most important thing in your life right now. Never show weakness, never show fear. As long as they refer to you as Hawk Heart Woman, you are safe."

"But I want to be more than safe," Rachel said. "I want to be free. Please, take me with you."

The old man shook his head.

"I can't do that, miss," he said. "If I tried, they'd have both our scalps."

"But they like you. I can see that."

"They like me because I am a trader. Trader Mike, I'm called. I bring them trinkets, as well as things of real value, in exchange for their animal pelts. I've been doin' this for thirty years. Fact is, I've got Indian grandchildren running around in half a dozen villages. If there was all-out war between the Indians and the whites, I could still come in here to trade my things. Do you understand what I'm tellin' you?"

Rachel shook her head. "No, I'm afraid I don't," she replied. "Except that it looks like you won't help me."

"I can't," Trader Mike said. "I can't do anything that

will change the way they see me. Right now I am nothing more to them than a part of the natural way of things. I am not a white man, not like other white men. I am a stream, a tree, a rock. I am a part of what they call their circle. If I help you, I'll be stepping out of that circle.''

"I see," Rachel said quietly. "I wouldn't want to do anything that would put your life in danger."

Trader Mike looked at her for a moment, then clucked his tongue and shook his head. "All right," he finally said. "I'll tell you what I will do. If you will write a letter before I leave here, I'll get it delivered."

"Oh," Rachel said, putting her hand on Trader Mike's hand. "Thank you, sir. Thank you very much."

"But I'll tell you right now, I don't intend to risk my life getting it through."

"I understand," Rachel said, and she hurried back to her tepee to compose the letter.

TO WHOM IT MAY CONCERN:

Help me, please! My name is Rachel A. Stewart. With my father and mother, I left Springfield, Illinois, several weeks ago to come West. My father had heard that there was free land, and we came to build a farm.

At Larned, Kansas, we departed the steam cars and began the final stage of our journey by wagon train, joining with five other wagons. The other parties involved were the Parkers, the Gibsons, the Millers, the Wilkersons, and the McKays. All were killed when Indians attacked the wagon train. Only I survived, and I am now being held a prisoner of the Cheyenne. I am being treated well for now, but I have been here for almost a month, and I long for my freedom and beg whoever receives this letter to set into motion events that will effect my rescue as quickly as possible.

If you cannot bring about my rescue, please be so

kind as to contact my Uncle, Raymond Foster, who
lives in Chicago. Tell him that the daughter of his
wife's only sister sends her love and begs him to buy
my freedom. I am told by Indian acquaintances I
have made here that prisoners are sometimes
ransomed free.

Sincerely, Rachel Stewart.

Nine

The social hub of Fort Hays was the Sutler's Store. Here, officers and men could buy anything from a razor to a can of peaches. The latest books and newspapers from the East were also on sale, and thanks to the railroad, the newspapers were never more than one week old.

Dances were held at the Sutler's Store on the first Saturday of every month, and as November 7 was the first Saturday, the meeting room in the back was turned over for the post dance. Hank was now an official member of the Fort Hays military family; therefore he was welcome to attend. The dances were somewhat restricted, owing to the lack of women. The wives of the post did their part by allowing their dance cards to be filled by the bachelor officers and men, and it wasn't all that unusual to see Libbie Custer, wife of the tactical commander of the 7th Cavalry, dancing with a young private.

There were a few single women, mostly laundresses, who lived on "Soapsuds Row," washing and ironing the post laundry. As a rule, the laundresses did not stay single very long. They were prime candidates for marriage to the noncommissioned officers of the post, and the salary of a laundress, combined with the pay and allowances of a sergeant, could give some of the senior NCO households incomes to be envied by all but the highest-ranking officers.

Even with the wives and unmarried laundresses, there
were still too few women at the post dances to go around,
so many of the younger soldiers would tie a handkerchief
around their left sleeve, indicating that they would be willing to be dance partners with the other soldiers. No one
thought the less of any soldier who did this. It was considered practical, not effeminate.

On the occasion of this dance, however, there was one
additional, young, very attractive woman at the fort. Her
name was Alice Patterson. Alice was the daughter of a con-
gressman and a special houseguest of General and Mrs. Custer. It had long been the custom of the Custers to invite a
young female for extended visits, not only because they enjoyed the interaction with someone from outside the military
family, but also to introduce a young woman into the social
mix of the fort.

Sometimes the young women who visited the Custers
would wind up married to one of the regimental officers,
and Miss Patterson had, in fact, been keeping company with
Lieutenant Murchison. Because of that, Hank maintained an
appropriate distance from her. When Alice asked Hank to
please put his name on her dance card, he was a little surprised. He acquiesced out of courtesy, not out of any real
interest.

When they began their dance, though, he felt a sense of
uneasiness. He realized at once that Alice Patterson was not
the sweet young ingenue Lieutenant Murchison imagined
her to be. She was, in fact, considerably more jaded than
Joe realized.

After their dance Hank took his leave of the Sutler's
Store. He didn't want to dance with any of the wives, and
he dared not dance with Alice again. She had a way about
her, a smile, a lingering touch, a provocative scent, that
managed to penetrate his carefully constructed reserve. He
was afraid that if he was around her too much, he would
wind up doing something that would rupture his newfound
friendship with young Murchison.

Hank walked out onto the quadrangle, then sat down by

the signal cannon and leaned back against the wheel. The music of the post band, playing now at the dance, floated across the quadrangle, and he sat in the dark, listening.

The band played "Lorena." "Lorena" had been one of the favorite ballads of the Confederate soldiers during the war, and as he heard it, he couldn't help but remember the hundreds of encampments and scores of campaigns in which he had heard this song being sung. Many who sang it were no longer alive, but he could never hear the tune without thinking of them.

Next the band played "Garryowen," a bouncy melody that Hank now knew had been selected by Custer to be the official regimental tune. It was also the signal that the dance was over, for "Garyowen" was the last piece played on any program involving the regimental band. Shortly after that, soldiers began filing out of the Sutler's Store, returning to their barracks as their laughter and loud talk drifted across the quadrangle. Though the air was more bracing than cold, it was cool enough that most of those leaving the dance hurried back to the warmth of their quarters. Hank wasn't quite ready to return to the BOQ yet, so he pulled up his knees in front of him and wrapped his arms around his legs for warmth. He looked around the post.

The hospital, commandant's quarters, and even Custer's house, which was the most substantial of all the married officers' quarters, gleamed white in the moonlight. All of the officers' quarters were well lit by kerosene lamps, and the windows were shining brightly, projecting squares of glimmering gold onto the ground outside. On the far side of the quadrangle the light was considerably dimmer from the enlisted men's barracks and from the married NCOs' quarters.

Hank was about to get up when he heard voices. Not wanting to expose himself just yet, he stayed where he was, sitting in the dark, leaning against the wheel of the signal cannon.

"Why are the lights so dim on that side of the post?"

Alice Patterson asked, pointing. "Is it to keep the Indians from seeing us?"

"No," answered Joe Murchison. "The army furnishes one candle per month per soldier, but lamps and kerosene must be bought, and that can get fairly expensive. Because of that, the enlisted men use candles almost exclusively."

"Oh, the poor things, to spend so much time in the dark."

"They don't seem to mind it too much," Joe replied, and as if to underscore his comment, a loud burst of laughter rolled across the parade ground from one of the barracks.

"May I call you Joe?"

"I would be most flattered."

"Do you like the army, Joe?"

"Yes, I do. I like it very much."

"What do you like about it?"

"I don't know that I can answer that," Joe replied. "A sense of belonging, I suppose. Although the army is not a surrogate for my family. I have a mother and father back in Illinois. But from the moment I set foot on the plain at West Point, I knew I had found my calling. I'll admit that's not much of an answer, but it is the kind of thing that, if it has to be explained, cannot be explained."

The chording of a guitar and the words and melody of a song, in four-part harmony, drifted across the quadrangle.

"Oh, listen to that. Isn't it beautiful?" Alice said.

"Yes, it is. Sometimes, even on these cool nights, I leave the window open in my BOQ room, and I am literally serenaded to sleep by the singing from the barracks."

"They are like children in a way, aren't they?" Alice asked. "The enlisted men, I mean. Happy-go-lucky . . . no cares or worries."

"I suppose one could be lulled into thinking that," Joe replied. "And perhaps some of the more patronizing officers truly believe it. But the truth is far different."

"What is the truth?"

"An army post is like a city. The officers are the city officials and the employers. The enlisted men are the employees and the citizens of the city. And like the citizens of any city, they are a diverse bunch. We have heroes and villains, courageous and cowardly, virtuous and evil, all living side by side, each with his own history."

"General Custer doesn't feel that way, does he?"

"Why do you say that? I think he has an enormous pride in the Seventh," Joe replied.

"Yes, in the Seventh Cavalry as a collective unit. Not in the individual soldiers. I have never heard him speak of individual soldiers as you just did."

"To be fair, he cannot think of them in the same way," Joe explained. "He must think of the Seventh only as it can be utilized tactically. If he starts thinking of the soldiers as individuals, he will lose his effectiveness." There was a small bed of chrysanthemums around the flagpole, and Joe bent to pick one. He handed it to Alice. "For you," he said.

"Why, Joe, what a sweet thought," Alice replied. "And what can I give you in return?"

Hank, whose position in the shadows of the gun-carriage wheel kept him from being noticed, could see Joe and Alice in silhouette only. They were backlighted by the glow from the officers' quarters. He saw Joe move toward her, then he saw them kiss. From Hank's perspective, it looked as if Joe's kiss was, at best, tentative, while Alice responded eagerly, pressing herself against him. Joe tried to pull away, but Alice plied herself to him even more tightly.

Finally they separated.

"I . . . I'm sorry," Joe sputtered. "I had no right to force myself upon you in such a fashion. Please forgive me."

Jesus, Joe, Hank thought. Do you really think you were forcing yourself on her? She was the one doing all the forcing.

"Joe, if I had not wanted you to kiss me, you couldn't have done it."

"Nevertheless, I feel I took an unfair advantage of you."

"So tell me, what are you going to do now?" Alice asked.

"I . . . I think I had better walk you back to the commandant's quarters. General and Mrs. Custer will be wondering what has happened to their houseguest.''

"All right, Joe. If you really think you must," Alice said, disappointment obvious in her voice.

Hank stayed perfectly still until both Joe and Alice were well across the quadrangle toward the Custer house. Then he got up, brushed off the seat of his pants, and walked through the dark to his own room.

There were six BOQ units at Fort Hays. Each unit consisted of a two-story building. On the bottom floor were two blocks of individual rooms, connected by a sally port. Every room had a private entrance. That was accomplished by having two squares of eight rooms each, the doors opening outward all the way around each square. Two rooms from each square opened onto the sally port. The same thing was true with the top floor. The two blocks were connected by a roof that spanned the sally port.

Hank's room was on the back side of the bottom floor, with the door opening toward the stockade wall that surrounded the fort. Because of the location, his room was the least desirable. It had no view, and though a breeze wasn't necessary at this time of the year, in the summertime his room could be stifling. However, its very undesirability was what ensured the room's availability when Hank signed on as a scout.

As soon as Hank was in his room, he removed his jacket, shirt, and boots. Then he stood at his chifforobe, bare-chested and barefoot, and bathed in the water basin. He was just finishing when someone knocked lightly at his door. Believing it to be one of his neighbors, Hank didn't bother to put on his shirt but just stepped over to the door and jerked it open.

Alice was standing outside the door, barely illuminated by the soft cast of light from Hank's room.

"What are you doing here?" Hank asked, surprised.

Alice smiled coquettishly. "Now, is that any way to greet a lady?" she asked.

"A lady wouldn't be visiting a man's room at this time of night," Hank replied.

"This lady would," Alice said, stepping into his room without being invited. "Of course, that might well raise the question as to whether or not I'm really a lady. Do close the door, would you? There is chill wind."

Hank closed the door. "You didn't answer my question, Miss Patterson. What are you doing here?"

"I have come for a tryst."

"A tryst? What is a tryst?"

"I believe Mr. Webster defines the word as a meeting between a man and a woman for the purpose of engaging in sexual intercourse."

"What?" Hank gasped.

Alice laughed. "That's a very sophisticated way to put it, don't you think? On the other hand, if I had just said that I was here to warm your bed, it would sound so whorish."

"Miss Patterson," Hank started, but Alice put her fingers across his lips.

"Really, Hank, we are about to make love. Don't you think you could call me Alice?"

"What makes you think we are about to make love?"

Smiling, Alice put her hands on the hem of her dress, then suddenly and unexpectedly pulled it over her head. This action left her totally nude.

"Because I'm quite determined to see this through," she answered. "And when I am this determined, I normally get what I want."

Hank looked at her, standing nude before him. She had a beautiful shape, and her skin, though unblemished, was at the moment pocked with little chill bumps in reaction to the cold air.

"Well, are you going to make me stand here and freeze to death?" Alice asked. "Or are you going to turn your bed back for me?"

"Miss Patterson ... Alice ... Joe Murchison is my friend. I don't want—"

"Oh, for crying out loud, Hank, don't you understand? You are *doing* this for Joe," Alice said.

"What?" Hank sputtered. He shook his head in confusion. "I know I'm not as sophisticated as you are, but I'll be damned if I can see how bedding another man's woman is doing a favor for that man."

"Think about it. Joe is a dear, sweet, wonderful young man. He is also a virgin. I, on the other hand, lost my virginity when I was fourteen. Lost it, hell, I gave it away. And I've been jumping into bed with every attractive man I've met ever since then."

"I see," Hank said.

"No, I'm not entirely sure you do see," Alice continued. She walked over to Hank's bed, turned the blanket down herself, then got in. "The only reason I'm here with you now," she continued, "is because I actually think Joe is trying to drum up enough courage to ask me to marry him."

"He wants to marry you?"

"Yes. Could you think of anything more disastrous for either of us? Lord, I can't picture myself as a junior officer's wife in some godforsaken remote post like this. I would go crazy. Not only that, I would probably wind up getting Joe killed nobly trying to defend my honor against someone's careless, but no doubt correct, remark."

"And so, somehow, going to bed with me is going to prevent all that?" Hank asked.

Alice turned back the corner of the bed, then patted the sheet beside her. "Yes, dear man, this is going to prevent it. Once you have been with me, and learned how . . . wanton"—she set the word apart from the rest of the sentence, speaking it in a low, husky way—"I really am, you will do everything in your power to discourage him from marrying me."

Hank felt a hollowness in the pit of his stomach and a weakness in his knees. Never in his life had he been so brazenly propositioned, not even by anyone who made a profession of such things. And Alice had been right when she'd said she normally achieved what she went after, for if her goal was to get him in bed with her, she was surely going to be successful. Hank began taking off his clothes. He didn't believe anything on earth could keep him away from her now.

Alice had also been right when she'd said she was wanton. She didn't need any preparation; she grabbed him and made the connection as soon as he was in bed. He felt as if he were being dipped into a vat of hot wax. She didn't just make love to him, she exploded around him.

When they were finished, Hank fell back onto his pillow, his senses jumbled by what had just happened. The one thing he did know was that Alice was right when she'd said she wasn't right for Joe. In his opinion, she would chew that young man up and spit him out in little pieces.

In the camp of Black Kettle on the banks of the Washita, a ring of campfires, all burning brightly, encircled the perimeter. A circle, Rachel now knew, was very important to the Cheyenne. Running Deer had explained it all to her, how the Cheyenne believed that the power of the world worked in a circle. Long before the Europeans had accepted the concept of the earth being round, Running Deer explained, the Cheyenne already knew it to be so. They reasoned that if the sky was round, the moon was round, and the sun was round, then the earth, too, must be round. This universal circle, they believed, was not without purpose.

The seasons also formed a circle: summer, fall, winter, spring, then summer coming back again. The nests of the birds were round, tepees were round and always set in a circle, and all meeting and ceremonies took place in the center of that circle.

Jumping Wolf led several warriors as they danced and chanted around a circle. Running Deer interpreted the song they were singing.

> *Listen, we are warriors.*
> *The God Dogs, our horses,*
> *Run swiftly*

Between our legs.
The arrow and the lance
Fly true in their path.
The blood of the toka, *our enemy,*
Stains the ground
Beneath the hooves of the
God Dogs.
We will have glory.
We will count many coups.
Listen, we are warriors.

"What does it all mean?" Rachel asked.

"Jumping Wolf is trying to convince the warriors to follow him onto the warpath," Running Deer explained.

"Will anyone follow him?"

"Yes, many will follow," Running Deer said. "I think that, after tonight, there will be no warriors left in the village. There will be only old men, young boys, and women."

Back in Fort Hays, Hank and Alice lay together in his bed. The air in the little BOQ room was redolent with the musk of sex.

"Now, Mr. Tyreen, you can't honestly say that you didn't like that," Alice finally said.

Hank said nothing.

"You are feeling guilty, aren't you?" Alice asked.

"I'm not very proud of myself," Hank admitted.

"Hank, I know you believe you have somehow violated a trust. But believe me when I tell you that there was no trust to violate. Joe is young and impressionable. Perhaps he believes that he is in love with me, but that's only because he has never been in love, and he doesn't know how it feels."

"Have you ever been in love?" Hank asked, although as soon as he said the words he wished that he had not.

"No," Alice said. "What you and I just had was as close to love as I have ever come, and as close as I will ever get."

"I see."

Alice raised herself up on one elbow and looked down at Hank. The action tended to flatten one breast while elongating the other.

"No, I don't think you do see. There was a reason I came to you tonight, and it was only obliquely connected with what just happened here."

"Obliquely?"

"Yes. I'm not denying that I seduced you. But the seduction was the means to an end, not the end. You see, what I really wanted was an ally."

Hank continued to look at her but said nothing.

"I don't know when the Seventh Cavalry will be going into the field again, but when it does Joe will go with it, and I shall be gone before he returns."

"Joe knows this?"

"No," Alice said. "If I tried to tell him, I'm afraid he wouldn't understand."

"I'm not sure that I understand," Hank said. "At least, not the ally part."

"Even though I have known Joe for only a short time, I believe I know him very well. His first thought is going to be to come after me. He may even want to resign from the army."

"He might," Hank agreed.

"That would be the worst thing he could do. He loves the army . . . much more than he thinks he loves me."

"And you want me to keep him from leaving the army and coming after you," Hank said. It wasn't a question, it was a declaration.

"Yes. You know what kind of woman I am, Hank. I have just given you a demonstration. I have absolutely no intention of altering my lifestyle to accommodate the virginal Lieutenant Murchison."

"Well, I'll be damned," Hank said. He chuckled softly.

"What is it?"

"Do you know Shakespeare?" Hank asked.

"Shakespeare?" Alice laughed. "Well, of course I do,

though I must confess to being a little surprised by your familiarity with the great Bard.''

"Who?"

"It's another name for Shakespeare," Alice explained. "But why do you ask?"

"Because someone quoted a line from one of Shakespeare's plays to me once. The line says that someone doth 'protest too much.' "

"I see. And you think that fits me?"

"You love him, don't you?" Hank said. "You would like nothing better than to accommodate the young lieutenant, but you are afraid."

"Afraid of what?"

"Afraid of being hurt . . . and of hurting him."

Alice was quiet. After a long moment she got up from the bed and padded naked in the moonlight to the small puddle of cloth on the floor that was her dress. She picked it up and put it on. When she came back to Hank's bed to look down at him, there were tears in her eyes.

"You are a more perceptive man than I imagined, Mr. Tyreen," she said. She kissed him lightly, then got up and turned toward the door.

Hank didn't answer, but he watched as she walked across the room, and then he closed the door behind her. In the tower nearest the BOQ, he heard the guard tolling off the hour.

"Post number five! Eleven o'clock, and all is well!"

Ten

When officers' call sounded the next afternoon, Hank joined the other scouts and officers who had assembled at regimental headquarters. Custer had a stern look on his face as he waited until all had arrived. Then he cleared his throat and began to talk.

"Gentlemen, you will remember, I'm sure, that a few weeks ago one of our patrols found the remains of a burned-out wagon train and the slaughtered civilians who were a part of that train."

The officers nodded in unison.

"You will also remember that one of the young women of that train had been keeping a journal. Indeed, many of you read her heartrending entries."

Again there were nods of agreement, though the expressions on the faces of some of the officers were beginning to reflect a shortening of patience. A few even wondered aloud, though only loud enough for their nearest neighbor to hear, where all this was leading.

"Today, a man known in these parts as Trader Mike brought us absolute proof that the young lady who made those journal entries is still alive and is a captive of the Cheyenne."

The assembled officers reacted in anger.

"Damn their hides!"

"Those heathen bastards!"

"How is she?"

"Has she been harmed?"

Custer held up his hand to call for quiet, and when the officers responded, he showed them a letter. "Trader Mike brought a letter from the young woman. I propose to read it to you."

The officers were absolutely quiet as Custer read from the letter he held. He read it quietly but dramatically, pausing at the appropriate places to allow his men to express themselves. When he finished, he looked up at them.

"Well, there it is, gentlemen, a call for help if there ever was one."

"General, what are we going to do about this?" Captain Hamilton asked.

Custer smiled, the first smile to cross his face since officers' call had sounded. "What are we going to do about it? Why, we are going after her. We are going after her, and we are going to destroy the Indian village where she is being held."

The officers roared their approval.

"Hurrah for the general!"

"Let the heathens feel some hot lead and cold steel, and it will be a while before they capture any more white women!"

"Gentlemen," Custer interrupted, "prepare your troops for departure first thing tomorrow morning. We will take food and equipment sufficient for a march of six weeks."

"Shouldn't we leave sooner than tomorrow, General?" Captain Benteen asked. "It would seem to me that every hour must count."

Custer shook his head. "She's been their captive for some weeks now," he said. "A few more hours won't matter. Tomorrow morning, gentlemen," he added by way of dismissal.

When the regiment left Fort Hays the next morning, the entire post was turned out to watch: officers' ladies, enlisted men's wives, unmarried laundresses, and Alice Patterson. Their dresses were covered with coats, blankets, and robes as they braved the cold to watch, standing on the porches and in the sally ports of the fort as the 7th made all preparations to leave.

There was a great deal of activity still going on. Men were riding at a gallop to and fro, delivering messages or attending to last-minute details. Aside from the rustle of horses and the murmur of men, however, the parade ground was relatively quiet.

Major Elliot, Custer's second in command, was already in position under the flagpole. Some of the messages were being delivered to him, and a horseman would ride up, salute, exchange a few words, salute again, then ride back, all at a gallop. Also at the flagpole, getting in position to play, were the members of the regimental band.

"Here comes the general now," someone whispered in the ranks. Hank overheard the remark, then looked toward Custer's quarters to see the general and Libbie, riding side by side. When they reached the edge of the parade ground, Custer continued on, while Libbie stopped and dismounted. A nearby soldier took the reins of her horse, and she joined some of the other ladies to watch the departure.

Custer rode to the flagpole, then received the salute from Major Elliot. He looked out over the parade ground at the assembled troops. A total of eleven companies were ready for the march, divided into three battalions.

From the regimental trumpeter came the clear, sharp notes of assembly.

Now the shuffling around stopped, and the regiment grew quiet. Custer stood in his stirrups and called to his battalion commanders.

"Form into line of march, column of fours to the right!" he shouted.

The battalion commanders issued the commands, and the entire regiment turned to the right.

"Guidons, post!"

The battalion and troop color bearers moved into position

at the heads of their respective units. The regimental color
bearer rode at a gallop to position himself to Custer's left.
For a long moment there was absolute silence as the horses
and men held their positions. The only sound to be heard
was the snapping of the guidons and the American flag.

"Battalion commanders, pass in review!" Custer ordered.

"Forward!" shouted the battalion commanders, and the
troop commanders picked up the supplementary commands.

"Forward!" the eleven troop commanders called, the
word echoing itself up and down the line.

"Ho!" called the battalion commanders, and as one, the
regiment began to move.

As the first horse stepped out, the band began to play.
The lead battalion did two left turns, then passed in review
with all officers rendering the saber salute to General Custer
as they rode by. The gates were opened, and the 7th left the
post to begin their march.

For miles piling upon miles, the 7th Cavalry moved south
toward the Washita, whereupon, according to information
they had received from Trader Mike, they would find the
Indian village. At each break the battalions would switch
positions so that the battalion in the lead would move to the
rear, the battalion in the middle would move to the lead,
and so forth.

After a full day's march covering some forty miles, a
scouting party was sent ahead to find water and wood, and
once a suitable place was located, the men established their
camp for the night. They ate beans and bacon and drank
coffee, then pitched their tents. Two troopers could bivouac
together to make a two-man tent by putting together the half
tent each of them carried. The officers shared the much
larger Sibley tents.

Because Hank was assigned specifically to Captain Hamilton's company, he shared the Sibley tent with Hamilton
and Joe Murchison.

"Are you sure I'm not overcrowding you?" he asked as
he threw his bedroll onto the ground.

"You aren't overcrowding us," Hamilton said. "We are used to having three men in here. Before you, there was Fred."

Hank knew Hamilton was talking about Lieutenant Fred Becker, the young officer who had been killed during the battle on the island that now bore his name.

By nightfall it was considerably colder than it had been, and a damp wind was coming down from the northwest. Inside the tent he was sharing with his two new friends, however, Hank was sheltered from the wind and warmed by his bedding so that he was, in spite of everything, quite comfortable.

"So, tell me, Joe," Hamilton said, "are you going to ask Miss Patterson to marry you?"

"Marry him?" Hank said. He laughed. "You are sort of pushing things, aren't you, Captain? You sound like the girl's father. Joe's a young man . . . let him sow a few wild oats in peace."

"Well, of course, I'm not trying to push anything," Hamilton said. "Sorry if I sounded that way."

"No," Joe said quickly. "Don't apologize. The truth is, I have been thinking about it."

"Thinking about what?" Hank asked. "Marrying that girl?" He snorted. "Joe, you can't be serious."

"Do you know of any reason why I shouldn't marry her?" Joe asked.

"No, of course not," Hank answered.

Although Joe's question wasn't sharp or particularly challenging, it was fraught with its own kind of danger, and Hank felt it would be best to change the subject as quickly as he could.

"Speaking as an outsider, I must say that I was impressed with the amount of ground the Seventh covered today. We made how many miles? Forty?"

"Oh, the drums would roll, upon my soul, this is the style we'd go. Forty miles a day on beans and hay in the regular army, oh!" Captain Hamilton sang.

Hank laughed.

"Hell, Hank, you aren't an outsider," Joe said easily, and the warmth of his comment cheered Hank because it let him know that Joe had already dropped his challenging posture with regard to Alice Patterson. What would Joe do, Hank wondered, if he knew that Alice had been in his bed last night? Challenge him to a duel? What had he been thinking when he let her in his room? He should have turned her out right then.

"Joe's right, Hank," Hamilton said. "You were at the battle of Becker Island with the rest of us. You've earned your place with us."

"Thanks," Joe said.

There was a long beat of silence, then Hamilton spoke again.

"Joe, how many people do you know at Fiddler's Green?"

"At Fiddler's Green, sir? Well, there's Lieutenant Becker, of course. And all the others who were with us at the island. Before that, there was a lieutenant named Canfield and a sergeant named Muldoon. Why do you ask?"

"Because by the time the regiment returns to Fort Hays, some of us will be at Fiddler's Green," Hamilton said.

"By some of us, you mean some of the regiment?"

"No," Hamilton said. "I mean some of the officers."

There was another beat of silence before Joe spoke again.

"Do you think about that much, Captain? Fiddler's Green, I mean."

"No," Hamilton said. "I never think about it. Do you?"

"No, sir."

"Good. It's good that you don't."

This was a conversation between two cavalrymen, and Hank felt that he had no place joining in. Had he been a party to the discussion, though, he would have asked a very obvious question. If neither of them ever thought of it, why were they discussing it now?

Lying in the cocoonlike warmth of his bedding, lost in his own thoughts, and with the gentle snoring of his two tent mates, Hank finally drifted off to sleep. The men of the encampment, exhausted by the hard day's march, were completely oblivious of the large flakes of snow that, just after midnight, began tumbling down through the blackness.

At Black Kettle's camp on the Washita, the snow drifted down from the black sky and added inches to that which was already on the ground. It fell silently, and its presence deadened all sound so that the movement of horses and the stirrings of villagers in their blankets were unheard.

The door flaps of all the tepees were laced tightly shut, and wisps of blue smoke curled up from the smoke holes, providing a scene of tranquillity to the village. The smell of a hundred simmering stews told the silent story of a night when no one went hungry and everyone was warm and snug against the elements.

Running Deer had come to build Rachel's fire for her and show her how to adjust the flap so that the smoke would curl up and out and not gather inside the tepee to choke her. Running Deer had also brought Rachel her share of meat and potatoes, and Rachel cooked a stew and invited Running Deer to stay and eat with her. Later, as the snow continued to fall and the temperature dropped, Running Deer accepted Rachel's invitation to stay the night.

Rachel was delighted that Running Deer accepted her invitation. Although at first she had been glad the Indians left her alone, she soon found herself growing lonely. And because Running Deer could speak English so well, she became Rachel's only contact with the outside world.

"Are you married?" Running Deer asked.

"No."

"The men who were killed when your wagons were attacked . . . were you promised to any of them?"

"No," Rachel answered again. "What about you?" she asked Running Deer. "I'm sure you aren't married, you are much too young for that. But do you have your cap set for someone?"

Running Deer laughed. "What does this mean? Have your cap set?"

Rachel laughed with her. "It means, do you have someone in mind that you would like to be your husband?"

Running Deer grew sober, then nodded. "I did," she finally said. "But I have him no more."

"What happened?"

"My man was Stone Eagle."

Rachel recalled the magnificent-looking Indian who had cut her restraints on that first day. Though her contact with Indians was limited, she was prepared to say that Stone Eagle was the biggest and most handsome representative of that race she had ever seen.

"Oh," Rachel finally managed to say. "I am so sorry, Running Deer."

"He was killed in battle," Running Deer said. "That means his spirit will live forever."

"But our religion teaches us that one's spirit will live forever anyway. It has nothing to do with dying in battle."

"You are talking about the white man's Jesus God, aren't you?" Running Deer said.

"Yes, I am. Do you believe in him?"

Running Deer nodded affirmatively.

"Good, good," Rachel said.

"Why is this good?"

"Because it is very important that you believe in the one way to the true God."

Running Deer shook her head. "How poor is the white man's religion, that you believe there is only one way to reach God. Many paths lead to the Great Spirit. The Jesus God is but one of those paths. The path taken by the Indian people is to live in harmony and balance with the circle of earth, wind, fire, water."

Rachel clucked her tongue and shook her head. "Our Father in heaven will not welcome you into His kingdom if you do not come to Him through the Son of God."

"You call Him our Father? Does that not mean we are all children of God?" Running Deer asked. "Are you not His daughter? Is Black Kettle not His son? Are earth, wind, fire, and water not His creations?"

Rachel thought hard, trying to remember all of her Sunday school lessons; but try though she did, no easy answer came to her.

"I cannot answer all of your questions. I can only tell you how things are," she finally said, hoping that Running Deer would accept her explanation and press the issue no further.

When "Reveille" sounded the following morning, the officers and men of the 7th, still some distance from the village, emerged from their own tents to a world covered in a pristine blanket of snow. There were no trails, no footprints, no hoofprints. It was as if man had never been here before.

Breakfast was a cup of coffee and a piece of hard bread. Then the trumpeter played "General," which was the call to strike tents, followed by "Boots and Saddles," which ordered the men to saddle their mounts, and finally by "To Horse." After that the orders "Prepare to Mount" and "Mount" were given verbally, and once again the 7th was on the march.

The march element was one battalion smaller this morning than it had been the day before, because Major Elliot and his squadron had left at three A.M. They were going ahead to make certain the Indians didn't get wind of the advancing cavalry, pull up their village, and leave.

Some distance south of the soldiers, in the very village that was their destination, the Indians were gathered around their fires to listen to Black Kettle. He had called them together to sing the song that had come to him during a dream.

A song that came in a dream, everyone knew, was very powerful medicine, so all gathered to hear Black Kettle sing. He paused for a moment, then began. The tune and the rhythm were different from any song they had ever heard before, and the words were powerful:

> *In this circle, hear what I sing.*
> *Where one knows of beauty,*

Already there is ugliness.
Where one knows of good,
Already there is evil.
Where there is,
There is also is-not.
Where there is easy,
There must be difficult.
Where there is before,
There is after.
Where there is the red man,
There is the white man.
Where there is life,
There is death.
Where there is white snow,
There is red blood.
Where there is the silence of the night,
There is the music of the soldiers' band.
Hear me in this circle I sing.

Many were puzzled by the meaning of the song. Running Deer, who had interpreted the words of the song for Rachel, was frightened by it. And Rachel, for some reason she couldn't understand, was also frightened.

The soldiers' march continued on through the day. Movement was much more difficult than it had been the day before, because they had to break the crust of the newly fallen snow, which quickly tired horses and men. Twenty minutes of every hour the men dismounted. During that break, they would lead their horses for ten minutes, then let them rest for ten minutes. Behind them, stretching now almost as far as the eye could see, was a long black smear across the plains, showing clearly the path they had taken through the snow.

"I have Major Elliot in front of us," Custer said. "If he locates the village, he will send a courier back."

"He won't try to attack without us, will he, General?" Lieutenant Keogh asked in his thick Irish brogue. "I mean, you do know Major Elliot. Sure an' he's just the kind of firebrand who would do something like that.''

"He has the strictest orders not to," Custer replied. He smiled. "But not to worry, gentlemen, we'll all get our chance.''

" 'Tis the lass the heathens have that I'm worried about. I hope we are there in time," Keogh said.

"Worry not, my lads," Custer said. "We'll be there in time." He stretched, then looked around at the men, who were in various stages of rest. "Give the word, gentlemen," he said easily. "We're moving on.''

"All right, boys, on your feet! Let's go!" Benteen shouted, and with a few groans, but with no grumbling, the men of the 7th mounted to resume the march.

It was nine o'clock in the evening when they caught up with Major Elliot. Elliot had halted near a stream of good water. He had selected the site well, because the valley nearby was quite heavily timbered. By building their fires so that they were sheltered by the riverbank, the men were able to prepare coffee without giving away their position to any Indians who might be looking. A handful of hardtack crackers supplemented the coffee and served as their supper. The horses were unsaddled, their bits were removed, and they were given a full portion of oats. The men began scraping out places in the snow, making ready to spend the night.

* * *

Eleven

There was to be no bivouac for the men of the 7th Cavalry. They rested for an hour only, then Custer gave orders that they were to resume the march. From here on there would be no bugle calls and no loud commands. Orders were given to tie down all loose equipment, thus minimizing the danger of being given away by making too much noise. The men were also forbidden to light their pipes, not only for fear the glow of fire might be seen, but also because the Indians might be able to smell the aroma of smoking tobacco. When they resumed the march, it had fallen to Captain Hamilton's troop to take the lead.

Hank and a handful of Osage scouts rode a quarter of a mile in front of the column. Custer was at the head of the column that followed behind him, silent save for the muffled crunch of the crusted snow.

Hard Rope, one of the Osage scouts with Hank, stopped and said something in Osage to the others.

"What is it?" Hank asked.

"Fire."

"You see fire?"

Hard Rope shook his head no. He laid his finger alongside his nose. "Smell smoke," he said.

Hank looked around, then in a nearby tree line he saw a faint glow of embers.

"I see it," Hank said. Quickly he rode toward it, Hard Rope and the other Osage scouts riding with him.

Hank dismounted, then knelt beside the fire. He examined the embers for a moment. No more than three or four of the glowing little coals remained.

"Can't be over a couple hours old," Hank said.

Hard Rope looked around. "I think young boys make fire to keep warm while they watch ponies," he said.

"Makes sense to me," Hank replied. "That means the village is close. I'd better go back and report."

Hank galloped back to the formation and gave Custer his report. Custer then signaled for the officers to come forward, and over the next few moments, the officers from the entire line of march moved to the front to confer with Custer.

"All right, gentlemen," Custer said when they were assembled. "The village can't be more than a couple of miles from here. Hank, you and the others go ahead to have a look. We'll wait here."

Hank nodded, then he and the Osage scouts went ahead. They had ridden at a trot for no more than ten minutes when the smell of smoke became very strong. Hank could smell not only smoke, but the lingering aroma of cooked meat.

"We're here, aren't we?" he said.

Hard Rope nodded, and they got down from their horses then sneaked ahead on foot. They reached the edge of a tree line, then looked across. On the other side of a small clearing, clinging to the banks of the Washita River, was a large village of many tepees. The tepees gleamed in the darkness, clearly visible because of the reflected moonlight from the snow. From nearly every tepee, a wisp of blue smoke curled, ropelike, into the sky.

The sleeping village was one of the most tranquil and picturesque scenes Hank had ever seen. For a moment he wished he could just turn around and go away, but he knew that he could not.

"Must tell general," Hard Rope said. "Heap many Indians down there."

"Right," Hank said as he and the others remounted for their ride back.

For a moment or two the moon was behind a cloud. When it emerged, it spilled its silver light onto a valley with a light so bright that even though it was just after midnight, the entire line of cavalry could be seen sitting motionless on their horses, awaiting further orders.

The order to march was transmitted by hand signals, and the soldiers moved on. A mile later they crested a hill.

"This is it, General," Hank said. "We saw the village from here."

"Show me," Custer said, dismounting.

Hank dismounted and led him up to the top of the hill. The scene was as pastoral as before, and Hank studied Custer's face to see how he would react to it. Would he find some compassion? Would he be as affected by the tranquillity of the village as Hank had been?

When Hank saw the smile spread across Custer's face, he knew the answer was no.

"By God, we've got the heathen bastards!" Custer said, opening and closing his hands in his excitement.

Custer hurried back to the column with Hank hustling alongside.

"Pass the word," Custer said quietly. "I want all the officers to report to me immediately. Tell them to leave their sabers behind. I don't want any sound."

It took almost five minutes before all the officers were assembled. Then Custer outlined his plan to them.

"I'm going to divide the column into four detachments of equal strength," he said. "Captain Barnitz, you will take one element to the woods below the village; Benteen, you take another to the timber to the right of it; Major Elliot, you occupy the crest just to the left; Captain Hamilton, your men will remain here with me. We will attack simultaneously."

"General, would you be for tellin' us our signal for attack?" Keogh asked.

Custer smiled. "I'll have the band play 'Garryowen.' That will not only provide everyone with a signal, it should also wake the heathens up."

Custer agreed to give the other detachments four hours to get into positions. In the meantime, Hamilton's troops were permitted to dismount, but they couldn't stamp their feet or even pace back and forth to get warm, for fear it might give away their position. Hank stayed with Captain Hamilton.

About two hours before dawn the moon went down, and the night, which had been so bright before, became pitch black. Suddenly a brilliant light appeared in the sky, and for a moment everyone thought it was a rocket. After looking at it more closely, however, they realized it was just a morning star.

"An interesting omen, don't you think?" Hamilton asked, pointing to the star. "But I don't know if it portends good luck or a terrible misfortune."

"What are you talking about?" Joe asked before Hank could mouth the question.

"The morning star," Hamilton explained. "It may be some sort of omen. Don't you know what the Indians call Custer?"

"No, sir," Joe said.

"Neither do I," Hank said.

"They call him Son of the Morning Star," Hamilton said.

Custer had long ago learned an interesting thing about Indians. Although Indians had "chiefs," the chiefs had no authority beyond what was allowed them by their people. A chief could make suggestions, but he could not give orders.

One of the orders a chief could not give was for someone to stand guard. If any Indian ever stood guard, it was as a volunteer only. On a night like this, when the snow was deep and the wind biting and cold, no one wanted to stay outside, therefore no guards were posted. As a result, the sleeping village was completely unaware that no more than two hundred yards away from its outer ring, in the lower reaches of a great pine forest, shadows were emerging from the darkness. The shadows that were emerging from shadows were long lines of riders, taking up their positions around the village in accordance with Custer's instructions. The horses moved silently, as if treading on air, and only their movement and the blue vapor of their breathing gave an indication of life.

A small, clinking sound of metal on metal came from the party, a sound that was unnatural to the drift of snow and the soft whisper of trees. In his tepee in the village, Black Kettle heard the sound while in the deepest recesses of his sleep, and his eyes came open and he lay beside his woman and wondered what could have caused the sound.

But the bed robes were too warm, and as he looked at his wife and saw that her sleep was undisturbed, he realized he must have dreamed the unusual sound, so he rolled back into the inviting curve of the sleeping form of the body of his woman and fell back to sleep.

Outside, the silent horses and the quiet men, now in position, waited.

"Captain Hamilton," Custer said.

"Yes, sir?"

"Have your men discard their overcoats and haversacks. It is time to go."

On the one hand, discarding the overcoat meant the men would be even colder and more miserable than they were now. On the other, however, it meant they were about to see action, and that had to be better than standing around waiting the whole night through.

A rifle shot echoed from the far side of the village, indicating that all troops were in place. Custer nodded toward the band director, and the night air was suddenly filled with the jubilant strains of "Garryowen."

Whether actually inspired by the music, or anxious to get moving at last, the soldiers from all four elements of Custer's command rushed forward, firing as rapidly as they could at the tents that rose up in the darkness before them.

Even though the Indians had not posted guards, Hank was

surprised at how rapidly they responded to the attack. From nearly every tepee in the camp, it seemed, men, and women, too, emerged with weapons in their hands: rifles, pistols, and bows and arrows. If Hank had thought the Indians would roll over for the slaughter, he was disabused of that notion by the ferocity with which the Indians were defending their village.

"Keep calm, men," Hamilton shouted to his troop. "Keep calm and fire low!"

Almost immediately following those words, as if punctuating the sentence he had just spoken, Hamilton gave a strange-sounding grunt.

Hank looked toward him and saw a torrent of blood pumping out from a hole in his tunic where a bullet had entered.

"Captain Hamilton!" Hank shouted.

Hamilton jerked convulsively, then stiffened out so that he was standing straight up in his stirrups. He was carried for a distance of several yards before he fell from his horse.

At almost the same time Hamilton was hit, Captain Barnitz, who had led one of the other elements, was engaged in a one-on-one skirmish with an Indian. They exchanged fire from point-blank range, and the Indian went down. Barnitz didn't go down immediately, though it was quickly obvious that he had been hit as well. The entry wound of the bullet was clearly visible because the Indian had been so close when he'd fired that the muzzle blast had scorched a ring on Barnitz's coat. He rode on for another two hundred yards, then calmly dismounted and lay down while the fighting raged around him.

A young Indian in his early teens suddenly burst out of one of the Indian lodges and jumped on an unsaddled and unbridled pony, obviously attempting to escape. Captain Benteen went after him. The boy wheeled his horse around and fired, killing Benteen's horse and dropping the officer into the snow. The boy fired twice more, missing both times, before Benteen returned fire, killing the boy with one shot from his revolver.

*   *   *

Rachel had awakened as quickly as the Indians. When she moved to the door flap of her tepee to look outside, she saw the swirling melee of soldiers and Indians. At first she was happy that the soldiers had come for her at last. But as she looked around the village she saw old men, women, and children going down under the soldiers' indiscriminate firing. These were people she had come to know over the last few weeks. Just yesterday a young boy had brought game, putting a rabbit on the ground before her tepee with a proud, shy smile. Now she saw that same young boy killed in a duel with a gray-haired soldier.

The woman who had given her a cooking pot was killed as she stood in front of her tepee, her blood staining the snow around her.

She saw Running Deer dashing across the circle.

"Running Deer, no!" Rachel shouted. "Come back! They won't hurt you if you are with me!"

Two soldiers on horseback caught up with Running Deer. With one soldier on either side, they were able to reach down and pick her up by grabbing the robe, and they carried her back toward the rest of the soldiers. Even above the screams and cries and crash of gunfire, Rachel could hear the two soldiers laughing.

"This here'n is a little hellcat, she is!" one of the soldiers said.

Suddenly Running Deer wriggled out of the buffalo robe she was wearing. Leaving the soldiers holding an empty robe, she started dashing, now stark naked, across the snow, headed for Rachel's tepee. Rachel could see the look of absolute terror on the girl's face, and she reached out toward Rachel, as if imploring her to help.

"No!" Rachel screamed at the soldiers. "Leave her alone! She is my friend!"

Whether they didn't hear her or didn't heed her, Rachel didn't know. She knew only that at least three of the soldiers aimed at her. Running Deer was hit in the back of her head, and she pitched forward. Her nude body lay facedown. The pristine white snow in front of Running Deer was sprayed red with blood, and Rachel suddenly recalled the song of red blood on white snow that Black Kettle had sung around the campfires the day before.

That was when she saw Black Kettle.

Despite the bullets flying around him, Black Kettle managed to get mounted. He galloped back to his tepee and shouted something. His wife darted outside and held up her hand. Black Kettle pulled her up onto the horse behind him, then kicked the animal's side, urging it into a run.

They made it as far as the river before several soldiers appeared in front of them. A bullet hit Black Kettle in the stomach, and he jerked the pony around. Another bullet hit him in the back, and he could no longer stay on his horse. At the same time Black Kettle was being shot, several bullets were slamming into his wife, and she, too, fell. The pony, riderless now, dashed off down the riverbank as the soldiers, looking for other targets, rode over the dead bodies of Black Kettle and his wife without so much as a second glance toward them.

"Oh, God in heaven, what is happening here?" Rachel cried, putting her hands in the air.

Hank was caught up in the fighting. To him the people he was shooting at were neither men, women, nor children. They were all Indians, and by now they were all armed and returning fire. A handful managed to get mounted, then they started downstream.

Seeing the Indians leave, Major Elliot held up a hand and shouted, "Some are getting away! Here's for a brevet or a coffin, boys! Who is with me?"

Elliot started after the Indians, and almost a score of troopers, including the regimental sergeant major, went with him. Hank saw Joe start after him as well, but at that same moment, Joe's horse was hit with an arrow. The animal broke stride, and Joe, realizing that any further riding might kill his horse, stopped and dismounted.

When the last batch of warriors fled downstream with

Custer in pursuit, the immediate fighting stopped.

At this point the soldiers began to look after their wounded. Hank saw Joe standing over the crumpled form of Captain Hamilton.

"How is he?" Hank asked.

Joe shook his head. "Dead," he answered. "Looks like he was hit in the heart and died almost instantly."

"I'm sorry," Hank said.

"He was Alexander Hamilton's grandson, did you know that?"

"No, I didn't know it."

"Knowing him was like knowing a little piece of our country's history."

"Hey, someone! Over here! Captain Barnitz is still alive."

Hank and Joe hurried over to Barnitz. The wounded officer was lying on the ground with a bullet in his stomach.

"Hank, get me one of those buffalo robes," Joe said, and Hank picked up the robe that had covered the young Indian girl whose nude body now lay in the snow. He took it back to Joe.

"Bless you, Mr. Murchison, Mr. Tyreen," Barnitz said. "But you lads are wasting your time. I'm gutshot. You ever know anyone who survived being gutshot?"

"Yes, I have," Hank said. "During the war I saw several men survive gut wounds."

"I'll be damned," Barnitz said. "Well, maybe I will and maybe I won't. Just in case, would one of you let me dictate a letter for my wife, then see that she gets it?"

"I'll write it," Joe promised. "But you can deliver it yourself."

As Joe was taking Barnitz's dictation, Hank wandered away to see what was going on elsewhere. The 7th was now going about the business of tending to the wounded and cleaning up the village. Included in this action was the shooting of several hundred ponies. It was a task the men undertook with little enthusiasm, but as Custer explained to them, it would make it more difficult for the Indians to make their raids against the innocent settlers next summer.

Hank didn't want to watch the ponies being killed, so he walked away. He saw a young woman in a deerskin dress standing over the body of the nude young girl. The woman was shivering in the cold. Hank saw another buffalo robe, picked it up, and draped it around the young woman's shoulders. She accepted it without a word.

"I know you probably can't understand me," Hank said. "But I'm sorry about the girl."

"What about the rest of it?" Rachel asked. "Are you sorry about it as well?"

"You speak English," Hank said in surprise.

"Yes, I speak English. My name is Rachel Stewart."

"Miss Stewart! Thank God you are alive! You are the reason we are here. We came to rescue you."

"And that's what all this slaughter was? A rescue? My God, I would have gladly been a prisoner of the Indians for another fifty years rather than witness all this."

"Perhaps, Miss Stewart," Custer said, coming over to join them then. "But let's not forget that you did write a letter, begging to be rescued."

"The letter," Rachel said. She sighed. "Yes, I did write it. And therefore I must share equal responsibility for this. I only pray that God will forgive me."

"I don't blame you for being disturbed by what has happened here," Custer said. "Even the most hardened soldier has a difficult time in the face of such slaughter. Unfortunately, Miss Stewart, it is the way of things in the world in which we have found ourselves. You'll feel better once you are safely back in civilization."

"Civilization, yes," Rachel said quietly. "I had nearly forgotten that we are the civilized ones." If Custer caught the irony of her remark, he said nothing.

Before they left the village, Custer called all his officers together.

"Gentlemen," he said, smiling broadly and rubbing his hands together in glee, "we have taught Lo a lesson he won't soon forget. We have recovered a white captive, and we have taken away the wherewithal for any nefarious activity the Indians might have planned for the future. The trains, stagecoaches, way stations, farms, and ranches of the white settlers in this part of the country are now secure, thanks to the Seventh Cavalry.''

The officers cheered.

"We are all saddened by the death of Captain Hamilton and the nineteen enlisted men. In addition, we have three officers and eleven enlisted men wounded. Is there any update to these figures?''

"What about Major Elliot?'' Hank asked.

"What about him?'' Custer replied easily.

"Hank's right, General,'' Joe said. "During the fight I saw him lead several troopers downstream after a group of fleeing Indians.''

"Aye, sir,'' Keogh added. "I saw him, too. And he took the regimental sergeant major with him.''

"Did he come back?''

"No, sir.''

"That's very odd. Does anybody else know anything about this?'' Custer asked, looking into the faces of all the men assembled.

None of them did.

Custer stroked his chin for a few moments, then said, "Then, gentlemen, it is my belief that Elliot has already returned to Camp Supply.'' Camp Supply was the interim post at which they were going to reassemble before going back up to Fort Hays.

"Don't you think we should go look for him?'' Benteen asked.

"What for?'' Custer replied. "Major Elliot is a big boy. He can find Camp Supply all by himself.''

"You mean we are just going to ride off and do nothing about him?''

"I told you, Captain, our business is finished here. If Major Elliot pursued the Indians for some distance, it would be an economy of movement for him to go directly to Camp

Supply rather than return here, and I would expect him to do just that.''

"General, if you'd like, I'll stay back and have a look around for him," Hank offered.

"No," Custer said. "I may have a need for you. And don't forget, we must get Miss Stewart back to . . ." He paused, then looked over at Rachel before he said the word. "Civilization."

With that, Rachel knew that he had caught the irony of her comment earlier.

"The poor woman has surely suffered enough," Custer continued. "Captain Benteen, prepare to move out."

"Yes, sir," Benteen replied. His tone of voice clearly showed that he would rather be leading a detail to locate Major Elliot.

Custer sent a courier ahead, carrying news of their victory to General Sheridan, who had promised to meet them at Camp Supply. Halfway there, a courier arrived from General Sheridan, bearing a message for Custer and the 7th. Upon reading the message, Custer broke into a big smile, then ordered the troops to be formed into a parade-front formation so he could read the message to them.

"Attention to orders, headquarters, Camp Supply," Custer began. "The energy and rapidity shown during one of the heaviest snowstorms known to this section of the country, with the temperature below freezing, the gallantry and bravery displayed, resulting in success, reflects highest credit on the Seventh Cavalry. The Major General, Commanding, expresses his thanks to the officers and men who were engaged in the Battle of the Washita, and extends his special congratulations to their distinguished Commander, Brevet Major General George A. Custer, for the efficient and gallant service opening the campaign against the hostile Indians."

Although there were too many men spread too wide for everyone to hear him, enough heard so that the message seeped through all the ranks.

"Gentlemen!" Custer shouted. "I salute the men of the

Seventh Cavalry! And when we return to Fort Hays, I promise you forty-eight hours without duties.''

"For the general!'' someone shouted. "Hip, hip . . .''

"Hooray!''

"Hip, hip . . .''

"Hooray!''

"Hip, hip . . .''

"Hooray!''

Doffing his hat, as he had so often during the Civil War, Custer returned to the front of the column.

"Bandmaster!'' he called.

"Yes, sir?''

"When we reach Camp Supply, the band will play 'Garryowen.' We shall return in triumph.''

"Yes, sir,'' the bandmaster agreed.

Twelve

Custer knew that General Phil Sheridan and the 19th Kansas Volunteers were waiting for him at Camp Supply, so when the 7th approached the gate he halted the column. There he orchestrated their entry in the way he wanted them to proceed for the pass in review.

The Osage Indian guides were moved to the front of the formation. They made quite a colorful sight, with their hair woven with feathers and silver ornaments. The Indian scouts carried rawhide shields, rifles, spears, and bows. Bloody scalps, recently gathered from the battle just fought, dangled from the spears. In addition, the flowing manes of the Indian scout ponies were trimmed with scalps as well as strips of red-and-blue cloth, cut from the Cheyenne blankets.

Behind the Indian scouts rode the three white scouts. The white scouts were Hank Tyreen, Jack Corbin, and Moses Embree Milner, who was known by the men as "California Joe." California Joe was the most colorful of the three, for he had lived among the Indians and could speak so many Indian dialects that he had already become a legend—a very dirty legend, since he didn't believe in bathing, but a legend.

The scouts were followed by the regimental band. Upon Custer's orders they began playing "Garryowen" the moment they passed through the gates of the stockaded post.

Custer rode behind the band. He was wearing dark blue

pants with twin gold stripes. These were actually the trousers of a general officer, and Custer, though he was called General, held the rank in brevet only and was not authorized to wear those trousers. However, he knew that no one would challenge him. He also wore a buckskin jacket and wide-brimmed hat, neither of which was part of the uniform. The buckskin jacket was trimmed in gold and festooned with the silver-leaf insignia of a lieutenant colonel.

Rachel Stewart rode behind Custer. She was wearing the white, beautifully trimmed deerskin dress the Cheyenne had given her, though because of the cold the dress was covered by a heavy buffalo robe. As she came through the gate and onto the post, Rachel looked neither right nor left, though from the corner of her eyes she could see that many were paying particular attention to her. Her cheeks burned as she realized they were contemplating her treatment at the hands of the savages. She had already experienced a little of that, as several of her "rescuers" had come up to her during the march back to ask whether or not the Indians had raped her. Some were genuinely concerned, but many, Rachel realized, were taking some sort of perverse enjoyment from the idea that she may have been used in such a way.

Behind Rachel rode fifty-three Cheyenne survivors of the fight at Washita, mostly widows and orphans. They were bundled up in blanket and robes, so well wrapped that only their eyes could be seen. Rachel knew that they expected to be killed, and after having witnessed the slaughter back in the village, she wasn't sure but that their fears might be justified.

The remainder of the regiment rode behind the widows and orphans. They were divided into companies, as if in line of march, each one behind their own fluttering guidons. The company-grade officers and noncommissioned officers rode in their accustomed positions.

When the entire regiment was inside the post, the massive gates were closed behind them. Custer halted his command, brought them around in parade-front formation, called them to attention, then galloped to the flagpole to render his report to General Sherman.

"Sir, the major general commanding announces to this command the defeat, by the Seventh Regiment of Cavalry, of a large force of Cheyenne Indians under the celebrated chief Black Kettle, reinforced by the Arapahoes under Little-Raven and the Kiowas under Santana, on the morning of the twenty-seventh, instant, on the Washita River near Antelope Hills, Indian territory, resulting in a loss to the savages of one hundred and three warriors."

Sheridan returned Custer's salute, then invited the commander to join him as the 7th passed in review.

On the next day Sheridan authorized one company of the 19th Regiment to be used to provide a guard detail for Rachel Stewart. Rachel was to be taken directly to Fort Hays, where she would be able to board a train and return to what remained of her family back in Illinois. Hank walked out to talk to her as the soldiers of the escort detail were making preparations to get under way. Rachel was standing next to the horse that had been provided for her.

"Are you all right?" Hank asked.

Rachel looked over at him. "Yes, thank you," she said. Her voice was flat and dispirited.

"Have you any family to go to?"

"I have family in Chicago," Rachel said.

"Is that where you'll be going?"

"I don't know. I haven't thought that far. For some time now, I've had no thought beyond the moment. It is easier that way."

"Yes, ma'am, I understand," Hank said. "That idea got lots of folks through the war."

"Prepare to mount!" called the commander of the company that would be escorting Rachel.

Rachel's horse holder held out the stirrup for her, and Rachel put both hands on the saddle pommel.

"May I help?" Hank asked. He made a stirrup with his hands and Rachel hoisted herself into the saddle, using his hands as a step up to the stirrup. When she was mounted, Hank took the reins from the horse holder and handed them to her.

"Thank you," she said quietly.

"Miss Stewart, I know you've been through a lot. First with your family being killed, then being a prisoner of the Indians, then getting caught up in the battle. But I've been watching you for the last several days, and I figure you've got the sand it takes to come through it all." Hank smiled. "Someday, fifty years from now, you'll be telling your grandchildren all about your great adventure."

"My grandmother told me about coming down the Ohio on a flatboat, Mr. Tyreen," Rachel said. "She described the beauty and serenity of the river. They were wonderful bedtime stories. I'm afraid I'll never be able to tell my stories at bedtime."

The commander ordered his troops forward, and Hank stepped back as Rachel, stoic as always, started out with them.

When Major Elliot did not show up at Camp Supply, Custer decided to route 7th Cavalry's return to Fort Hays through the site of the Washita battle. General Sheridan, who was anxious to see the spot of Custer's triumph, accompanied the regiment. The 19th Kansas Volunteers joined them as well, so that the column was twice as large now as it had been during the battle.

When the marching column reached the crest of the hill from which Hank had first observed the peaceful scene of a sleeping village, Custer called a halt. There, while the men rested their animals, General Sheridan and several of the officers from the 19th Kansas followed Custer up the hill and out to the edge of the tree line. From that vantage point Custer pointed down into the valley as he animatedly described the tactics he had used during the attack. Hank wasn't close enough to overhear the conversation, but he could see the excitement in Custer's eyes and the eagerness with which Sheridan and the curious, and somewhat envious, officers received the briefing.

After a few minutes Custer and the others returned to the body of troops, remounted, then rode down the side of the hill and out into the place where the village had been. The village was gone now, with only blackened circles to indicate where tepees and hogans had once stood. Several Indian bodies were still lying around, most of them frozen to the ground in the same position in which they had fallen. Some of the bodies had been lifted up and put into the forks of trees, some had been wrapped in blankets, and some had been covered with straw, but most lay exposed to the elements.

One exposed body was that of the nude young girl Rachel Stewart had been standing over when Hank found her. Running Deer, as Rachel had called her, was lying facedown with a gaping black hole in the back of her head. And though some of the other bodies were showing evidence of flesh-eating scavengers, Running Deer's body was still without a blemish, other than the bullet wound that had killed her.

Hank found a buffalo robe. Most of the robes had been taken by the surviving Indians and by the soldiers, but this one had been left behind because it was partially burned. He spread it over her. He knew it wouldn't protect her from the carrion, but somehow it seemed proper. The least he could do now, he thought, was provide her with a little dignity.

"It's eerie, isn't it?" Joe Murchison said, coming over to stand beside him.

"Yes," Hank agreed.

"Is this what the battlefields were like after a battle?"

"Somewhat, I suppose," Hank answered without elaboration. He thought of some of the battles he had been in: Shiloh, Antietam, Lookout Mountain, Franklin, Saylor Creek. There had been thousands of bodies scattered across those fields, and many more thousands of men who had been wounded. After one day of fighting at Antietam there were so many dead in the cornfield, Union and Confederate alike, that a man could walk from one side of the field to the other without his feet touching the ground.

For the most part, however, the ghosts of those battle-fields had been young men, armed soldiers who were killed in the fight. An unusually large number of these bodies were old men, women, and children. Out of slightly over one hundred bodies, he could see only a dozen or so of warrior age. Upon casual observation, it might appear as if the battle here had been little more than wanton slaughter. But only those who did not participate in the fight could come to such a conclusion.

In truth, on the morning of the attack, age and gender had meant nothing. It did not keep them out of the battle, and despite the fact that the field looked unbalanced now, Hank was well aware that nearly everyone here had been wielding a gun and holding their own.

"Mr. Tyreen," Captain Yates called, "would you accompany me up this creekbed to search for Major Elliot, sir?"

"Yes, of course, I'd be glad to," Hank replied, turning away from Running Deer's body. He swung into his saddle, then followed Yates and ten of his men up the creekbed.

They had ridden for just under a mile when they saw the first soldier's body. There was no uniform to identify him as a soldier, but he had obviously been a white man. He was on his back, with a dozen or more arrows sticking out of his body. His right hand, left foot, and penis had been cut off. There were long gashes in both legs, and the wounds were blue-gray rather than red.

"Captain Yates, up here, sir!" shouted one of the men in advance. "We've found Major Elliot and the others!"

Hank spurred his horse to a canter and followed Captain Yates up the gulley for another two hundred yards.

"Oh, God," Yates said. "Look at that."

"Father in heaven!" a soldier gasped.

Elliot's men were on the ground, lying with their feet together, facing out in a circle as if they were spokes in a wagon wheel. This was obviously the site of Elliot's last fight. It had not been a very well-chosen defensive position, because there was high ground all around them.

"They must've put up one hell of a fight," one of the soldiers said. "Look at all the empty shell casings."

Major Elliot and all the men with him were as badly mutilated as the soldier they had found two hundred yards back.

"Some of the Indians we captured told us there were three more camps up this way," Yates said. "We didn't know it at the time, but there were probably another five thousand Indians camped along this creek. Elliot never had a chance."

"We should have come after him," Lieutenant Weir said.

"Didn't you hear what I said, Weir? There were five thousand Indians up here. If we had come after Major Elliot, we would all be lying here now," Yates suggested.

Weir chuckled. "Captain, are you trying to tell me that a bunch of Indians, no matter how many there might be, could do something like this to an entire regiment?"

"We were, how many? A little under six hundred? The Indians had us outnumbered almost ten to one. If you ask me, we were lucky that Elliot and these men were all that we lost."

"What are we going to do with them?" Weir asked.

"Get out picks and shovels and break them loose from the ground. We'll take them all back down the creek to where General Custer and the others are. We'll bury them there, I suppose."

"Elliot, too? He's an officer."

Yates stroked his chin, then wiped a cold, dripping nose with his sleeve. "No, I imagine we'll take him all the way back to Fort Hays with us. Then, more than likely, the army will ship his body back to his people."

"Major Elliot and Captain Hamilton killed. And Barnitz, too, probably," Weir said.

Yates shook his head. "Don't count Barnitz out. He's a tough old bird. It wouldn't surprise me if he pulls through this."

Weir chuckled. "Yeah, he was sure giving them what for

back at Camp Supply, wasn't he?" Then, turning to the others, Weir gave the order. "Let's go, men, let's get these bodies broken loose. They deserve a decent burying."

Just before dark Hank stood with Lieutenant Joe Murchison, Lieutenant Weir, Captain Yates, General Custer, and the others from the 7th and the 19th as the bodies of the slain troopers were wrapped in blankets and lowered into a large, common grave. With heads bowed, they said good-bye to nineteen enlisted men, including the regimental sergeant major. The men were buried on top of the hill, overlooking the valley, where two weeks earlier they had stood anxiously, awaiting Custer's orders to attack.

"Shouldn't we fire a volley or play 'Taps' or something, General Custer?" Captain Benteen asked.

Custer shook his head. "We'll send them off with our prayers," he said. "No need to be firing volleys or playing 'Taps' right now. Only two weeks ago there were over five thousand Indians right here, against our six hundred, yet we were victorious. Who is to say that the heathens aren't nearby, just waiting for a chance to have their revenge?"

"It just doesn't seem proper," Benteen grumbled.

"It's proper enough," Custer replied. He looked at the men who were gathered around the large open grave, though not in any particular formation. "Officers and men of the Seventh and Nineteenth, hats off."

Hank, Joe, and the others doffed their hats. They all stood silently for a moment, then Custer said: "Amen."

"Amen," several repeated.

"Officers of the Seventh, prepare your men to move out. We are going to Fort Hays. General Sheridan, officers and men of the Nineteenth, we bid thee adieu."

By the time the Seventh returned to Fort Hays, Rachel Stewart was already gone. Alice Patterson, true to her word, was also gone. Hank had expected this, of course, but Joe was caught by surprise, and he moped around for a few days, drinking more heavily than usual and talking about resigning from the army so he could go after her.

"That would be the dumbest thing you ever did," Hank said as the two men drank beer in the back of the Sutler's Store.

"It's obvious to me, sir, that you have never been in love," Joe slurred. "If you had, you wouldn't say anything like that."

"I thought I was in love, once," Hank said.

"What happened?"

"When I came back from the war she was married to someone else. A Yankee carpetbagger, in fact."

"What did you do?"

"I left town."

"I mean, what did you do to the Yankee carpetbagger who married your sweetheart?"

"I didn't do anything to him," Hank answered. "I told you, I left town."

"Then you weren't really in love with her," Joe said, taking another swallow of his beer.

"That's my whole point, Joe," Hank said. "I thought I was in love with her, just as you think you are in love with Alice Patterson. But I wasn't, and you aren't."

"What makes you think I'm not in love with Alice Patterson?"

"Because you are good man. Much too good a man to waste yourself on a woman like that."

Joe looked up in confusion, then quick anger. "What did you say? What do you mean, when you call her 'a woman like that'?"

"I think you know what I mean."

"Careful, Mr. Tyreen."

"Joe, I didn't want to be the one to tell you this, but Alice Patterson is no damned good. She is a tramp who will sleep with any man who asks her."

Joe stood up so quickly that the chair he was sitting in fell over with a loud clatter. He pointed accusingly at Hank. "Mister, I could kill you for that!" he shouted.

Joe's explosive condemnation of Hank brought the conversation of the others in the room to a complete halt. As ragged sentences hung incomplete in the air, everyone looked toward Joe and Hank to see what was going on. They saw Joe standing on one side of the table, glaring in anger at Hank. Hank was sitting calmly on the opposite side, both hands on the table. The scene held their rapt attention.

"Joe, do you think I enjoy telling you this?" Hank asked. Because the room had grown deathly quiet, his words were heard clearly by all. "I said what I said for your own good."

"Mister," Joe said, pointing at Hank, "you have insulted the woman I love. I demand satisfaction!"

"Hold it, Lieutenant Murchison, you don't want to do that," Captain Benteen called over to him. He had been sitting at a table on the far side of the room, writing a letter to his wife back in St. Louis. Like the others in the room, he had interrupted his activity to observe the drama unfolding before them. "It is a court-martial offense for an officer to participate in a duel."

"With all due respect, sir, my disagreement with Mr. Tyreen is none of your business," Joe said coldly.

"That's where you are wrong, Mister Murchison," Benteen answered forcefully. He stood up and walked toward the two men. The others continued to watch in silence. "You are an officer in the United States Army. Mr. Tyreen is an employee of the United States Army. I am superior to both of you in rank, and that makes any disagreement between the two of you my business."

Hank was still seated, and he looked up at Joe to see the hurt and anger in the eyes of the young officer who had been his friend.

Hank sighed. "Lieutenant, I had four years of killing men who were wearing uniforms exactly like the one you are wearing now," he said. "And now I find that I am in the killing business again. I don't know about you, but I take no pleasure from killing. I don't enjoy killing my enemies, I won't kill my friends, and I damned sure don't want any of my friends to kill me." He smiled as he made the last comment, hoping to elicit a smile from the scowling young officer. His attempt at humor was unsuccessful.

"You should have thought of that before you passed that remark," Joe said angrily.

Hank stood up. "I'll tell you what," he said. "I am going to apologize to you in front of all these people, and then I am going to leave Fort Hays. Captain Benteen, I hereby tender my resignation. Please give my regards to General Custer."

"Your apology isn't accepted," Joe said angrily. "Not unless you withdraw the comment you made about Miss Patterson."

Hank looked at Joe for a long moment, and the silence was almost palpable. Finally he sighed. "Very well, Mr. Murchison. I withdraw my comment about Miss Patterson. Upon further reflection, I find that I now feel she is too good for you."

Without giving Joe a chance to react, Hank left the Sutler's Store. He walked quickly over to his room, where, from behind a loose board, he removed the money he had thus far earned as a scout for the 7th. It took only a moment to pack his few belongings into his roll and saddlebags. After that he went to the stable, saddled his horse, and started out.

As he rode by the chapel, he heard the congregation singing Christmas carols. It wasn't until that moment that he thought about it.

It was Christmas Eve.

Thirteen

Hank had carried the saddle for nearly two miles, and when he reached the railroad track he dropped his load with a sigh of relief. He climbed the small grade and stood in the middle of the track, scratching the beard he had let grow during his weeks out on the prairie. He looked toward the west at the spreading color of the setting sun.

Hank had been living in Ellsworth for nearly two years now, working at odd jobs in between buffalo herd migrations. At the moment, he was waiting for them to come back down from the summer migration to the north. Last year had been a good one for him. He had made over $6,000 hunting buffalo, providing meat to the railroads and hides to the processors back east.

But buffalo hunting was seasonal, and when the herd went back north, Hank, like all the other buffalo hunters, had to subsist on his savings or take on odd jobs.

Fortunately Ellsworth was a bustling town. It was an important railroad hub, it was the headquarters of buffalo hunters who were waiting for the season to begin, and it was a terminus of several of the large cattle drives from Texas. As a result, there were many ways a person could earn a living, and at one time or another over the past two years, Hank had tried them all.

The occupation that best suited him, though, was hunting

buffalo. And it wasn't only the money, though it did pay better than anything else Hank could imagine. It was the activity. He enjoyed the hunt, and he enjoyed the isolation.

It was now late fall, and soon the great herd would be coming south to its winter feeding area. Their arrival could not be kept secret, but whoever spotted it first would have a distinct advantage over all the other buffalo hunters, for he would get a head start. That was what had brought Hank out onto the prairie two days ago. But late this afternoon, his horse had stepped in a gopher hole and broken his leg.

Reluctantly, though without a choice, Hank had destroyed him. He was better than twenty miles away from town when it happened, but only a few miles from the railroad. He could only hope that the train from Abilene would stop for him.

Hank knelt by the track and put his ear to one of the iron ribbons. He could hear the faint humming of the track that told him the train was just over the curve of the horizon. He knew he was lucky, because had he missed it, another wouldn't be due until the next morning.

Hank looked around until he found a couple of branches that were just about the right size to make a torch to signal the train. He wrapped sage grass around the end of the branches when he saw the first wisp of smoke from the train, then he waited as the train approached. He knew that it was running at thirty miles an hour, but the vast openness of the plain gave the illusion of slowness to its approach. Against the gold-and-red vault of the late afternoon sky, the train appeared little larger than a crawling insect.

Hank lit the sage grass, and the torch began smoking. He stepped up to the side of the track and watched as the train grew nearer. He could hear the chugging of the engine as it labored, pulling the train across the vast open prairie, and he started waving the smoking torch back and forth to signal the engineer.

A moment after he began waving the torch, the engineer blew his whistle and Hank knew he had been spotted. He ground out the fire on the end of his torch, then walked back

down and picked up his saddle and gear. He knew now that
the engineer had not only seen him, but planned to stop, for
he heard the steam valve close as the engineer braked his
train.

As the engine drew very close, Hank was able to put into
perspective just how vast this country was, for the train that
had resembled an insect but moments before was now a
behemoth lurching toward him. It ground to a chugging,
squealing, squeaking halt, puffing black smoke, wreathed in
tendrils of white steam that purpled in the light of the setting
sun as it drifted away.

A conductor stepped down from one of the cars and, seeing Hank, came toward him.

"Did you signal the train to stop?" he asked.

"I did. I lost my horse. I need a ride into town."

"It'll cost you two dollars."

"Two dollars? Isn't that a little steep?"

"Railroad rules," the conductor replied. "Anyone who
boards the train during an unscheduled stop will be charged
the fare from the previous scheduled stop. That would be
Abilene. The fare from Abilene to Ellsworth is two dollars.
Like I say, it's the rules."

"Rules? It's robbery," Hank said, growling as he took
out the money.

"You can always walk into town," the conductor suggested.

"No thanks. I'll pay the robber baron that owns this railroad his fee."

"Very good, sir. Now, if you would, please, get on board
quickly. This stop has thrown us off our schedule," the conductor said.

The conductor went back to the last car, but Hank went
into the first one. He dropped his saddle in the vestibule,
but because he thought it unwise to leave his rifle unat-
tended, he slipped it out of the saddle holster and carried it
with him as he went inside. The rifle was a genuine buffalo
gun, a Sharps fifty-caliber, half again as large as an ordinary
rifle. It could throw a quarter-pound projectile for over a

mile, and though buffalo would sometimes continue to run after being hit with one, two, or even three normal-size bullets, one bullet from a Sharps 50 would bring the beast down in an instant.

There were half a dozen people in the first car, and they looked at him nervously. Hank realized that they were frightened by his unexpected appearance, especially as he was carrying such a large rifle. Some might even think he was a train robber.

"I'm sorry about making the train stop, folks," Hank said. He held up the rifle. "I'm a buffalo hunter. My horse went lame, and I needed a ride back into town, that's all."

Hank touched the brim of his hat, then sat near a window as the train, with bumps and jerks, started rolling again. Soon they were back up to speed, and Hank watched the countryside roll by as the light dimmed and finally changed to darkness. The conductor came through the car and lit the overhead gas lamps. Patches of yellow were projected from the windows of the train onto the ground below.

It was very dark by the time the train reached the station, but the station platform was so brightly lit by nearly a dozen gas lamps that it shone like a golden bubble. Hank got off the train, then walked up to the engine to thank the engineer for stopping.

"My pleasure, mister," the engineer said. "Wouldn't want to leave a man afoot out there."

Hank carried his saddle over to the livery stable.

"Where's your horse?" the liveryman asked.

"He broke his leg in a gopher hole," Hank said grimly. He didn't have to say anything more, because the liveryman understood exactly what had happened to him.

"That's a shame," the liveryman said. "I know you set quite a store by that horse."

"He was a good horse," Hank said.

A couple of people ran by in front of the livery stable.

"They're on the other side of the track!" one of them called.

"Bat and Ed have gone after 'em," the other man shouted back.

Hank saw a crowd of people gathered around a small shed on the other side of the track, and he stepped out into the street to look down that way.

"There were a couple of drunken cowboys shooting up the place a few minutes ago, just before the train arrived," the liveryman volunteered. "They told some people in the saloon that if any of the marshals come after 'em, they was gonna kill 'im."

Suddenly four or five gunshots erupted from the other side of the track, and Hank heard someone shout. He started toward the track on the run, then he saw young Ed Masterson coming out of the darkness toward him.

"Ed! Ed, what is it? What's going on?" Hank asked.

Hank saw a peculiar glowing, then he realized that it was a circle of fire. Ed's coat was burning.

Ed looked at Hank with a half smile on his face, then fell facedown to the ground. Hank ran over to him and rolled the young marshal over. He patted out the ring of fire on his jacket. That was when he realized what had caused the fire in the first place. Ed Masterson had been shot at point-blank range, and the powder blast from the revolver had set his jacket ablaze.

"There he goes, Sheriff!" a man's voice sounded from the dark on the other side of the tracks. Hank instinctively drew his pistol and peered into the darkness.

A figure suddenly appeared on the railroad track, having run up the slight grade from the dark on the other side. He was tall and rangy, with a bushy, walrus-type mustache. He was wearing a high-crowned hat of the type favored by the range cowboys, and Hank saw a flash of light from one of the rowels on his spurs. The man was carrying a pistol, and Hank saw him pointing it back toward the dark from which he had come. The gun in the man's hand boomed three times, and in the light of the muzzle flash, Hank could see the almost demonic features of his face.

His three shots were answered by three shots from the

darkness, coming back so quickly that had it not been for the sharp definition of sound, Hank would have thought they were echoes. The gunman on the track suddenly threw up his gun, then fell backward, sliding headfirst down the railroad embankment on the near side. Hank ran over to him and saw bubbles of blood coming from his mouth. He was trying hard to breathe, and Hank heard a sucking sound in his chest. He knew then that at least one bullet had penetrated his lungs.

"Oh, damn," the cowboy said. "Oh, damn, I've been kilt, haven't I?"

"Is the son of a bitch dead?" a calm voice asked from the track. Hank looked up to see Bat Masterson standing there with his gun in one hand and his cane in the other.

"He will be shortly," Hank replied.

"Where's Ed?" Bat asked, looking around. "I saw him coming this way. I don't know, I think he may have been hit."

"He's over there, Bat," Hank said, pointing toward the still form of Bat's brother.

"What?" Bat gasped. "No, he wasn't hit that badly! He couldn't have been!" Bat ran toward his brother's body, then dropped to his knees beside him. By that time more than two dozen people had climbed the railroad embarkment from the dark on the other side of the track.

"There he is," someone said, pointing to the dead cowboy at Hank's feet. "Bat got both of 'em, slick as a whistle."

"This'n ain't dead yet," someone else said.

"Let's string 'im up!" another suggested.

"No need in that," Hank said.

"You planning on being the one to stop us?"

"Won't have to stop you," Hank said. "He'll be dead before you can find a rope."

"Hank's right," the doctor said. "This fella doesn't have more'n a minute or two left."

By now nearly a hundred people had collected around these two bodies, and Hank gathered from the conversation that there was another body on the other side of the tracks. Several more people came hurrying toward the commotion from town, and Hank could hear the clomp of boots on boards as they ran down the wooden sidewalks, drawn to the excitement.

Hank looked toward Bat and saw him squatted beside his brother, holding his hand over his eyes. His pearl-handled, silver-plated gun was lying in the dirt beside him, totally forgotten in his sorrow. The doctor had left the outlaw and was now checking for Ed's pulse.

"I'm sorry, Bat, he's gone," Hank heard the doctor say quietly.

"Hey, Doc, this here'n just died."

The doctor looked back toward the man Hank had seen shot. "I figured he would," he said.

There were even more people coming to the scene now, and Hank felt the urge to leave, to disassociate himself from the morbid curiosity that was running so rampant.

It had been his original intention to go straight to his room after dropping off his saddle, but now he decided he would stop by the Lucky Lou Saloon and have a beer instead. He felt unique. He was the only one walking toward town, whereas he passed dozens of people coming away from town.

"What is it?" they would ask as they passed him by.

"What happened down there?"

"Has there been a killing?"

The questions were all shouted by passersby, but Hank made no effort to answer any of them.

The Lucky Lou Saloon was midway down the street on the left. It was easy to find, because of all the golden patches of light that spilled through the windows and doors of the buildings, the brightest patch lay in the street in front of the Lucky Lou. Hank pushed through the swinging doors and walked inside.

Normally, at this time of night, the saloon would be very busy. But the excitement at the other end of town had drawn everyone away, so it was actually very quiet inside. The piano player was sitting with his back to his instrument, drinking a beer and looking out at the nearly empty saloon. The bartender was making lazy swipes across the top of the bar with his towel, and a couple of the girls were sharing a table with a single customer. The customer was Wild Bill Hickok.

"Hank!" Hickok called, smiling broadly when he looked up to see him. "Come and join us. These two young ladies are new to our city, and I'm doing my civic duty by welcoming them. What was all the commotion?"

"A gunfight down by the switching shack," Hank answered. He took a beer from the bartender, then carried it over to sit at the table.

"Bat and Ed get it taken care of all right?" Hickok asked. "I offered my services, but Bat told me to stay here."

"Ed was killed."

The smile left Hickok's face. "Killed? Damn, I should've gone with them, no matter what Bat said. Killed, you say? I never expected anything like that, certainly not from a couple of drunken cowboys. What about Bat?"

"He's all right. He killed the two men who killed his brother."

"Well, I'm glad for that, at least. Oh, was it a fair fight? I mean, Bat didn't just shoot them down, did he? He won't be in any trouble?"

"I don't know about the first one," Hank answered. "But I saw the second man killed. He was standing on the track, shooting at Bat, when Bat shot him."

"Good. Bat's going to have a hard enough time of it, dealing with his brother being killed. He doesn't need to be going to court, defending what he did. Say, what are you doing back here, anyway? I thought you were out looking for the herd."

"I was."

"Did you find it?" Hickok asked excitedly.

Hank shook his head. "Didn't see any buffalo, didn't see any sign."

"Then why did you come back so fast? You just went out a few days ago, didn't you?"

"Lost my horse," Hank said.

"You going back out?"

"Not for a few days. I think I was out there too early," Hank said.

"See any Indian sign?"

"No," Hank answered.

"Well, I don't think we're going to have any problem with them north of the Arkansas River. But I sure wouldn't want to be wandering around south of the river without an army escort."

"With Custer back east for a while, they are getting a little bolder," Hank said.

"Say, what about that young lieutenant you befriended? What was his name? Murchison?"

"Yes, Joe Murchison."

"How is he getting along?"

"I haven't heard from him," Hank said. "Though I understand he's in Europe now."

"Europe? What's he doing over there?"

"He is a military observer of the Franco-Prussian War."

"That seems like a damn fool thing to do," Hickok said. "Don't we have enough wars over here without having to send someone to Europe just to watch one?"

"You would think that, wouldn't you?" Hank said.

"I swear, if I'm not feeling positively ignored," one of the two women said.

Hickok chuckled. "Forgive me, forgive me, my dear," he said. "Hank, you haven't had the privilege of meeting our town's two newest and loveliest citizens, have you? They arrived just yesterday."

"No, I haven't had the pleasure," Hank admitted.

"Then allow me to remedy that. The young woman to your right is Kate. Isn't she lovely?"

Kate, who was the more attractive of the two, beamed under Hickok's praise.

"Kate allows as how she is practically a virgin, since she

will only go to bed with gentlemen for whom she feels a particular affinity.''

"What does that mean?" Kate asked.

"It means people you like," Hank explained easily.

Kate put her hand on Hank's hand and squeezed it lightly. She was a soiled dove, but she couldn't have been in the business very long, for she hadn't yet taken on that dissipated look so common to women of her profession. The other woman, Hank noticed, did have that look.

"Molly, our redheaded friend, is considerably more democratic than her younger sister," Hickok said. "She will hop in bed with anyone who has the price."

"We aren't sisters," Molly said quickly.

"I meant the term figuratively," Hickok explained. Then, to Hank, he added, "Molly, you see, believes devoutly in the biblical commission to 'love thy neighbor,' and she does her best to accommodate as many of her neighbors as she can. She has even been known to share her bed with a buffalo hunter or two. Or is it with a buffalo?"

Molly laughed good-naturedly. "You are really a card, you know that, Mr. Hickok?"

"So I have been told," Hickok replied. "At any rate, I'm about ready to call it a night. I would be honored, my dear, if you would call it a night with me," he added, holding his arm out toward Molly.

"Why, I would be very pleased to go with you, Mr. Hickok," Molly replied.

"What your friend said about me is true," Kate said after Hickok and Molly were gone. "I will only go to bed with people I like."

"I see," Hank said.

"I like you."

"Do you?"

"I do indeed. And I have a room upstairs. You could come up with me if you want to."

"So early? Don't you have to wait until eleven o'clock?"

Kate laughed. "No," she said. "Molly and I have an arrangement with the owner of the saloon. We will help him sell drinks, but other than that, we are in business for ourselves.''

"Then, yes, I think I would like to come up with you," Hank said. He was surprised at just how quickly his sexual appetite had been stimulated.

"It's the third door down on the right," she said. "You go on up and wait for me there. I'll get us a bottle."

Hank started up the stairs. By now several more of the saloon's customers had returned, and snatches of their conversations reached him. They were talking about the shooting, and Hank couldn't help but think of the corpses of the three young men who were now lying in the morgue just down the street. They would never again be with a woman. The thought made him feel a little uneasy, so he pushed it aside as he hurried up to Kate's room to wait for her.

When Kate knocked on the door a moment later, Hank smiled at the idea of her knocking on her own door.

"Come in, by all means, come in," he called.

Kate slipped through the door, then closed it behind her. She stood in front of it and smiled self-consciously at Hank.

"Why did you knock?"

"I don't know," Kate said. "It just seemed to be the right thing to do." She held up a bottle. "I hope you like this. It is real Tennessee mash, not some local rotgut."

"I'm sure that I will like it," Hank said. He reached for the bottle, but when he saw no glasses in her room, he pulled the cork and drank right from the bottle, never taking his eyes off the girl.

Kate undid the ribbon that held her hair and shook her head to let it tumble down. That simple act created the amazing illusion of transforming her from a prostitute to an innocent young girl, and for a second Hank hesitated. He had no intention of being a despoiler, but that was exactly what he felt like.

"Anything wrong?" she asked, noticing the expression on his face.

Hank took another drink straight from the bottle, then shook his head to clear the image. "No, nothing is wrong."

Kate moved closer, then reached out to touch him with cool, soft hands. Hank put his hand on hers and held it for just an instant. His need for her grew stronger, and he moved his hand from hers up to the top of her dress. Holding it there for a moment, he could feel her warm, heavy breasts through the material.

"I'll get undressed now," Kate said.

She looked at him through smoke-gray eyes and began removing her clothes, pulling the dress off her shoulders and pushing it down her body.

Hank slipped out of his own clothes quickly and stood there naked as he watched Kate continue to undress, fascinated by the almost languid way she did so. Her studied actions had the effect of inflaming his desire to an even greater pitch.

Kate folded her clothes very carefully and placed them, one item at a time, on the chest near the water basin. Then she turned to face him once more. Her body was subtly lighted by the lantern that burned on her dresser. The area at the junction of her legs was darkened by the shadows and by a tangle of hair that curled at her thighs.

"Shall we?" Kate invited, moving her arm toward her bed. Though they were both naked and the bed beckoned, the invitation was as guileless as if she had just asked him if he wanted a cup of tea. It made the moment all the more erotic.

Once in bed, Kate came to Hank with a kiss. This in itself was unusual, Hank knew, for soiled doves rarely kissed their customers. They tended to guard the kiss as the last vestige of their privacy.

Kate opened her mouth on his, and Hank sent his tongue darting against hers as he rolled on top of her. Kate received him easily, wrapping her legs around him, meeting his thrusts by pushing against him. Hank lost himself in the pleasurable sensations until a few minutes later, when Kate began a frenzied moaning and jerking beneath him. He let himself go then, thrusting against her until at last he played out his own passion.

Fourteen

From June until October of 1871, only one inch of rain had fallen on Chicago. The prolonged drought, which had left animals out on the prairie dead and dying around dried-up mud holes, had been nearly as brutal to the three hundred thousand people who lived in the city. The vast majority of Chicago's dwellings were wood, and the wood had dried and cured in the sun so that the slightest spark could ignite a fire. And though it was only one week into October, the number of fires had already equaled the highest number of fires in any previous month. The overworked fire department was battling fires at the rate of ten per day.

Most of the fires occurred in the shanty towns, the immigrant areas of town where people could least afford insurance, so that every fire was a disaster. In these parts of the city there scarcely seemed enough time in one day for the poor people to earn their bread. So, long before the sun rose, they would be out working, trying to stretch the hours to meet their needs.

Fishmongers, their wagons loaded with yesterday's catch, pushed their carts through the narrow, twisting back alleys. They moved through the garbage and sewage, hawking their wares, protected from the stench by the peculiar odors of their own profession.

With the fishmongers went the vegetable peddlers, the

bread sellers, the milk dealers, all filling the air with their calls, given in a distinctive singsong voice that identified them to their personal customers.

At the other end of the day, when the sun went down and the more affluent part of Chicago went home to family or out to restaurants and saloons to relax and play, Chicago's poor continued their labors. Someone had to drive the hacks, work in the kitchens, and stock the merchants' shelves so the next day could begin all over again.

Rachel's time in the city had been equally as hard, and she related to those people who struggled to survive.

It wasn't always like this. When Rachel had arrived in Chicago almost three years ago, she was hired as a schoolteacher. And though teaching school was not a high-salaried position, it did pay enough for Rachel's simple needs, and it was a position of respect. It was also something that she very much enjoyed.

Rachel was quite comfortable with the idea of being a schoolteacher for the rest of her life. But that all ended when the school board president, Mr. Lyman Tanner, sent her a letter, suggesting that she resign.

"Why should I resign?" Rachel asked when she took the letter to his office to inquire about it.

"I had hoped you would have the good grace not to bring the matter to a head-to-head confrontation," Tanner said. He was a small man, about an inch shorter than Rachel. He had very thin, light brown hair, which he combed across the top of his head in an attempt to conceal his baldness. His watery blue eyes seemed enlarged by the glasses he wore.

"You are asking me to give up my livelihood, and walk out on the children, without even questioning it?"

"I suppose it was foolish of me to think you would do the right thing now, when you have shown a disinclination to do so in the past. Please, Miss Stewart. For the good of the children, won't you just leave quietly?"

"What do you mean, 'for the good of the children'? It is for the children that I intend to stay. I am a good teacher, Mr. Tanner. You have written letters of commendation in which you say so yourself. I've also received similar letters from the parents of the children.''

"It is not a question of your teaching abilities, Miss Stewart,'' Tanner said.

"Then I don't understand. If not my teaching, what?''

"There is also a moral consideration.''

Rachel gasped. "What? You are questioning my morals? Has someone brought a charge against me? If so, what is the charge?''

"We have just learned that you lived with the Indians for a period of time. Is that true?''

"Yes.''

Tanner cleared his throat. "Then by your own admission the accusation is true. And, that being the case, we . . . that is, the school board and I . . . feel that your continued presence around the children would constitute a moral liability.''

"That is ridiculous. I was a *captive* of the Indians, not a guest,'' Rachel said resolutely.

"Yes, so we have been told. And that is all the more reason for concern,'' Tanner replied. "Miss Stewart, it is our belief that you lost your innocence to the savages.''

"My innocence? You are concerned with my innocence?''

"Well, after all, the fate of white female captives of Indians is quite well documented. You were their prisoner. They must have, uh . . .''

"They must have what?''

"I think you know what I mean, Miss Stewart. It shouldn't be necessary to spell it out.''

"Yes, it is necessary. As I told you earlier, this is my livelihood we are talking about. I want you to spell it out.'' Rachel was upset, and though she knew she was already fighting a losing battle, she didn't intend to make it easy for him.

Tanner pinched the bridge of his nose and frowned in irritation. "Very well, Miss Stewart, you leave me no choice. I had hoped we could deal with this in a civilized manner, but given your moral character, I suppose a confrontation was inevitable. I *shall* spell it out. Did the Indians . . . use you? By that I mean, did they . . .''

"Are you asking me if I was raped, Mr. Tanner?"

"Yes," Tanner replied. "I am asking if you were raped. I'm sorry for the indelicate question, but you have left me no choice."

"Why do you need to know that?"

"Because, whether or not you were raped goes directly to your morality, and to the corrupting influence your continued presence would have on innocent children."

"How could a rape victim have a corrupting moral influence on innocent children? On anyone, for that matter?" Rachel asked. "If a woman is raped, she is not a participant *in* the act, she is a victim *of* the act. An *innocent* victim, I might add."

Tanner cleared his throat. "Technically, I suppose she is innocent," he said. "In that she did not initiate the action. Although a woman who allows herself to be raped does create a situation of doubt."

"I see."

"So I ask you again, Miss Stewart. Were you raped?"

"I refuse to answer that question, Mr. Tanner. Whether or not I was raped should have no bearing on my ability to teach school."

"I'm sorry, but we feel that it does, and if you refuse to resign, we shall be forced to dismiss you."

Harboring the unreasonable hope that the school board would reverse Mr. Tanner, Rachel refused to resign. Her dismissal came with the next post.

Rachel's aunt Maybelle and uncle Raymond knew that she had not been raped, because when she had first returned to Chicago, she'd told them everything. She'd even told them that she had befriended the Cheyenne girl Running Deer and had mourned her loss, as well as the loss of several of the other Indians.

"Why didn't you tell the school board that you weren't raped?" her uncle Raymond asked. "It seems to me like a simple enough thing."

"It wouldn't have made any difference. They were bound to dismiss me anyway. Besides, it's not simple," Rachel replied. "Don't you see? Why should I be considered innocent just because I wasn't raped? I would be no more guilty if I had been . . . especially as I had no control over either outcome."

"That's just the way things are, dear," her aunt Maybelle said.

"Well, they shouldn't be that way."

"And you shouldn't have let the Indians capture you," said her uncle Raymond.

"*Let* the Indians capture me?" Rachel said in a shocked tone. "What do you mean by that? Do you think I volunteered to go with them?"

"Yes!" Raymond shouted, bringing the argument to a close. "You volunteered to go with them the moment you decided not to shoot yourself, as any decent, God-fearing, and innocent woman would have done."

Rachel was so stunned by her uncle's declaration that she was silent for a long moment. Then she asked very quietly, "Is that what this is all about? Do you actually resent me because I didn't shoot myself when the Indians attacked the wagon train?"

"It's not enough that you debased yourself," Raymond said. "You also managed to bring disgrace upon your family, and since we are the only family you have left, that means you have brought disgrace upon us. My God, I can scarcely hold my head up among my friends and business associates."

"Well, I'll try not to humiliate you any further," Rachel said. "I'll move out of your house today."

"Rachel, no, he didn't mean that," her aunt Maybelle said. "You're welcome to stay as long as you like."

"I *have* stayed for as long as I like, Aunt Maybelle," Rachel said.

Rachel moved out of her aunt and uncle's house, got a room of her own, and went through a succession of jobs, leaving whenever someone discovered the secret of her scandalous past as a captive of those "dirty, smelly Indians." Actually, for a resident of the city of Chicago to call any place or person "dirty or smelly" seemed to Rachel to be the ultimate irony.

With her current job, however, things seemed to be looking up somewhat. She was a seamstress, and it was a position she enjoyed. She was employed by Mrs. Mollie O'Connor, who owned a dress shop on De Koven Street. Mrs. O'Connor did a brisk business, supplying ball gowns to Chicago's wealthiest citizens.

Rachel not only enjoyed her work, she dearly loved the woman for whom she worked. Molly O'Connor had taken a personal interest in Rachel, teaching her not only how to sew, but how to design, and Rachel was beginning to have dreams of perhaps owning her own dressmaking business someday.

One of the things Kate liked most about her employer was the fact that Mrs. O'Connor knew all about Rachel's experience with the Indians but treated it as a nonevent.

"Heavens, child," Mrs. O'Connor said when Rachel told her of her experience, "how on earth could anyone fault you for whatever did or did not happen? I think it speaks well of your courage and determination that you survived such an ordeal. You are to be admired, not vilified."

October 8, 1871, was a Sunday, and though Mrs. O'Connor did not require Rachel to work on Sunday, Rachel had come to the shop on her own. She was working on the first dress that was entirely of her own design, and she wanted to be able to show it to Mrs. O'Connor first thing the next morning.

Rachel was in the back of the little shop when she heard the front door open. For a moment she thought she might have forgotten to lock the door, and she started toward the front to see who had come in. That was when she saw Liam O'Connor and half a dozen of his friends.

Liam, Mrs. O'Connor's son, worked as a drayman. He was two years older than Rachel, and though Mrs. O'Connor had tried a little matchmaking early on, her efforts hadn't taken. Liam was too intense a young man, too deeply immersed in the politics of the "Irish Brigade," as he called his group. The Irish Brigade met often and spoke passionately about the need for all Irish of the city to band together to ensure fair treatment.

Rachel had once asked, in all innocence, how the Irish were mistreated. Her question was met with stony silence and glaring stares on the faces of Liam and all his Irish friends.

"Sure'n you're a Scot and not Irish, so there's no way you'll ever understand it," Liam said finally.

"We're welcome in the back doors of any place in Chicago," said one of Liam's friends. "But not at the front doors."

"Aye. And have you not seen the signs, 'Coloreds, Irish, and Dogs Not Allowed'?"

"I'm sorry," Rachel said. "I guess I never paid that much attention to it. I see what you mean."

Fortunately for Rachel, her social relationship with Liam had no bearing on her working relationship with Mrs. O'Connor. Rachel was a hard and conscientious worker, Mrs. O'Connor was a fair and honest employer, and the two got along famously.

When Rachel saw that it was only Liam and his friends who had come into the store, she withdrew quietly to the back of the shop where she had been sewing. As Liam explained to his mother once, he and the Irish Brigade often met at the shop because it was a place where words spoken in honest passion would not be overheard by the wrong ears.

Satisfied that the group would not interfere with her, Rachel picked up the dress and resumed her sewing. As she worked, bits and pieces of the conversation drifted to the back of the shop, but Rachel was so intent upon the task at hand that she just let the words wash over her, with no attempt at deciphering the meaning.

" 'Tis a risky game we've been playin', Liam," one

brogue-thick voice said. "I fear we can't continue without suffering some consequences."

"Aye, but would you be tellin' me what has ever been gained without a bit o' risk? Besides, no one has been hurt."

"True, no one has been hurt. So far. But with the dryness of the weather, these buildings are all like tinder now. 'Twould be a disaster if things got a bit out of hand."

"And 'tis our own who are mannin' the hoses and pumps. 'Tis our own who are putting life and limb in harm's way," another voice said.

"And 'tis our own to whom the people are beholdin' for savin' life and property," Liam insisted. "We can't quit now, lads. But a few more wee candles here an' there, and Chicago will never again speak of the Irish and the colored folk in the same breath. For they'll be knowin' 'twas the Irish kept them safe from the devil's own fire."

The meeting continued a little longer, but the conversation grew quieter, and Rachel couldn't hear. She didn't try to hear, because in truth she had no interest in their political shenanigans anyway.

It was a little after eight o'clock that evening when Rachel finished the "Opera Toilette" she had designed and made. There was no particular customer for the dress, but Mrs. O'Connor had assured her that they would be able to sell it. And when and if they sold it, she promised to give Rachel half the profit.

The dress consisted of an underskirt of blue faille, trimmed with a gathered flounce, surmounted by a bias fold and pleating. The overdress was of apricot faille, trimmed with ruches of blue faille and edged with lace around the neck. The sleeves of apricot faille were slashed and under-laid with white silk, while the bodice was also of white silk, forming a square neck with the overdress and trimmed with ruches of blue faille and lace. The overdress was looped much higher on the left side than on the right.

Rachel didn't care if it was her creation. It was the most beautiful thing she had ever seen.

She locked up the shop, then walked down De Koven to her apartment on Van Buren Street. Her apartment was reached by a dark, narrow stairway, which had a toilet niche on every landing, though there was sufficient olfactory evidence to suggest that everyone used the walls instead of the toilets.

Too tired even to light a candle, Rachel undressed in the dark and went straight to bed.

Rachel had no idea how long she had been asleep when she heard the clanging of a firebell and the hooves of galloping horses. She also heard several loud voices, and when she looked toward the window she could see a wavering orange glow.

Thinking the fire must be very close, she stepped to the window for a better look.

Rachel was absolutely astounded by what she saw. The sky over Chicago was yellow orange with fire and vaulted with smoke. The fire leaped and curled around every building she could see, from the ones down by the river all the way back to the most distant structures in the business district. The dry tinder of the wooden buildings were feeding flames to the adjacent buildings, then leaping to the next, and the next, as fast as a man could walk.

At first Rachel thought the fire was spreading from building to building only, and she believed the firemen would be able to control it. But a large, blazing piece of timber got caught in an updraft, climbed several hundred feet into the air, then fell onto the towering steeple of a wooden church building several blocks to the north, and within moments it, too, was blazing. Thus the fire was spreading even beyond its confines.

As she stood at the window, Rachel saw firebrands falling all around her, and a moment later she heard someone within her very building screaming that they were on fire. Rachel turned back to look inside her room for something to put on. She didn't even have to think about lighting a candle, for by now the glow coming in through her window was as bright as any lantern.

She dressed as quickly as she could, then ran down the stairs. Already she could feel heat in the stairway, and by the time she reached the second floor, the stairway was filled with smoke. With her eyes smarting and her lungs burning from the smoke, Rachel managed to make it down the rest of the stairs, then out into the street, where she coughed and gasped for breath.

By now the conflagration had created a firestorm, whereby the fire was heating the air, which then rose, bringing in fresh air to make the fires even hotter. No street was wide enough to act as a firebreak, and when the flames advanced to the street, they merely leaped across, as if the very air itself were on fire. Indeed, some of those gathered in the street thought that was the case.

"The air is burning!" someone shouted. "If all the air catches fire, what then?"

"It will burn us all!" another replied, and several began crying out in fear.

Rachel saw people running through the streets of the burning city. She could hear screams and wails and curses as the black shadows appeared, backlit by the hellish orange glow.

"We've got to get out of here!"

"Look at how fast it's coming! In another few minutes, this will all be a sea of fire!"

As Rachel stood in the street with the others, she overheard a conversation that told how the fire started.

"The fire started in a barn on the west side, and before the alarm could be given, it was already spreading."

"Whose barn?"

"The O'Leary barn, down on De Koven."

"Did you say the fire started at the O'Leary place?" Rachel asked.

"Aye. 'Twas the worst place to start, too. Narrow streets and alleys, buildings all of wood, one and two stories high, and all with barns and sheds in the alley."

"What I can't figure out is how a fire started in a barn," someone said.

"It can't start in a barn, unless someone starts it."

"Who would be in a barn at this time of night besides horses and cows?"

"Maybe Mrs. O'Leary's cow started it," someone suggested, and the others laughed.

Suddenly Rachel remembered the bits and pieces of conversation she had overheard Liam and his friends discussing earlier in the day.

"*'Tis a risky game we've been playin', Liam,*" one brogue-thick voice had said. "*I fear we can't continue without suffering some consequences.*"

"*Aye, but would you be tellin' me what has ever been gained without a bit o' risk? Besides, no one has been hurt.*"

"*True, no one has been hurt. But with the dryness of the weather, the buildings are like tinder, now. 'Twould be a disaster if things got a bit out of hand.*"

Rachel put her hand to her mouth. "Oh, Father in heaven, surely not," she said.

"What is it, girl? You see something?" one of the others asked, curious about her strange outcry.

"No," she said. "I .... I was just referring to the fire."

The *Chicago Tribune* published its first edition on the following Wednesday.

During Sunday night, Monday, and Tuesday, this city has been swept by a conflagration which has no parallel in the annals of history for the quantity of property destroyed and the utter and almost irremediable ruin which it wrought. A fire in a barn on the West Side was the insignificant cause of a conflagration which has swept out of existence hundreds of millions of property, has reduced to poverty thousands who, the day before, were in a state of opulence, has covered the prairies, now swept by the cold southwest wind, with thousands of homeless unfortunates, which has destroyed public improvements that it has taken years of patient labor to build up, and which has set back for years the progress of the city, diminished her population, and crushed her resources.

Though she shared her speculation with no one, Rachel was more convinced than ever that Liam and his Irish Brigade were the cause of the fire. But if so, it would never be known. Even if his hand were discovered, Liam would never be held accountable for it, for he had already paid the supreme penalty.

Liam was one of the more than three hundred souls killed by the fire. He had been killed, it was said, fighting bravely, almost maniacally, against the encroaching flames.

"He seemed more horror-stricken than anyone at the enormity of the disaster and fought against it as if possessed by demons," an eyewitness said.

The store of Liam's mother was destroyed, as was, of course, the beautiful dress Rachel had designed and made. Mrs. O'Connor was not hurt, though she was distraught over the death of her son. Rachel saw her in one of the undamaged school buildings that had been turned over as a shelter for the homeless. Ironically, it was the same school from which she had been dismissed as a teacher some time earlier.

Rachel comforted Mrs. O'Connor as best she could, but she felt totally inadequate to the task—partly because she held Liam responsible for the fire. She walked away from Mrs. O'Connor and looked out over the hundreds of homeless people who were gathered in the school.

The fire victims all had the same look of shock on their faces. Many of them had been affluent before the fire, with large, comfortable homes, fine furniture, and adequate food. Others had been so poor as to exist on a day-to-day basis. Now, however, they were equal in their misery, and she could see men sitting on the floor, leaning against the wall,

wearing soot-darkened suits of the finest cloth and latest cut,
sharing a crust of bread with laborers dressed in homespun.

"Can you read, miss?" a soldier asked, coming over to
her. The army had been called out to maintain order, and
the young man who had addressed her was one of a dozen
soldiers who stood by, looking on in sympathy at those in
his charge.

"Yes, I can read," Rachel answered.

"If you don't mind, then, I'll be sending some folks who
can't read over to you. I'd be obliged if you would read this
proclamation to them."

The soldier handed Rachel a broadsheet. At the top of the
sheet, in sixty-four-point bold type, was the word "PROC-
LAMATION."

Within a few minutes twenty or thirty people had gathered to hear Rachel read. It was the first official response to
the fire, and the people, mostly poor laborers, were hungry
for any type of direction, information, or reaction that could
begin to restore some order to their shattered lives.

Rachel began to read:

"Whereas, in the Providence of God, to whose
will we humbly submit, a terrible calamity has
befallen our city, which demands of us our best
efforts for the preservation of order and relief of
suffering, be it known that the faith and credit of the
City of Chicago is hereby pledged for the necessary
expenses for the relief of the suffering.

"Public order will be preserved. The police and
special police now being appointed will be
responsible for the maintenance of the peace and
protection of property.

"All officers and men of the Fire Department and
Health Department will act as special policemen
without further notice.

"The Mayor and Comptroller will give vouchers

for all supplies furnished by the different relief committees.

"The headquarters of the City Government will be at the Congregational Church, corner of West Washington and Ann Streets.

"All persons are warned against any act tending to endanger property. Persons caught in any depredation will be immediately arrested.

"With the help of God, order and peace and private property will be preserved.

"The City Government and the committee of citizens pledge themselves to the community to protect them and prepare the way for a restoration of public and private welfare.

R. B. Mason, Mayor.''

After Rachel finished reading the proclamation, she walked outside. Though the fires were out, the air smelled of smoke and burnt wood. It was cold outside, and she pulled the shawl around her for what warmth it could provide. She was wearing the only clothes she was able to save from her room, but her dress had been augmented by a shawl she'd taken from one of the several clothing barrels set up inside the various relief centers.

She had no idea whether her aunt and uncle had survived the fire or not. Their house had been destroyed, she knew that, but as to their safety and or whereabouts, she knew nothing.

She was cold, hungry, and totally dispirited. She walked over to the corner of the school building, leaned her head against the brick wall, and began to cry.

"Here, now. You survived the Indians. Surely you aren't going to let something like this get you down," said a soothing voice. The same person gave her a handkerchief. She thanked him and used it before she turned to her benefactor. She was surprised to see that it was General Sheridan.

"You *are* Rachel Stewart, aren't you?" General Sheridan asked. "Or, perhaps you have married now, and the name is no longer Stewart."

"It's still Stewart. I'm amazed that you remember me."

Sheridan laughed quietly. "Well now, Miss Stewart. There were nearly a thousand soldiers at Washita, but only one beautiful white woman. Did you really think I could forget?"

"It's good to see you again," Rachel said. "Not under these circumstances, of course." She took in the fire-blackened city with a sweep of her arm. "But it is good to see you."

"You lost your house?" Sheridan asked.

"It wasn't a house," she replied. "It was a room in an apartment building, and yes, I lost it. Also my place of employment."

"What will you do now?" Sheridan asked.

Rachel shook her head. "I don't know. For myself, I haven't thought that far ahead. The magnitude of this disaster seems too overwhelming for a person to be caught up in her own troubles."

"Indeed it does," Sheridan said. "You have family here, I believe?"

Rachel shook her head. "No. Not anymore," she replied.

"Lost in the fire?"

"Yes, I lost them in the fire." It was easier to say that than to explain the circumstances that had brought about the family rupture so long ago. And in truth they were lost, at least to the degree that she now had no idea where they were. "I will probably leave Chicago."

Rachel hadn't even thought of that until this moment. But having spoken the words, she knew them to be true.

"Have you enough money for train fare? The trip?" Sheridan asked.

Rachel shook her head. "I have no money at all, now. Everything is gone."

Sheridan took out two twenty-dollar bills and handed them to her. "Take this," he said.

"No, General, I can't do that," Rachel said, waving aside his gift.

"Of course you can. That's why I'm here," Sheridan said. "I'll get reimbursed by one of the relief committees."

"I don't know how to thank you," Rachel said.

"Well, you won't get far on forty dollars," Sheridan replied. "But perhaps this will help." He took out a notebook, and on paper that bore the printed notice of the ARMY OF THE MISSOURI, he began to write. "Take this to any railroad station in Chicago, and present it to the ticket agent," Sheridan instructed. "Tell him where you want to go, and he will issue the ticket."

He tore the page from the notebook and handed it to her.

"Thank you, General," she said.

"Where will you go, by the way?" Sheridan asked.

"I'm going back to Kansas," Rachel said. As before, it was a decision that wasn't made until she actually spoke the words, but once spoken, it was resolute.

"Good for you," Sheridan said. "Kansas is still one of our frontier states. Such places need women of courage and tenacity. It is my prediction that you will do well there."

Fifteen

Hank found a buffalo stand and moved into position. It was the winter of 1873, and he was now an old hand at the hunt. In the past he would have started shooting as soon as he arrived, but now he knew that selecting the correct buffalo for the first kill was very important in making the others remain. In order to ensure that, he spent more than half an hour studying the herd before he determined which one to take down. His target was a huge brute of a bull who had positioned himself just upwind of the small stand in his charge.

This was the king buffalo, the bull from whom the others took direction. If he moved, they moved; if he stopped, they stopped. As if fully cognizant of his responsibilities, the bull would graze for a few moments, then lift his shaggy head to sniff the air. Finding no scent of danger, he would go back to his meal. The others, dependent upon their leader for warning, made no effort whatever to sniff for trouble. They continued to graze, totally unconcerned about potential danger.

The big Sharps buffalo gun roared and kicked back against Hank's shoulder. Two hundred yards away a puff of dust and a misty spray of blood flew up from just behind the left shoulder of the big bull. The buffalo went down without a sound.

Hank waited for a moment, just to make certain his selection had been right. The last echo of the gunshot died, and once again there was nothing but the soft sigh of wind across the plains. The buffalo continued their grazing, unaware of the demise of their leader.

Hank slid another bullet into the breach for his second shot. Although one could buy factory-made ammunition, Hank preferred to do his own loading, though he did buy the cartridge cases, powder, and bullets. He did his own assembly, pouring in 110 grains of powder and tamping it down with a paper wad. After that he would dip the base of the bullets into melted beeswax, then slide them down into the cartridge case and seat them with a small tap. It might have only been his belief, but it seemed to him that the bullets he assembled flew more accurately and hit the target with greater impact than the ones he could buy.

His second shot brought down another bull, this one some three hundred yards away, and he smiled because he knew he had successfully locked the herd in place. Now he could shoot leisurely, taking the time to select only those bulls with the finest hides.

He killed thirty-five before he stopped. After that he walked out to them and began marking them as his own by putting little green flags on each carcass. Then, leaving them where they lay, he started back to camp to bring up the two wagons and his cutter and skinner. The previous three weeks had already produced over four hundred hides, and they were now cut and stacked back in the two wagons that accompanied him.

Hank knew that he was lucky to have cutters and skinners like Elmer True and Ben Spicer. They were experts with the knife and could take a hide off quickly and cleanly, doing so in such a way as to allow the hide to begin to cure naturally. A botched job could ruin the hide, if not immediately, then soon after, for if it began to rot instead of cure, it could also affect other hides it came in contact with.

True and Spicer also knew the country, they were sober

and intelligent, and Hank was convinced that True was one of the best cooks he had ever encountered.

It had been unseasonably warm yesterday, and it was still warm this morning. Now, however, as he rode back to camp, a chill wind began blowing from the north. At first he thought he would be able to make it back to the camp without having to take out his heavier coat, but the temperature kept dropping. It finally reached the point where he had to stop and pull out his buffalo robe.

He had not remembered riding this far in search of the herd, but he must have. He knew that he wasn't lost; he was navigating with a compass, and he saw several landmarks that he remembered seeing during the ride out. It was just that he was busy then, looking for sign, and hadn't paid that much attention to the distance he was covering. Now all he wanted to do was get back to the camp, get something hot to eat, then get the wagons moved back to the site so they could begin harvesting the hides.

The day had started out not only warm, but also bright and cheery. Now it was dark and dreary, so heavily overcast that the position of the sun couldn't be made out, even by a faint glow. He was sure it had been in the sixties in midmorning; now he was equally sure it was in the twenties, and the temperature continued to fall. How could the temperature fall so far so quickly? he wondered.

It began to snow, going within minutes from a few flakes to a blizzard so heavy that Hank couldn't see more than ten feet in any direction. Now he had to depend entirely upon the compass, for the landmarks could no longer be seen.

The horse kept trying to turn his back to the freezing wind, but that would have taken them away from camp, so Hank finally dismounted and led the animal. By now the snow was beginning to pile up, and Hank moved on as best he could, plunging into drifts that were sometimes waist deep, urging his horse on. He had moved from the head back to the side of the horse, feeling somewhat guilty about keeping the poor creature between him and the wind.

It was nearly dark by the time he reached the encampment. True and Spicer had pulled the two wagons together, then stretched the hides from the bottom of the wagons to the ground. The result was a very low shelter, no bigger than the area covered by the two wagons. But the hides made a great windbreak, and a little curl of smoke told Hank that the men had built a fire inside their shelter.

Hank breathed a prayer of thankfulness at reaching the camp and had to fight the urge to go inside right away. He forced himself to take care of his horse first, and he led the animal around to the side of the wagons to give him the most protection from the wind. There he tied him off with the mules, putting him in between them, thinking in that way to give him a little more protection.

"Sorry, mules," he said as he worked. "But my horse needs a windbreak more than you do. He brought me back through all this." Hank chuckled. "Well, that's not quite true. I reckon I brought him back, but he's been out in it, and you haven't. So he gets the best place."

Hank's hands were so frozen that the simple act of removing the saddle and tying the horse to the wagon proved to be almost impossible. He called out to True and Spicer, but the icy wind was at near hurricane velocity by now, and his voice sounded so thin that he could scarcely hear himself. Finally, with the horse secured, Hank began fumbling around with the hide covers, trying to find one to lift so he could crawl inside.

They were frozen so stiff that he couldn't lift them. He tried as hard as he could, working his frozen fingers around until he could find what he thought was the edge. He pulled, but the hide didn't move.

"Dear God," he called out. "Have I come this far, to die outside the shelter because I can't get inside?"

The sharp ice crystals adhering to the buffalo hides cut his hands and fingers, but he couldn't feel it. His hands and feet were so numb that he could no longer feel anything.

He tried for several more minutes but was no closer to getting inside. In fact, the longer he went, the weaker he became, and he realized with a sinking feeling that if he had not been able to move the hides earlier when he was relatively fresh and strong, there was no way he was going to be able to move them now.

Dejected, he stepped away. To have come so close, only to freeze to death just inches away from safety, seemed to him the cruelest blow of all. It would have been better to have died out on the prairie. At least there he would not have gotten his hopes up.

He shouted again, but by now his voice was growing weaker. They couldn't hear him. He wasn't sure they could even hear a gunshot.

"A gunshot!" Hank said aloud. "Why didn't I think of that before?"

Hank pulled his pistol and pointed it in the air. He pulled the trigger. The resultant bang could barely be heard above the howl of the wind.

"My God! That sounded like a pop gun!" he said. "Is this wind so strong that not even a gunshot can be heard over it?" He sighed. "I'm going mad. I'm talking to myself."

Hank fired three shots in quick succession, thinking that even if they heard one pop, they may not realize what it was. But three quick pops would have to get their attention.

Nothing.

Because he normally carried an empty chamber under the hammer, he now had only one bullet remaining. He had more ammunition in his saddlebag, but he honestly didn't know if he had enough strength or flexibility in his fingers to reload.

"If I had two bullets left, I'd shoot both you bastards for not hearing me!" Hank screamed at the shelter.

Then, suddenly, he got another idea. They couldn't hear the shot from out here. What if he shot inside the wagon?

He thought of it a minute. Where would he shoot? He had to be careful not to hit either of them, but he had to get close enough to them for them to know what it was. The question, of course, was, where were they?

The fire. They had to be sitting by the fire.

Hank stepped back away from the wagons to look once more at the smoke. It was hard to determine exactly where the smoke was coming from, because the wind was whipping it about so. But he knew that it had to be coming up from an opening between the two wagons.

There was no ground-level separation of the wagons. So skillfully had the hides been applied that the wagons were little more than a framework. Looking at the shelter from outside, a person could see only one solid structure.

Finally Hank decided to take a chance. He knelt down so he could get the angle he needed, and he pointed the gun up. What he planned to do was shoot a hole through one of the hides. The bullet would then pass through the hide and out the roof, which was actually the wagon floor. Surely they would be able to hear a bullet passing through the very center of their shelter.

Hank put the gun right against the buffalo hide, and fired. The shot left a little blackened ring and a puff of smoke around a bullet hole. The bullet went inside, just as he wanted. The question was, where did it go, and did they see it?

As it happened, his question was answered a moment later when one of the hides bulged out, then separated from the hide nearest to it. Hank saw True's head poke outside and look around in curiosity.

"True!" Hank shouted, and to make certain that he wasn't overlooked, he moved quickly over to put his hand on True's head.

"Boss, what you standin' out here for?" True asked. "Get in out of the cold."

True opened the hide a little wider, and Hank lunged his body through.

"Spicer," Hank heard True call, "get over here and help me with the boss. He's in a bad way."

Hank had no idea how long he had been sleeping. When he opened his eyes he saw that he was inside the shelter. In addition to the buffalo hides that formed the wall of the shelter, hides were covering the ground. Hank was lying on a pile of them, covered by warm woolen blankets. There was an orange glow from the fire that burned cheerily in the middle. He could also smell coffee and some sort of a stew.

"How long have I been asleep?" Hank asked.

Spicer laughed. "Is that what you call it? Sleep? Me'n True thought maybe you was dead. You sure didn't make no moves once we got you wrapped up in them blankets."

"Is it still snowing?"

"Not now, it ain't," True answered. "It quit snowin' yesterday afternoon."

"It quit yesterday afternoon? You mean I slept all day yesterday?"

"All night, all day yesterday, and all night again last night. Like I told you, boss, me'n True was gettin' some worried about you," Spicer said.

"Are you hungry?" True asked.

"Yes. I am."

"Well, that's a pretty good sign, I reckon. Leastwise, I'd be worryin' more if you wasn't hungry."

True brought Hank a plate of steaming stew and a cup of hot coffee. He had to crawl, because the wagon was so low over their heads.

Hank sat up. It was amazingly warm inside, almost too warm. He noticed then that both True and Spicer were wearing only their longjohns.

"You folks look comfortable," he said.

"Yeah," Spicer said sheepishly. "We figured we should keep it really warm for you, which made it too hot for us, so we stripped down to our longhandles."

"So I see," Hank said with a little chuckle. He reached for the cup, and when he held it, his hands stung. He winced, then pulled one of his hands away to look at it.

"I don't think you got the frostbite," True said, answering the unasked question. "But somehow you cut your hands up pretty good."

"What does it look like outside?" Hank asked as he drank his coffee. "Can we get out of here?"

"I reckon we can," True said. "We just been waitin' on you to give us the word."

"Then let's do it."

It took a couple of hours to take down their shelter, load the hides, and connect the teams. But by early afternoon, in a sunlight so bright that the reflection off the snow was nearly blinding, they began the trip back to Hays City.

The load was bulky and awkward, and movement was very difficult because the mules had to break through the snow as they walked. Going was a little easier for the second wagon, however, so every hour they would take a ten-minute rest period, then switch the wagons around before continuing.

At one point they started down a long, rather steep slope, and the freezing mules pulling the front wagon suddenly and unexpectedly broke into a gallop. The trailing team followed, and the two wagons careened down the snow- and ice-covered hill, and it was all True and Spicer could do to keep the wagons upright.

When they reached the bottom of the long hill, the teams slowed, then halted. Hank, who was on horseback, caught up with them.

"Them sons of bitches're tryin' to kill me!" True swore. "For two cents I'd shoot both their miserable hides and put 'em out of their misery, right now."

"And leave yourself stranded out here?" Hank asked.

True spat a wad of tobacco, leaving a brown stain on the pristine white snow alongside the trail. "That's the only damn thing keepin' 'em alive," he said with a growl.

"Let's take a double-length breather this time," Hank said.

"I'm for that," Spicer said. "But we can't stay here too long. If the mules get too cold and too stiff, we won't get 'em movin' again."

Hank looked back behind the wagons. A long, deep, black scar cut its way across the prairie and down the hill, marking the way they had come. Hank stuck his hands under his armpits to warm them. He didn't think he had ever been in a cold this bitter. When he looked at True and Spicer, he saw that the beards and mustaches were covered with ice, brought about by the condensation of their breath. Their eyelashes were frozen, too, and though Hank had no beard to catch the ice, he knew that his eyelashes were probably no different from those of his men.

Hank took out his compass and got a couple of readings.

"Can you tell where we are with that thing?" True asked.

"I've got a pretty good idea," he said. "Why, don't you know where we are?"

"Not really," True admitted. "I've been over this ground dozens of times . . . but damn me if it don't look all different, covered over with snow like this."

"How much farther do you figure it is into town?" Spicer asked.

"I'd say about twenty miles."

"Damn. No chance of makin' it today, is there?"

" 'Fraid not," Hank answered.

Spicer sighed. "All right, we'll just go as far as we can tonight so that we're sure to make it by mornin'. That all right with you, boss?"

"That's fine with me," Hank said, thankful that he wasn't going to have to persuade them to move on. If they thought it was their idea, then that was all the better.

They had been going about another hour when Spicer, who was now in the lead, stopped his wagon. True stopped as well.

"Boss!" Spicer called. He stood up and pointed. "Boss, look over there!"

Hank looked in the direction Spicer had pointed. There he saw signs everywhere of an enormous number of buffalo, the snow cut and worn, the long bottom grass flattened wherever it was exposed, the willows cropped close by the weary, starving animals. Also, in every direction were the thawed, brown, icy spots where the buffalo had bedded for the night. Then, just over the ridge, he saw a magnificent sight.

As far as he could see, there was one solid mass of buffalo, dark and mysterious-looking under the enormous breath cloud that hovered over them. They were grazing quietly on the mesquite grass that had been exposed by hundreds of thousands of scraping hooves.

"Boys," Hank said with a happy smile, "we have hit the mother lode."

Hank was not the only one to have discovered the herd. On the other side of the herd Jumping Wolf and four Indians, in violation of the military orders to stay south of the Arkansas, had also discovered the herd.

Jumping Wolf and the others had come through the same blizzard as Hank, True, and Spicer. They'd had no wagons to use in the construction of a shelter, but they had used a time-proven trick of survival. Each had carried a buffalo robe. When caught out, they'd wrapped the robes around themselves and dug in under a protecting bank somewhere. With the rifle set up, and the barrel acting as an air vent, they'd let the snow drift and pile over them. That had helped insulate them, and they'd been able to last out the blizzard quite easily.

When the storm had abated, Jumping Wolf had taken a count, determined that all who had come with him were still there, and suggested they move on. They had found the herd about two hours before Hank. Now they were engaged in an intense conversation, trying to decide how best to proceed.

"Perhaps if we do nothing, the herd will go into the Territory by itself," Lame Bear suggested.

"We will not wait for the herd to go into the Territory. We will return to our village and gather a hunting party," Jumping Wolf said. "We will bring them up here and hunt."

"Jumping Wolf, we can't do that," Black Bird said. "If we do, it will anger the soldiers, and they will punish us."

"And you fear the soldiers?"

"I do not fear the soldiers in battle," Black Bird said. "But I fear what the soldiers will do to our people. They are cowards, and they attack our villages when the warriors are gone. You remember Black Kettle, and the village at Washita.''

"Black Bird is right," Lame Bear said. "Besides, if we honor the treaty, even if the herd does not come south far enough for us to take our needs, the agents will give us beef. They will not let us starve."

"Bah," Jumping Wolf said, making a spitting sound to show his disdain for the caution suggested by Black Bird and Lame Bear. "You would have us wait for the white man to give us a few head of beef?"

"It is in the treaty," Lame Bear said. "They must feed us."

"I am a man, not a child, and not a woman who has no man. I will not be fed cow meat the way a baby suckles at its mother's breast. There are buffalo here . . . more buffalo than I have seen in a long time. I think it is a sign. It is a sign that we should go back to our old ways."

"What old ways?" Black Bird asked.

"The way it was before the white men came to break our sacred circle."

"Perhaps there is another way," Lame Bear suggested. "Perhaps we could go to the white man in peace. We would tell him that we mean no harm and want only the right to hunt the buffalo."

"Foolish one, do you think the whites will listen?" Jumping Wolf asked.

"We will tell them that the buffalo are a gift from the Great Spirit. It is a sacred thing. I think they would listen to a sacred thing."

"The white man does not understand things that are sacred. He mocks even his own Jesus God."

"But someday, someone must listen," Lame Bear insisted.

The discussion continued far into the day as each held to his own idea as to what should be done. The question was still unresolved by sunset.

Sixteen

Just before dark that evening, Hank and his little party stumbled across a much larger hunting party. They had not started on their hunt as early as Hank, so when the blizzard hit, there were still enough of them together to form a hasty though quite comfortable camp, which they were calling Fort Necessity.

Wild Bill Hickok and Bat Masterson turned out to greet Hank, True, and Spicer as they arrived.

"Well, look what the storm blew in," Bat teased. He grabbed Hank's hand in a hearty handshake, and when Hank winced, he jerked it back quickly. "What happened to your hand?"

"The boss was caught out when the storm hit," True said.

"Let me see your hands."

Hank took off his gloves, and Bat, who fancied himself something of a doctor, examined them closely. "You were lucky," he said. "You nearly got frostbite."

"Yeah, I know."

"I've got just the thing for that," Bat said. He went into his tent for a moment, then came back with a little jar of salve. He rubbed the salve liberally on Hank's hands. The salve gave off a terrible smell.

"What the hell is that stuff?" Hank said, screwing up his face in protest.

"It's called Dr. Spears' Wonder Salve," Bat said. "I bought it off a traveling medicine show. I swear, that woman he had traveling with the show was the most beautiful creature I ever saw in my life."

"So you bought it because she was pretty."

"Well, yes," Bat admitted. "But the stuff really does work. Dr. Spears claimed you could put it over a bullet wound and it would suck the bullet right out of your body. I've never tried that, but I have used it for cuts, burns, and the like, and it works well for that."

"Tell us about your adventure," Hickok said.

"Not much to tell. I was caught in the storm, I got cold, but I made it back to camp and I survived," Hank said. "What I would rather tell you about is what we saw this afternoon, not more than two hours from here."

"What was that?"

"The biggest herd of buffalo I've ever seen in my life."

"Yeah, well, you haven't been out here all that long. Wouldn't take a lot of buffalo to be the biggest herd you ever saw."

"What about me?" True asked. "I've been out here for nearly twenty years."

"Well, that's different," Hickok said. "If *you* say it was the biggest herd you ever saw, I'd be pretty impressed."

"Well, I am saying that. Matter of fact, it's two, maybe three times bigger than any herd I ever seen before," True said.

"Hot damn!" Hickok said with a whoop. "Boys, did you hear that?" he called to the others. "We've found the herd!"

Hickok's call brought the other hunters over, and for a few minutes they listened excitedly as first Hank, then True, then Spicer, described the herd. After that they began a frenzied discussion as to what would be the best way to handle it. Should they go in as one large body and start shooting them? Or if the herd really was as big as reported, maybe they should take positions all the way around the herd?

"Hey," someone called out. "Hey, fellas, they's some Indians here."

All conversation stopped then as three Indians came riding slowly into the camp.

"Will you look at them redskin bastards?" one of the hunters said. "Riding in here like they owned the place."

The Indian in the middle held up his hand, palm out, the universal symbol of peace.

"What do you want?" Hickok asked.

The Indian replied in his native tongue, and the hunters looked at each other in confusion.

"Any of you folks speak Cheyenne?" Hickok asked.

No one did.

"Lame Bear, how will we ask them to allow us to take some buffalo from the herd, if they do not understand our language?" Black Bird asked.

"We will make them understand," Lame Bear replied. *"We will show them that we come in peace, and that we are hungry."*

"Hey, what the hell are they doing?" one of the hunters asked. "When they're talking to each other like that, and we don't know what they are saying, they could be making some sort of plan."

Hickok shook his head no and pointed at the Indian who seemed to be their leader. "Don't you heathens be talking to each other," he said. "You talk to us, not to each other, do you understand? We don't want you making plans."

"I don't think they mean any harm," Hank said. "If they did, they wouldn't come into a camp this large. Not just three of them."

"There's no tellin' how many of them might be out there somewhere," Hickok said.

"We are hungry," Lame Bear said in his own language. Then he rubbed his hand on his stomach to pantomime eating.

"Hungry?" Hank asked, not understanding the language

but recognizing the gesture. He repeated the motion.

Lame Bear nodded, then said in English, "Yes, hungry."

"Hell, they just got caught out in the storm, same as I did," Hank said. "Give 'em something to eat, and they'll go on their way."

"All right," Bat said. He pointed toward a nearby campfire. A coffeepot and a stew kettle sat on a small grill to the edge of the fire. "You boys get yourself something to eat, then get on your way."

"See. They are going to give us food. I think we can make them understand," Lame Bear said. *"You stay on your horses. I will get some food, and they can see that we mean no harm. Then we can talk."*

"Hey! If they're so hungry, how come only one of them got down?" Hickok asked. "You two, get down. Get down from your horses."

"Lame Bear, he speaks in anger. What does he say?" Black Bird asked.

Lame Bear was halfway toward the fire. He stopped and looked at the angry white man, trying to decide what he was saying.

"Take your rifles from their sheaths and hold them pointing down. That will show them that we have come in peace," Lame Bear suggested.

Black Bird and Little Whistler did as Lame Bear suggested. They pulled their rifles from the beaded buckskin sheaths that held them.

"Look out!" Hickok shouted. In a lightning, reflexive action, he drew his pistol. He fired three times, and all three Indians went down. The entire incident was over in less than three seconds, and the white hunters were as shocked by the sudden turn of events as the Indians would have been, had they lived long enough to realize what was happening. In fact, all three were dead before the echoes of the three shots died out, for not only was Hickok fast, he was deadly. Every bullet had been a killing shot.

"Damn, Bill! What the hell did you do that for?" Bat shouted in a shocked voice.

"Didn't you see them? They were going for their guns."

"You don't think they really intended to shoot us, do you? My God, there were just three of them," Bat said.

"I don't know what they intended to do," Hickok said. "But it has long been my policy to never allow any adversary to pull a gun on me. How else do you think I have managed to stay alive this long?"

The hunters gathered around the three bodies and looked down at them as if unable to believe what they had just witnessed.

"What are you goin' to do with them now, Hickok?" one of the hunters asked.

"What do you mean, what am I going to do with them? What am I supposed to do with them?"

"Dress 'em out and cut 'em up as meat, or bury 'em, it don't make no nevermind to me. But you ain't goin' to leave 'em here in the middle of our camp."

"I see. And you are giving the orders around here now, are you?"

"I'm tellin' you to get them damn Indians out of here," the hunter said.

"You think you can back those orders up?" Hickok asked. He turned menacingly toward the hunter and let his hand hover over his gun.

"You planning on killing one of our own now, are you, Bill?" Hank asked.

"Because if you are harboring such plans, I think you should know we won't let you get away with it," Bat added.

"Well now, is that so?" Hickok asked. "I know you're fast, Bat, but do you really think you can beat me?"

"He won't have to beat you, Hickok," one of the other hunters said. "If you shoot Dobbins, or Bat, or anyone else . . . by God, the rest of us will kill you."

"The rest of you, huh?"

"Yes, the rest of us," Hank said. "You might get one or two, or maybe even three of us. But in the end, we'll get you."

"I can't believe this," Hickok said. "I can't believe that my own friends are turning on me because I killed these Indians."

"Killing these Indians may wind up getting some of us killed," Bat said.

"Yeah, well, I'm sorry. I told you, they went for their guns. I didn't know what they were going to do."

"That part's over and there's nothing we can do about it. Now, you do what Dobbins told you to do," Bat ordered. "You get these bodies the hell out of this camp."

"How?"

"I don't care how. Just do it."

Hickok stared sullenly at the others for a long moment, then nodded. "All right. Will someone help me lift them? I'll tie them on their horses, then send the horses out of here."

"I'll help," Hank offered.

The rest of the hunting camp stood around in silence as Hank, True, Spicer, and Hickok put the bodies of the Indians belly down across the backs of their horses. The bodies were tied on securely, then Hickok slapped each of them on the rump, sending them away at a gallop.

There was great excitement in the village when Jumping Wolf returned to tell of the great buffalo herd he, Lame Bear, Black Bird, and Little Whistler had found.

"There are more buffalo than the stars in the sky," Jumping Wolf said.

"Is the herd as large as that?" Spotted Tail asked. "Not since the days of my grandfather has there been a herd so large."

"Where are they now?"

"They are north of the Arkansas River," Jumping Wolf said. "I have left Lame Bear and the others to keep watch over the herd so that we do not lose it."

"North of the Arkansas?"

"Yes. I left the others to keep watch. Spotted Tail, we must put together a hunt," Jumping Wolf said. "It will be the biggest hunt ever. We will return with meat and robes and horns and hooves."

"I agree," Spotted Tail said. "We will have a great dance in preparation. How close to the Arkansas River are the buffalo?"

"They are far north of the Arkansas," Jumping Wolf said. "They are near the Cimarron."

"The Cimarron? That is far north indeed," Spotted Tail said with concern.

News of the great buffalo herd had spread rapidly, and from all over the village people were hurrying to the inner circle to join the discussion. This was the happiest news any of them had ever heard, and already plans were being made for the great feast of celebration they would have after the hunt. But the news that the buffalo were north of the Arkansas River, and might not come south at all, caused Spotted Tail to sound a precautionary note.

"Do not get drunk with joy, for if they do not come south of the Arkansas, we will not be able to hunt them at all," Spotted Tail warned.

"We will hunt them where they are," Jumping Wolf said.

"You know we cannot, Jumping Wolf. We have signed a treaty with the white man. We are not allowed north of the river."

"A treaty with the white man," Jumping Wolf said angrily. "The treaty means nothing to them, why should it mean anything to us?"

"Would you have us go to war with the white man?" Spotted Tail asked.

"If there is to be war, let it be," Jumping Wolf said. "I have fought the white man before. I will fight him again. If the fight is to be over the buffalo, then I say there is no better reason to fight, and there is no better day to die."

"Yes, you have fought the white man before," Spotted Tail said. "You fought the white man at the battle where

the river divided. It was there that many of our people were
killed. It was there, too, that Stone Eagle was killed. Tell
me, Jumping Wolf, was there glory that day?''

"Our people fought bravely," Jumping Wolf insisted.

"Yes, I agree, they fought bravely. Yet even the bravest
warriors, led by the ablest war chief, were unable to find
victory.

"And what of Black Kettle and those who were killed at
Washita?'' Spotted Tail continued. "They were brave, too,
but they died, and they found no victory in death. No, Jumping Wolf. I say we do not go north of the Arkansas River.''

"But surely, Spotted Tail, you must see that this is a
sign?'' Jumping Wolf pleaded. "For many years, there have
been very few buffalo. Is it for nothing that they suddenly
appear? I say the Great Spirit sent us these buffalo. Would
you deny the Great Spirit by not hunting what has been
provided?''

Spotted Tail held up his hand. "I have listened to your
words, Jumping Wolf,'' he finally said. "Perhaps they are
wise words, I do not know. Tonight, I will go into the sweat
lodge and I will think on these words. If it is as you say,
that the Great Spirit wants me to take our people north of
the Arkansas River, I will know. And if the Great Spirit
wants me to honor the treaty and remain south of the Arkansas River, this I will know as well. I will make no decision now, until I have the wisdom.''

With that, Spotted Tail made no further contributions to
the discussion. He had turned it all over to a spirit force
outside himself.

Jumping Wolf, however, wasn't quite ready to put the
decision in other hands. He insisted to all who would listen
that tomorrow, with or without the blessing and approval of
Spotted Tail, he would return to the herd and begin the hunt.

"Those who would provide for your families and for the
widows of our people, build fires, paint your bodies, make
your dance. Tomorrow, we hunt!''

"Eeeiii!'' one young man shouted, and his excited outburst was infectious. Soon dozens and then scores of young

men were whooping and shouting. The flames in the center circle fire grew higher as, one by one, the painted young men joined the dance ring.

It snowed again during the night.

When Spotted Tail emerged from the sweat lodge the next morning, the meadow was clean and white and the snow was unbroken. It was a good sign, for with all tracks obliterated, any mistake or wrongdoing Spotted Tail had ever committed had been erased as well. But it meant that his good deeds and heroic achievements were erased as well, and thus he was starting fresh, the rest of his life to be measured from this moment of this day.

As he was contemplating the meaning and the opportunity of this, he saw Lame Bear standing by the sweat lodge. He was surprised by this, because he hadn't noticed him before now, and he hadn't seen him approach. Lame Bear was dressed in ceremonial robes and wearing his finest headdress of feathers and beads.

"Lame Bear."

Lame Bear said nothing.

"I am glad you are here. I know that you were with Jumping Wolf. Is it true? Has the herd returned?"

"Yes," Lame Bear said.

"And is the herd as large as Jumping Wolf says?"

"The herd is as large as in the days of our grandfathers."

Spotted Tail sighed. "And in the days of our grandfathers, this would be a cause for rejoicing. But if the herd remains north of the Arkansas, it will be as if it had not come at all. Even so, Jumping Wolf wants to lead the young men in a great buffalo hunt."

"And what about you, Spotted Tail? What do you wish to do?"

"My heart tells me to hunt the buffalo, but my mind tells me we should heed the lessons we learned at Sand Creek and Washita. There, without reason, the soldiers came and killed many of our people. How many more would they kill if they had reason?"

"Already in the village, the young men are preparing for the hunt," Lame Bear said.

"I know. Jumping Wolf has inflamed their passions. The need for food and the desire for the hunt is strong. It will take very powerful medicine to stop them, and I do not have such medicine. I came seeking wisdom and praying for a vision. But wisdom did not occur, and a vision did not appear."

"Perhaps you have the wisdom but do not know it, possess the medicine but cannot use it, have observed the vision but would not see it."

"I don't understand."

"There are colors that blind a man's sight, songs that deaden a man's hearing, and tastes that spoil a man's tongue. You are the finger that touches but touches not itself, the eye that sees but sees not itself."

"You speak in riddles, Lame Bear," Spotted Tail said in frustration. He turned his head and studied his visitor. "I am puzzled. Did Jumping Wolf not say he left you with the others to watch the herd?"

"Yes."

"Then why have you come to see me?"

"I have come to say good-bye."

"You have come to say good-bye? I don't understand."

"When you know, you will know."

Spotted Tail held up his hand. "Wait, I will get my things from the sweat lodge and we will walk to the village together."

Spotted Tail reached into the sweat lodge for his bow, knife, and buffalo robe. "You are not wearing a robe," he said over his shoulder. "How is it that you are not cold?"

Spotted Tail retrieved his belongings, then stood up and turned around. He gasped. Lame Bear was not there.

That was when he saw the clean, white, unbroken snow. There were no footprints anywhere, not even where Lame Bear had been standing.

*   *   *

By the time Spotted Tail returned to the village, he was filled with wisdom. He was ready to counsel against the hunt, and he knew now that he had the medicine to make them listen. But he was almost too late, for the young men were painted and armed for the hunt and already gathering their horses.

"Wait!" Spotted Tail called. "Wait, listen to what I must say to you!"

"It is Spotted Tail," one of the hunters called to the others.

"Do not listen to him. He is a foolish old man," Jumping Wolf said. "Come, we must go now."

"I want to hear what he has to say," the hunter said.

"So do I," another added.

"Spotted Tail," the first hunter called to him, "did you find the wisdom you sought?"

"Yes," Spotted Tail said.

"We will listen," the first hunter said, and when he started toward Spotted Tail to hear his counsel, the others followed.

"Don't listen to him! He is a frightened old woman!" Jumping Wolf yelled. When the others didn't turn back from Spotted Tail, Jumping Wolf, who was still mounted, reacted in anger, jerking his horse around in a circle, the horse's hooves tamping down the snow.

"And what is that wisdom? Are we to hunt?" asked one of the hunters.

"We will not hunt north of the Arkansas River," Spotted Tail replied.

Jumping Wolf pointed at him. "You counsel our young men to be cowards!"

"Caution and prudence should not be confused with fear," Spotted Tail replied easily. "We need but a little patience, for already the herd is moving south. When the snow falls twice more, the herd will be south of the Arkansas River. Then we will have a glorious hunt."

"The herd has not moved," Jumping Wolf said. "If it had, Lame Bear would have come to tell us."

"Lame Bear cannot come to tell us," Spotted Tail said. "He is dead."

When the people heard him say that Lame Bear was dead, they gasped.

"Lame Bear is not dead!" Jumping Wolf said. "Lame Bear, Black Bird, and Little Whistler are watching the herd. This I know, because I left them there."

"All are dead. They were shot by the white man who wears his hair in long curls. The one called Hickok."

"How do you know this?"

"I know because I know."

Now the wives of Lame Bear, Black Bird, and Little Whistler began to cry, for their hearts told them that Spotted Tail's words were true.

"Do you think by your lies you will get the people to listen to you?" Jumping Wolf asked. "I will go get Lame Bear, Black Bird, and Little Whistler. I will bring them back so that all can see that you do not tell the truth." Jumping Wolf pointed to himself. "Then I will lead the people on the hunt. And if any whites try to stop us, we will kill them!"

Several of the young men, who were bordering between following Jumping Wolf and listening to Spotted Tail, were moved by his thrilling words, and they cheered. Then one of the women saw something moving on a long slope on the other side of the valley, and she shielded her eyes against the glare of the snow and studied it for a moment. When she realized what it was, she called to the others.

"Look!" she shouted, pointing north.

When the villagers looked, they saw three horses coming toward them, their approach as visible as black ink on white paper. The ponies were walking in single file, leaving behind them a long, dark scar on the face of the white field.

When the horses reached the village, the people could see that each was carrying a body. They hurried out to catch the animals and relieve them of their sorrowful burdens.

"It is Lame Bear, Black Bird, and Little Whistler," said

one of those who reached the ponies first. "Spotted Tail was right, they are all dead."

"Then he had truly been given the wisdom. That means he is right about the hunt as well. We will wait until two more snows. Then the herd will be south of the Arkansas, and we can hunt without fear."

"But wait!" Jumping Wolf shouted. He pointed to the bodies. "What of these men? The man named Hickok killed them. Do we stay here like women and do nothing? Is no one to answer for them?"

"Their blood is not on Hickok's hands, Jumping Wolf. Their blood is on your hands," Spotted Tail said. "You took them north of the Arkansas, and you left them there. If anyone is to answer for them, it should be you."

"Then I shall answer for them," Jumping Wolf said. "I will answer for them by taking the scalps of many white men. I am leaving. Who will go with me? Who will avenge our brothers?" he challenged.

Several of the young men, still in hunting paint, looked at each other.

"Do not come if you are a coward. I want no cowards," Jumping Wolf said. "Do not come if you are a weak heart. I want no weak hearts. Do not come if you are a woman! I want no women. Come only if you would be a warrior!"

Without looking back, Jumping Wolf started riding out of the village. For a moment it looked as if he would ride alone, but first one young man, then another, and another still, jumped on their horse until at least a score of young men were riding after him. Not until he reached the outer circle of the village did Jumping Wolf turn. When he saw that many more had responded to his call than he expected, he let out a tremendous war whoop. The others yelled as well, and continuing their yells, they joined together and galloped as a rather substantial band across the meadow, the hooves of their horses churning up the snow as if it were another blizzard.

"Spotted Tail, what will become of this?" someone asked.

Spotted Tail watched the young men ride away, and though he would not give in to it, or admit it to any of his people, a part of his soul yearned to ride with them.

"We cannot worry about this," Spotted Tail said. "Now we must prepare for the hunt."

Seventeen

Old-timers agreed that the fall and winter season of 1873 was the best buffalo hunting anyone had experienced since before the war. The boom of the big Sharps fifty-caliber rifles, the crack of the Henry and Winchester repeaters, even the pop of pistols from those hunters brave enough to ride right up beside the animals and shoot them with handguns, all took a large harvest from the great herd.

And as Spotted Tail had predicted, after two more snow-falls the herd did move south of the Arkansas River. Thus, for the first time in several years the cooking pots were filled with buffalo meat and the lodges with warm robes.

Always before when the buffalo went south of the Arkansas, there would be a few white hunters who would defy the restrictions and venture into Indian territory. There they would poach from what, by treaty, had become the Indians' herd. But this hunting season been so successful that not one white hunter ventured into Indian territory. For once there were enough buffalo to satisfy everyone.

The white hunters busied themselves with skinning and baling hides and cutting meat, which they sold to the Santa Fe and Kansas Pacific Railroads. These two railroads were pushing steel highways farther and farther across Kansas. In so doing, they were also bringing new settlements into being.

Once such settlement began when a man named Charley Meyers established a little trading post just west of the military reservation of Fort Dodge. Railroad construction workers were the first to pitch their tents on the grounds near the trading post, then a few buffalo hunters made camp there, and they started calling the place Buffalo City.

A liquor dealer named Hoover saw the potential for profit, so he set up a tent, built a bar, and opened a saloon. Shortly thereafter two whiskey wagons came into town, and the wood from the wagons was used to construct a second saloon. Then Charley Rath brought in a general store, and Bob Wright started a freighting outfit. The buffalo hunters built several pole-and-sod corrals, which were soon piled full of hides waiting to be shipped out on the railroad. Evidence of the successful buffalo hunting season just past could be seen in the great white ricks of buffalo bones. These bones stretched for a mile along either side of the tracks coming into and leaving town.

The Mooar brothers came in to open a buffalo-hide processing and tannery operation, and they were followed by a meat packer, then a gunsmith shop, until finally at least a dozen traders were doing business. Cattle and hide buyers, land speculators, and traveling salesmen started arriving by train from the East, and a two-story hotel and a back-east-type restaurant had to be built to accommodate them.

With the influx of merchants came merchants' families, and the tents of the first settlers were quickly replaced by dugouts and shacks. The dugouts and shacks were then replaced by wood-frame houses as lumber and building materials became one of the principal products brought into town by the daily trains.

A post office was built, and that changed everything. Now the settlement was no longer just a camp, it was a real town, recognized as such by the state of Kansas and the United States government. But Kansas already had a Buffalo City, and a town called Buffalo, so the government, without petitioning the citizens of the new town, renamed it. It was no longer Buffalo City, it was now Dodge City. And Dodge

City, the newest town in Kansas, became the center of all buffalo trade, shipping out more than two hundred thousand hides in its first fall and winter of operation.

While many new settlers were coming into Dodge City, Wild Bill Hickok was making up his mind to leave. Despite the fact that the reservation Indians under Spotted Tail were content with their lot because of the successful hunting season, there had been an increase in the number of Indian depredations against the whites in southwest Kansas. The motivation for the Indian raids was a mystery to the army, but it was no mystery to the buffalo hunters. To a man, they believed the Indian problems were the result of Hickok's gunning down the three braves who had come, peaceably, into the hunting camp last winter. They didn't share that information with the army, or with any other authority, but they were not shy in letting Hickok know that they blamed him.

Hickok tried to claim that he had killed the Indians in self-defense.

"They pulled their guns," he said. "I thought they were going to start shooting. It wasn't my own life I was worrying about. I was concerned for all of you."

Hickok's explanation fell on deaf ears, because he was trying to convince people not to believe what they had seen with their own eyes. Hickok was miserable with his sudden and unexpected ignominy. He was a man who needed popularity, who reveled in being a bigger-than-life hero, and when he saw that he could no longer enjoy that kind of support in Dodge City, he made plans to leave.

He announced several times that he was considering leaving Dodge City.

"I thought maybe I'd take a look around in Cheyenne, or maybe Deadwood," he said. "There doesn't seem to be any reason for me to stay here."

He thought that someone would try to talk him into staying. But when even his friend Bat Masterson didn't try to stop him, he knew that his reign in Kansas was over. He left town early one morning, riding out without so much as a glance back.

Few lamented his departure, and the recently established newspaper editorialized that it was a good thing he had left:

> When a man is as fast with a sidearm as is Mr. Hickok, and as willing to use this engine of death as is Mr. Hickok, then his continued presence becomes an impediment to tranquillity and the peaceful pursuit of commerce.
>
> While Mr. James Butler Hickok will no doubt leave friends behind, this editor and the people of our vibrant community should welcome the departure of such a notorious gunman.

With hunting season over, Hank faced a long period of unemployment. Most of the buffalo hunters used this time to spend their money in high living, but Hank had other things in mind. Few who knew him realized it, but Hank had already put away a rather sizable sum in a savings account at a bank in Topeka.

He had spent a lot of time alone over the last several years, and during that time he'd occupied his mind with a growing dream. He was now very close to being able to achieve that dream. After one more hunting season he was going to quit the business and locate a good piece of land. Then he planned to buy a seed bull and a few heifers and start his own cattle ranch.

In the meantime he needed some form of gainful employment, and for that he didn't have to look far. In fact, he didn't have to look at all, because the job came to him. The newly convened town council of Dodge City asked him to be their very first duly constituted town marshal.

The little town was less than a year old when Hank accepted the job, but Dodge City had already achieved a dubious national distinction for wildness and violence. Men were being killed in the saloons and dance halls, in the street, and on the prairie. Twenty-five were killed in the first year alone, shot or knifed in drunken brawling, in anger, or in robbery. Sometimes innocent bystanders died as well, hit by stray bullets.

Early one morning, not long after Hank was appointed marshal, two sets of brothers from Missouri, George and Billy Wales, and their cousins Matt and Luke Dobbs, broke into the house of Angus Pemberton, one of Dodge City's most successful businessmen. The four men, who during the war had ridden for Bloody Bill Anderson, killed Pemberton and his sixteen-year-old son, then they raped and killed Pemberton's wife and fifteen-year-old daughter, each man taking turns with each one of them. After that they helped themselves to the breakfast Mrs. Pemberton had prepared, then they stole the money that Pemberton kept in his house and rode off into the prairie without so much as a challenge.

Hank was just finishing his own breakfast, eating off the desk at a jailhouse that was so new, it still smelled of green wood, when one of Pemberton's neighbors brought him the news. He had seen the Wales and Dobbs boys leaving Pemberton's house, and because he knew them to be men of the most unsavory reputation, he was concerned enough to check it out. When he didn't get an answer to his hails, he went into the Pemberton house. Shocked by what he found inside, he informed his other neighbors, then ran down to the marshal's office.

Hank and several members of the town council hurried down to the Pemberton house. By the time they arrived, news of what had happened had spread to the rest of the town, and scores of angry citizens were milling about, inside and outside the house. All were demanding swift and extreme justice.

It was bad enough to see Pemberton and his young son lying dead on the kitchen floor. But when they went into the bedroom and saw the naked bodies of Marsha Pemberton and her young daughter, Linda, it was enough to make even those with the strongest stomach ill. The throats of mother and daughter had been cut, and the bed on which they were lying was red with their commingled blood.

Several men came up to Hank and volunteered to be a part of the posse, but Hank turned them all down, saying he would rather trail them himself.

"Are you nuts? Those men rode for Bloody Bill Anderson during the war. They don't give one whit for a life. Why, they can kill a person as easily as stepping on a cockroach."

"As far as I'm concerned, they *are* cockroaches," Hank said. "I'll find them quicker if I go alone, and the way I see it, they are cowards, so one to four should be just about the right odds."

With the town wishing him good luck and godspeed, Hank started after George and Billy Wales and Matt and Luke Dobbs.

George Wales lay on top of a flat rock, looking back along the trail over which they had just come. He saw the single rider following them.

"Is he still there?" Billy called up to him.

"Yeah," George growled. "I believe that son of a bitch could track a fish through water."

"What'd you say his name was?"

"Tyreen. Hank Tyreen. He's the new marshal back in Dodge."

"Who would've ever thought Dodge would get a marshal?" Matt asked.

"Where'd this fella come from? Has he marshaled before?" Luke asked.

"I don't know," George said. "Only thing I know about him is, when he's not marshaling he's buffin'."

"Well, what are we goin' to do about him? We can't shake him off," Billy said.

"I've got an idea," Matt Dobbs said. "Let's go up into that draw." He pointed.

"That's a dead-end canyon," Luke said. "Don't you 'member that, Matt? Me'n you was up here last year."

"I know it's a dead-end canyon," Matt said. "But it's

got two or three good places in there where we can hide. All we got to do is let him follow us in there, then ambush him.''

''What if he don't come in? What if he just stays back at the mouth of the canyon and waits us out?'' George asked.

''Hell, there's only one of him. There's four of us,'' Matt insisted. ''If he don't come in, we'll just come out and get him. How much trouble can a buffalo hunter give us?''

''Matt's right,'' George said. ''Let's just kill the son of a bitch and get it over with.''

''Come on, I know the perfect spot to bushwhack him,'' Matt said.

Hank had been to the canyon before, and he knew it was a dead end. He stopped at the mouth of the canyon and took a drink from his canteen while he studied it. He was pretty sure that the Wales and Dobbs boys knew it was a dead end as well, so why would they want to go into it?

Then he answered his own question: They figured they would be able to draw him in, then set up an ambush for him.

Hank hooked his canteen back onto the pommel and pulled his rifle from the saddle holster. This wasn't the Sharps 50 he used for hunting; this was a Winchester .44-40 repeating rifle. He jacked a round into the chamber, then walked into the canyon, leading his horse.

The horse's hooves fell sharply on the stone floor and echoed loudly back from the canyon walls. The canyon made a forty-five-degree turn to the left just in front of him, so he stopped. Right before he got to the turn he slapped his horse on the rump and sent it on through.

As he thought it might, the canyon exploded with the sound of gunfire when the Wales and Dobbs boys opened up on what they thought would be their pursuer. Instead of killing him, however, their bullets whizzed harmlessly over the empty saddle of the riderless horse. The missiles raised sparks as they hit the rocky ground, then careened off into empty space, echoing and re-echoing in a cacophony of whines and shrieks.

From his position just around the corner from the turn, Hank located two of his ambushers. They were about a third of the way up the south wall of the canyon, squeezed in between the wall itself and a rock outcropping that provided them with a natural cover. Or so they thought.

The firing stopped, and after a few seconds of dying echoes, the canyon grew quiet.

"Where the hell is he?" one of the ambushers yelled, and Hank could hear the last two words repeated in echo down through the canyon.

Hank studied the rock face of the wall just behind the spot where he had located two of them, then he began firing. His rifle boomed loudly, the thunder of the detonating cartridges picking up resonance through the canyon and doubling, then redoubling, in intensity. Hank wasn't even trying to aim at the two men but was instead taking advantage of the position in which they had placed themselves. He fired several rounds, knowing that the bullets were splattering against the rock wall behind the two men, fragmenting into deadly shrapnel. He emptied his rifle. Then, as the echoes thundered back through the canyon, he began to reload.

"Matt!" called a strained voice. "Matt!"

"What is it?" another voice answered. This voice was from the other side of the narrow draw, halfway up on the opposite wall.

"Matt, we're both killed."

"What?"

There was no answer.

"George?" And again, the echo: *"... George?... George?"*

Silence.

"Billy?... Billy?... Billy?"

More silence.

"George, Billy, are you all right?... *all right?... all right?"*

There was still no answer.

Hank changed position, then searched the north canyon wall. There was silence for a long time, then, as he knew they would, his quarry began to get anxious. He saw first one and then the other pop up to have a look around.

"Matt, Luke? . . . *Matt, Luke? . . . Matt, Luke? . . . Matt, Luke?*"

Hank called out to the two outlaws, the canyon echo repeating his call.

"What do you want? . . . *want? . . . want? . . . want?*"

"I want you to throw your guns down and give yourselves up," Hank said.

"Why should we do that?"

For his answer, Hank raised his rifle and shot at the wall just behind Matt and Luke, creating the same effect he had with George and Billy. The only difference was that he shot only one round, and he placed it in a way that would give a demonstration of what he could do . . . not in a way that would kill.

"Son of a bitch!" one of the two men shouted.

"I can take you out of there just the way I did George and Billy," Hank said. "Or I can let you wait up there until you run out of water. You didn't take your canteens with you, did you?"

Hank was running a bluff. He couldn't see well enough to determine whether they had their canteens or not. He would bet, however, that if they thought they would be able to ambush and kill him quickly, then they didn't think to take the canteens with them. It was actually a double bluff, because even as he was threatening them, he recalled that just before he sent his own horse through, he had hooked his canteen onto the saddle pommel.

There was no response from the two men, so Hank waited for a few minutes, then fired a second time. The boom sounded like a cannon blast, and he heard the scream of the bullet, followed once more by a curse.

"By now you've probably figured out that I can make one bullet do the work of about ten," Hank said. "If I shoot again, I'm going to put them where they can do the most damage . . . same as I did with George and Billy. You've got five seconds to give yourselves up, or die . . . *or die . . . or die.*''

Hank raised his rifle.

"No, wait! . . . *wait!* . . . *wait!* . . . *wait!*'' The terrified word echoed through the canyon. "We're comin' down! . . . *down!* . . . *down!* . . . *down!*''

"Throw your weapons down first.''

Hank saw hands appear, then pistols and rifles started tumbling down the side of the canyon, rattling and clattering until they reached the canyon floor.

"Put your hands up, then step out where I can see you,'' Hank ordered.

The two men, moving hesitantly, edged out from behind the rocky slab where they had taken cover. They held their hands over their heads.

"Come on down here,'' Hank invited.

Stepping gingerly, the two climbed down until, a moment later, they were standing in front of Hank. Hank handcuffed each of them.

"What are you goin' to do with us?'' Luke asked.

"I'm going to take you back to Dodge City to stand trial,'' Hank said.

"How we goin' to ride like this? We can't stay in the saddle with our hands handcuffed behind us like this. We'll fall off.''

Hank smiled at them. "Well, stay on as long as you can, boys,'' he said. "And when you fall off, I'll help you on again.''

The two men were tried the next day, their trial taking place in the Red Rooster Saloon. There was no disrespect for the law implied in choosing the saloon. It was selected because it was the largest building in Dodge.

It took less than an hour to try them and less than fifteen minutes of deliberation for the jury to find them both:

"Guilty as hell, Your Honor. By God, there wasn't nary a one of us thought otherwise.''

Judge Craig, who had been summoned from Hays City

by telegraph to handle the case, took off his glasses and polished them as he studied the two prisoners before him.

"Matthew and Lucas Dobbs, you have been found guilty of the crimes of murder, rape, and robbery. Before this court passes sentence, have you anything to say?"

"Yeah," Matt snarled. "Pemberton's wife was fine." He rubbed himself.

"And the fifteen-year-old girl was better," Luke put in.

The court gasped, then several men shouted out in anger.

"Hang the bastards! Hang 'em right here!"

Judge Craig pounded his gavel again until, finally, order was restored. He glared at the two men for a long moment, then cleared his throat.

"Matthew Dobbs and Lucas Dobbs, it is the sentence of this court that you be taken from this place and put in jail just long enough to witness one more night pass from this mortal coil. At dawn's light on the morrow, you are to be taken from jail and transported to a place where you will be hanged."

"Your Honor, we can't hang 'em in the mornin'. We ain't built no gallows yet," someone said.

The judge held up his hand as if calling for silence, indicating that he had already taken that into consideration.

"This court authorizes the use of a tree, a post, a hay-loading stanchion, or any other device, fixture, apparatus, contrivance, agent, or means as may be sufficient to suspend your carcasses above the ground, bringing about the effect of breaking your neck, collapsing your windpipe, and in any and all ways squeezing the last breath of life from your worthless, vile, and miserable bodies. And not even God will have mercy on your souls, you sorry sons of bitches."

Eighteen

"Rachel, I am facing a crisis. A genuine crisis," Joel Demmings said. "Silky is leaving us to get married. Can you imagine that? She and her husband-to-be are going to open a trading post at a place called Adobe Walls. You ever heard of it?"

"No, I've never heard of it," Rachel said.

"I've never heard of it, either, but I gather that it is in some dreadful, godforsaken place down in the extreme southwest part of Kansas. Surely the only customers they could expect down there would be buffalo hunters and maybe a rancher or two."

"So she is going through with it?" Rachel asked. "Silky is actually getting married?"

"You mean you knew about it?"

"Silky and I have become great friends. She tells me everything," Rachel said.

"I just wish she had been more open with me. When she came here from Leavenworth, I thought she was going to stay from now on. I had no idea she was planning such a thing. I can't believe she would actually be insensitive enough to marry a customer. And I can't imagine a customer marrying one of my girls. The only reason I can think of is that perhaps he wants her to whore for him out in Adobe Walls."

"Have you stopped to think that they may love each other?"

Joel chuckled. "Love? Oh, my dear, disabuse yourself of the idea that someone could ever love a whore. No one ever falls in love with a prostitute. Why would anyone be willing to buy what they can rent?"

Rachel let the insult slide by her. "When is Silky leaving?"

"Tonight. Isn't that an awful thing to do to me tonight? And here I am, expecting a very special and high-spending customer. Silky was my number one girl. I was really counting on her. She is young and pretty, and she has experience."

"You are very resourceful, Joel. I'm sure you'll come up with something," Rachel said.

"Well, I'm going to have to, that's all there is to it. You're young and pretty, but you don't have much experience."

"I don't have much experience, but I haven't had any complaints," Rachel said.

Joel folded his arms across his chest, then raised one hand and extended his forefinger, pressing it into his cheek as he studied her.

"Come to think of it, you haven't, have you?" he said. "All right. As of now, you are my number one girl. I'll be sending the special customer to you tonight. Just remember, he's paying a lot of money for your services. I want you to be uncommonly good." He smiled at her. "After all, you will be getting thirty percent, so it's to your advantage, too."

"I *am* uncommonly good," Rachel said. "Though that's not anything you'll ever know, is it?" she teased.

"Don't be a smart aleck, my dear. No one likes a smart aleck."

Rachel laughed at Joel's reply. When she'd first come to work at the Golden House of Pleasure, she'd fully expected Joel to sample the merchandise. But after several weeks of anticipating an event that didn't seem to be happening, she'd asked Silky when she could expect a visit from Joel.

Silky laughed at Rachel's question.

"What is it? What's so funny?" Rachel asked.

"Honey, I thought you knew. You won't ever get a visit from Joel. You don't have the right equipment."

"The right equipment?" Rachel asked, confused by Silky's reply. "What do you mean?"

"I mean down there," Silky replied, pointing to the junction of Rachel's legs.

Rachel was confused for a moment longer, then her eyes grew wide in shock. "You mean he . . ."

"I mean he would rather hear a fat boy fart than listen to a pretty girl sing," Silky said. "I thought you knew that."

"No, I had no idea," Rachel said. She had no idea because she had never encountered a homosexual before. In fact, Rachel had had no sexual experience of any kind until fairly recently.

After the great Chicago fire, she accepted General Sheridan's gracious offer of money and a train ticket. Without trying to locate her aunt and uncle, she left the burned-out city to begin a new life. She got off the train in Lawrence, Kansas.

If she had reasoned that leaving Chicago would be the beginning of a bright new future, she quickly discovered the error of her thought. It proved to be much more difficult than she had anticipated to find employment in Lawrence. She applied for a job teaching school, but no teaching positions were available. She asked the local seamstress if she could work for her, but the seamstress declared there to be barely enough business to support herself, and she had no intention of subsidizing someone who might someday start her own dress shop in competition.

After several unsuccessful days of hunting for work, and when the last of the money General Sheridan had given her was just about gone, she managed to get work as a hotel maid. It was not what she wanted for herself, but at least it was employment. The work was brutal, the hours were long, and the pay was minuscule.

Shortly after she began working at the hotel, the desk clerk, a man in his mid-thirties, started showing a lot of interest in her. Bruce Kindig wasn't exactly a lady-killer, but because Rachel was lonely and desperately in need of something, or someone, she was particularly vulnerable to his attentions.

Bruce took her virginity one evening in one of the un-rented hotel rooms, and Rachel was convinced that what they had done was a mutual expression of love. She was sure that he would soon propose to her. She even began designing the wedding dress she would make herself.

After several evening couplings in unrented hotel rooms, Bruce asked her to meet him in the middle of the afternoon. Since they normally met only in the evenings, this was a change in their routine, and Rachel believed she knew why. She was certain that he was going to ask her to marry him.

Rachel arrived at the appointed time, then knocked lightly. The door opened from inside. Bruce had beaten her there, and Rachel smiled at his anxiousness. She decided he had probably been rehearsing what he was going to say to her.

Bruce held up a bottle of champagne, and Rachel was almost giddy with happiness. He poured her a glass, and they toasted each other. She drank all of hers, not noticing that he drank none of his.

Almost immediately after consuming the champagne, Rachel went numb. She was still conscious, but she was unable to speak or move. Nothing like this had ever happened to her before, and she was frightened.

She sat on the bed, then fell back. She saw Bruce wave his hand in front of her eyes to see if she was still awake. She knew he must be terribly worried about her, and she wanted to tell him that she was conscious—and perfectly aware of what was going on—but she was unable to move or speak.

She thought he would go get a doctor for her, but to her complete shock, he began taking off her clothes. At first she thought he might be doing it to provide some sort of medical attention to her, but then he began making love to her.

It wasn't until that moment that she realized she was in the state she was in because of the drink he had given her. So now she knew what happened to her, she just didn't know why. After all, they had been making love for several weeks now. If he wanted her, all he had to do was ask. He didn't have to put something in her drink.

Bruce began to make love to her, but it wasn't like anything he had ever done before. He was rough with her, and he said nothing to her. Then, when he was finished, he looked down at her without a flicker of emotion of any kind. The change in his demeanor frightened her almost as much as her current physical state.

Bruce put his own clothes back on, and she wanted to ask him to help her get dressed as well. Try as she might, though, she was still unable to speak.

As soon as Bruce was dressed, he opened the door and let three strange men come in. Rachel was shocked by his action. What was he thinking? Couldn't he see that she was still naked?

"Did it work all right?" one of the men asked.

"Yeah, she's still conscious, but she doesn't know a thing," Bruce answered. He pointed over to the bed where Rachel lay, naked, with her legs still splayed. "What did I tell you?" he asked the men. "Is she not the most beautiful woman you have ever seen?"

"Oh, my, yes. She is very beautiful," one of the men said. He gave Bruce some money. "I don't know about the other two, Mr. Kindig, but I accept your offer."

The other two paid as well, then Bruce and two of the men left the room. The one who stayed behind undressed, then with absolutely no preliminaries began using Rachel.

Rachel was fully aware of what he was doing but was completely unable to resist. When the first man finished, another came in, then another. Rachel had to endure them all, including a second visit from Bruce, the man she had thought she loved.

When the men were satiated and gone, and mobility had

at last returned to Rachel, she dressed, left the hotel, and took the first train out of Lawrence. Sometime later she got off the train in Wichita, and there she asked the first person she met where she could find the local whorehouse. Surprised at the boldness of her question, the man directed her to the Golden House of Pleasure. Unlike her previous experience of seeking work only to be rejected, Rachel's offer to be a whore was immediately accepted by Joel Demmings.

That had been three months ago, and already Rachel was being promoted to the position of number one girl. That was genuine progress, she told herself. She had, indeed, found her calling.

On the evening of the day Rachel was promoted to the position of number one, she was in the kitchen having a cup of tea. Joel came in to speak to her. "That special customer I told you about this morning is here," he said.

Rachel put down the cup and stood up. She made a minor adjustment to the scoop neck of her dress, pulling it in such a way as to afford a more generous view of the creamy tops of her breasts.

"Where is he?" she asked. "In the parlor?"

"No, he has already gone into the suite."

"The suite? Ooh la la," Rachel teased. "He must be a big spender."

"Yes, one of our best. I told you, he is a very special, very well-paying customer, so be good to him," Joel said.

"Don't worry about that, honey. I'll be very good to him."

"Wait," Joel said as Rachel started to leave the kitchen. "You'll need to stop by your room and change dresses first."

"Change dresses? Joel, what are you talking about? This is the most provocative dress I have. What else would you have me wear?"

"Your apparel is laid out on your bed," Joel said. "Perhaps I had better come with you. Your customer has rather strange tastes. I will need to explain them to you."

"Strange tastes? What does that mean? Joel, you won't let him get rough with me? You won't let him hurt me, will you?"

"Heavens, child, don't worry about that," Joel said, putting his hand reassuringly on her shoulder. "I promise you . . . you won't be harmed in any way."

Joel followed Rachel into her room, and she began immediately to take off her dress. She was soon totally naked in front of him, but she had absolutely no qualms about that. He had seen her nude many times before. In fact, he had seen all the girls this way, because they frequently paraded naked through the upstairs halls. Having Joel here seemed little different from being naked in front of one of the other girls. He never showed more than a clinical interest in the nude forms of his girls.

"The dress he wants you to wear is in that box," Joel said.

With a shrug, Rachel padded naked over to the bed and opened the box. When she pulled out the dress, she gasped. She had seen it before . . . or at least, she had seen many just like it. The dress was high-necked and full-sleeved. It had very narrow blue and white pinstripes, with a plain, square fichu to be worn over the top. It was, in fact, the prescribed apparel for female teachers in half the school districts in the country.

"This can't be right," she said, turning toward Joel and holding out the dress for him to see. "This isn't at all attractive."

"Nevertheless, it is what your customer wants you to wear," Joel said. "He also wants you to put your hair up in a bun, and you are to have no lip rouge or face paint of any kind."

"Hmm, he sounds very strange," Rachel said as she began putting on the dress.

"Wait until you go in there," Joel said. "It will get stranger."

*   *   *

A few minutes later, Rachel, now looking every bit the schoolteacher she once was, knocked lightly on the door.

"Come in," a voice called from within.

Rachel stepped into the room. It was nearly dark, the lantern flame having been turned way down.

"I'm over here," a voice said.

Because of the shadows she was unable to make out his features, so she walked over to the lantern and turned it up. As the room brightened, she could see him more clearly. He was a small man, about an inch shorter then she was. He had very thin light brown hair, which he combed across the top of his head in an attempt to conceal his baldness. He also had watery blue eyes that were greatly enlarged by the glasses he was wearing.

She gasped, then smiled, but said nothing.

"You are my teacher, and you have kept me after school," the man said. He took off his glasses, folded them very carefully, and laid them on the bedside table. Then he picked up a paddle and handed it to her. "And you should have kept me after school, because I have been a very bad boy."

The man undid his belt and dropped his pants. Then he leaned over the bed so that his bare butt shone in the light of the lantern.

"I want you to tell me that," he said. "I want you to tell me I have been a very bad boy, then I want you to paddle me. Do you understand what I want of you?"

Now Rachel's smile was so broad, she could barely hold back the laughter, but the man who had been the president of the Chicago School Board, the man who had once fired her for being a poor moral influence, couldn't see that she was trying to hold back the laughter, because his head was buried in a pillow.

"Oh yes, you have been a very bad boy," Rachel said, bringing the paddle back to strike a blow that would release four years of suppressed anger at this man. "I understand perfectly . . . Mr. Tanner."

"What? My God, do you know me?" a startled voice asked.

At that moment Rachel delivered a swat that could be heard in every room of the top floor of the Golden House of Pleasure.

Three days later Joel called a meeting of his girls. Twelve of them, in various stages of dress, were sitting around in the parlor to hear what he had to say. The front doors were not only locked, a "Closed" sign was posted. Some of the older girls said that this was the first time "the House," as they referred to it, had ever been officially closed.

"I wonder what this is about?" one of them asked.

"Maybe we're going to host a private party for the entire Chicago School Board," another suggested, and all laughed, because by now everyone knew of Rachel's recent customer and her past association with him.

All speculation ended when Joel came into the parlor a few minutes later. A younger, rather effeminate-looking man dressed in lavender and lace was with him. He was, Rachel knew, Joel's boyfriend.

"Ladies," Joel said, "I know you have all been wondering what this is about."

All conversation stopped as the girls paid close attention to the announcement Joel was about to make.

"I have recently learned of a great economic opportunity," he said. "There is a new town west of here called Dodge City. Dodge City is growing faster than toadstools after a rain. It is near Fort Dodge, so there are hundreds of soldiers there; it is also the rail head for cattle drives up from Texas, so there are hundreds of cowboys there; and it is the place where all the buffalo hunters congregate, so there are many of them there as well. Do you get the picture, ladies? It is filled with men."

"I don't know why that should have you excited, Joel. I doubt that any of them are your kind," one of the girls said, and the others laughed.

"You would be surprised where-all I can find my kind

of men,'' Joel answered without embarrassment. ''But that's not what I'm talking about. What I'm talking about is the opportunity this provides for a business like ours. We can charge two, three, maybe four times more money there than we can here. Two years there, and we will all be rich.''

''What are you saying? That you want to move the House there?'' someone asked.

''No. I see no reason to close the House,'' Joel replied. ''We are an old, established, and—dare I say it?—respected business here, in Wichita. What I am proposing is to keep this establishment in operation here, while at the same time opening a new place in Dodge City. A saloon.''

''A saloon? Not a whorehouse?'' one of the girls asked.

''We'll have rooms upstairs, of course,'' Joel said. ''That way, you'll double your opportunity to make money. You will get a percentage of the drinks we serve downstairs, as well as your share of any business you might conduct upstairs.''

''Not for me,'' one of the girls said. ''I've hustled drinks before. You get pinched, patted, squeezed, and puked on by drunks. I'm satisfied with where I am.''

''Well, that's fine,'' Joel replied. ''Some of you—most of you, in fact—will have to stay here to keep the House going. But I shall ask a few of the more adventurous of you to move farther west.''

''I'll go,'' Rachel said.

Joel looked at her in surprise, then stroked his cheek. ''Rachel, you are my number one attraction here,'' he said. ''I expected you would want to stay. In fact, I hoped that you would.''

''I'd much rather move on,'' Rachel said.

''If you're going to make the new place successful, you are going to need someone as pretty as Rachel,'' one of the other girls said. There was absolutely no false vanity among any of the girls. They all knew that the work they were doing was taking its toll on their looks, and they knew that even someone as pretty as Rachel would not keep her beauty long. There was no jealousy. On the contrary, having a very pretty girl among their lot helped all of them.

"All right," Joel said. "Rachel, you can go."

A few days later Joel and his party made a fine show as they came up Front Street, the dusty road that was the main avenue of Dodge City. They arrived in ten wagons, and because Joel believed in advertising, the canvas sides of the wagons were rolled up to show what he was bringing into town.

There were barrels of beer and cases of bottled whiskey and wine. And there were the girls, five of them, including Rachel.

The girls were dressed in their most provocative outfits, and they rode in an open carriage, showing bosom and calves and smiling sweetly at the crowd of dirty, bearded, gun-packing men who ran alongside. The girls shouted at the men, joked with them, and teased them by pulling their skirts up to show even more of their legs. One of the girls even pulled the top of her dress down far enough to let a nipple peek out and by that action started a near riot as the men rushed toward the carriage. For a moment Rachel was frightened that they might overturn it.

Dodge City was still growing, and there were half a dozen buildings in various stages of construction. One building had been framed up but not finished, and when Rachel looked toward it she gasped. She sat down quickly, shocked by the two objects she saw hanging in the half-finished building.

Two men, with their necks stretched grotesquely, and their faces reflecting the horror of their last moments, were swinging gently from ropes which were tied to the overhead beams. A large, hand-lettered sign was propped up beneath them.

THESE TWO MURDERIN' RAPIN' BASTARDS
MATT AND LUKE DOBBS
ARE THE FIRST EVER HUNG LEGALLY
IN DODGE CITY

"Oh, my," Rachel said.

One of the men who was walking alongside the wagon noticed what Rachel was looking at, and he chuckled.

"Yeah, we hung 'em this mornin'," he said. "We're a real town now."

At the same time Rachel and the others were arriving in Dodge City, Hank was at the Railroad Cafe in Hays City, having dinner with Joe Murchison. Joe, a captain now, was recently returned from Europe, where he had been an observer of the Franco-Prussian War. He had returned to duty with the 7th Cavalry, but the 7th was relocating to Fort Abraham Lincoln in the Dakota Territory. Joe was detailed to remain behind until the last element had pulled out, then he would join them.

Hank and Joe had not seen each other since their near confrontation in the rear room of the Sutler's Store at Fort Hays over four years ago. For most of that time Joe had been in France, then, more recently, he'd been in Washington, D.C., so it wasn't as if the opportunity had been there. But recently Joe had written a letter to Hank, informing him that he was leaving for Dakota Territory. He asked Hank if he would come to Hays City to see him before he left.

Hank wondered what it was about. He was sure that enough time had passed since their last meeting to smooth over any difficulty that might have sprung up. And as it turned out, the meeting was very amicable. Hank found himself wishing that he had taken the initiative to reestablish their friendship as soon as Joe had returned to Kansas six months ago.

Joe told Hank about a young Frenchwoman, a ballerina, with whom he had fallen in love. Her name was Monique Mouchette, and she had been killed when her building was destroyed by the German shelling of Paris.

"There was no military justification for the Prussians' attack upon civilians, other than to create panic," Joe said.

"But how could they get their guns close enough to shell

the city?" Hank asked. "Couldn't the French cavalry dash out and spike them?"

Joe shook his head. "Hank, the world has never seen guns such as these. They were able to throw two-hundred-pound explosive shells from the Châtillon heights all the way to the Île-Saint-Louis. That is a distance of over eight miles!"

Hank shook his head. "I'm glad we didn't have guns like that during the War Between the States."

"And I'm glad I graduated from West Point too late to fight in that war," Joe said. "I think I have a little idea now of what you fellas went through. On both sides. Besides, I would have fought for the Union, and you did fight for the South. That means we might have stared at each other over the ends of our guns. I'm glad that never happened."

Hank chuckled. "Oh, but it did happen," he said.

Joe looked confused. "What happened?"

"We did stare at each other over the ends of our guns."

Joe shook his head. "If you are talking about my foolish reaction to that business with Alice Patterson, I beg you to forget that."

"No, that was just a discussion, and I did forget that, a long time ago," Hank said. "I'm talking about the time we ac'.ily did stare over the ends of our guns at each other. In .act, you went so far as to pull the trigger, and if your pistol had not misfired, you might have shot me."

Joe studied Hank in total confusion for a long moment, then suddenly realized what he was talking about.

"My God," he gasped. He pointed at Hank. "On the road in Arkansas. You were the one who robbed the money shipment."

Hank nodded.

"I can't believe this. That was you?"

Hank chuckled. "Sorry about sending you off in your longjohns," he said.

"I'll be damned," Joe said. "You know, I could have you arrested for that."

"I know," Hank said. "But you won't."

"What makes you think I won't?"

"I just know that you won't."

Joe drummed his fingers on the table for a moment, then shook his head and chuckled. "You're right," he said. "I won't. But don't think you'll ever get away with anything like that again," he added. "At least around me."

"Don't worry. I'll never try anything like that again," Hank said. "Especially around you."

In the distance they heard a train whistle.

"That'll be my train," Joe said. The two men stood up. Joe started to pay for his meal, but Hank stopped him.

"Let me get it," he said. "In a way, I owe you."

"I'll say you do."

Hank paid for their dinner, then they walked out onto the platform. The train was in view now, smoke billowing from the stack, steam gushing from the drive cylinders, the bell clanging. It slowed for its approach into the station, and the engineer could be seen leaning out of the cab, looking ahead down the track as he brought it in. It finally squeaked to a stop, and the conductor stepped out onto the platform. "Well, I guess I'd better get on board." Joe reached for Hank's hand, and Hank took it in a firm grasp.

"Listen, you be careful up there in the Dakota Territory," Hank said. "Custer is something of a glory hunter, and glory hunters always find trouble."

"I'll be careful. Besides, I'll have the entire regiment with me. You're the one I'm worried about. They say that Jumping Wolf has over a hundred warriors in his band now. He's not paying any attention to treaty restrictions, he's going anywhere, anytime he wants to. When you go back out after the buffalo . . . stay alert."

"Don't worry about me," Hank said. "If I see Indians a mile away, I'm pulling out."

"Good."

"Board!" the conductor called. The engineer rang the bell, then gave a short toot of the whistle. Hank watched until Joe was on board, then he walked back across the street and went into the saloon. As the town marshal, he felt it wouldn't bode well for him to spend too much time in the saloons back in Dodge City, except in his official capacity. Therefore any card playing, drinking, and womanizing he needed to take care of should be done over here in Hays City, where he was just another paying customer.

☆ ☆ ☆

Nineteen

Rachel climbed down from the seat and stood alongside the wagon. It had been three months since she'd moved with four other girls from Wichita to Dodge City. Of the five original girls, only two remained. One of the girls had died when she stole wolf poisoning from the pocket of a buffalo hunter and took it, thinking it would cure her headache. A second girl left to go into business for herself. Rachel was the third girl to leave Joel. She left the business because she was pregnant.

Right now her back was hurting, but she didn't know if it was the normal back pain of pregnancy or a new pain brought on from sitting too long on the hard plank seat.

"I'm going to check the harness. Don't you go wandering away, Mrs. Smith," Mr. Wade said as he, too, climbed down.

"I'm not going anywhere," Rachel replied.

Rachel hadn't expected to get pregnant, though she knew it was a risk of her profession. When she thought about it she realized that she was lucky to have been in the business as long as she had been without getting pregnant before now.

She had no idea who the father of the baby might be, nor did she want to know. Joel had told her that there were ways to end the pregnancy, though he admitted that there were risks involved. When she said she didn't want to do that, Joel told her she could stay on as long as she wanted to and wouldn't even have to work until after the baby was born.

Rachel didn't want to do that, either. The idea of giving birth in a whorehouse didn't appeal to her. She wrote a letter to Silky, who, with her husband, Carl Oldham, ran a saloon and trading post in Adobe Walls. Rachel asked if she could come down there and stay until the baby was born.

Silky's answer was an enthusiastic yes. She was the only woman for miles around, and she would dearly welcome the company of an old friend. Silky reminded her, however, that it was a difficult trip for a woman to make alone, especially if the woman was pregnant. She suggested that Rachel get someone to bring her.

Joel found Mr. Wade, a teamster who worked for Bob Wright's freight outfit, and paid him a handsome sum to take Rachel to Adobe Walls. Wade was a good man for the job, not only because of his experience in driving a wagon, but also because he was a sober, industrious person who had never once set foot in a saloon or whorehouse. In fact, when Joel told him that the woman he would be transporting was Mrs. Smith, the young widow of an army officer, Wade believed him because he had never met Rachel at her work.

"Got the harness all straightened out. We can go now. Back still botherin' you, is it?" Wade asked as he climbed back onto the driver's seat.

"Yes."

"I remember when my missus was carryin'," Wade said. "Her back used to bother her somethin' fierce."

"What did she do about it?"

"Well, ma'am, at nighttime, she'd have me rub it."

"Oh, I think that would feel heavenly. Maybe you could rub my back tonight."

Wade blushed, then coughed in embarrassment. "No, ma'am, I don't reckon it'd be fittin' for me to do that," he said. "See, for it to work, you got to rub right against the skin."

"That would be all right."

"No, ma'am! That wouldn't be all right a'tall!" Wade insisted.

"All right, if you say so," Rachel said. She put her hands on the top of the wheel and, using the spokes of the wheel, climbed back onto the seat. "I guess we should get on, then."

Wade was rubbing his left arm. "Yes'm, I spec's we had," he said.

"Your arm still hurting?"

"Yes, ma'am. Been botherin' me for two or three days now. Don't know why. I ain't done nothin' to strain it."

Rachel chuckled. "With your ailing arm and my aching back, we're quite a pair to be making such a long journey, aren't we?"

"Yes'm, we truly are," Wade said. He snapped the reins and clucked at the team, and the mules started forward.

Rachel fixed her body on the seat in as comfortable a position as she could and steeled herself for the journey. According to Mr. Wade, it would be five more days before they reached Adobe Walls.

Hank Tyreen examined the buffalo chip, then, seeing that it was an old one, kicked at it in disgust. "Hell," he said out loud. "For all I know, this chip was here before Columbus discovered America."

He walked back to his horse, pulled down the canteen, and took a drink as his eyes searched the terrain from horizon to horizon. His stint as marshal of Dodge City was finished. It was early June now, and he was back in the field for his last buffalo hunt, but he was a little frustrated. It was time for the Texas herd to be moving up through Kansas on their summer migration, but so far there wasn't a buffalo to be seen.

Hank had talked to several of the other hunters and knew that they had not had any luck, either. Last week Bat Masterson had crossed the Canadian to the great tablelands, where turkey and quail were thick along the creeks and prairie chickens were in the sand hills. Bat said that the prairie was cut by hundreds of buffalo trails, some as deep as a foot, so there had been a great herd there not too long ago. But not one buffalo was there now.

Hank made a wide swing around the region, riding along the higher ridges so he could scan the country, not only for buffalo, but also for any Indian sign. He was being particularly cautious about the Indians because Jumping Wolf was getting bolder and bolder. Hank had not run across his band, but some said he now had as many as two or three hundred warriors riding with him.

Behind Hank, and lower down, Ben Spicer was driving the wagon. Hank had been signaling him around arroyos and washouts by waving his hat. Somewhat farther back, and off to his right, Elmer True was on horseback, rifle in scabbard, also looking for the elusive herd. Sometimes the three men would go for several days without seeing any movement other than their own on the wide plain.

Hank was heading gradually toward Adobe Walls. The hunters had all agreed to meet there and share any information they might have gathered that would give some indication as to when the Texas herd would be making their move. It was impossible to believe that the great herd had vanished, but there was no way to hasten whatever impulse, instinct, or intelligence that set the herd in motion twice a year. They went south in the late fall and early winter, then north again in the late spring or early summer.

Hank figured that many of the hunters were probably already at Adobe Walls, playing cards, drinking whiskey, racing their horses, and shooting at targets. Hargroves would be there with his fiddle, and there might be dancing for anyone willing to dance with a bearded, smelly buffalo hunter. There were no women there, except for Mrs. Carl Oldham.

Hank smiled as he thought of Mrs. Carl Oldham. She was the onetime prostitute Silky Sommers. Hank had met Silky first in Leavenworth, then he'd run across her again after she'd moved to Wichita. It was while she was working as a whore in Wichita that Silky met and married Carl Oldham.

Hank wasn't the only one who knew about Silky's past. Bat Masterson and a few of the other, older hunters who would be at Adobe Walls knew that about her as well. Most of the younger hide hunters, however, knew nothing of her past. Those who did know were following an unspoken pact of silence. They figured that whatever life Silky might have led before she'd come here was her business. She was Mrs. Carl Oldham now, and she would be treated with all the respect a married woman could expect.

Hank's musings were interrupted when he saw a wagon about a mile ahead. At first he thought it was his own wagon, but he was confused as to how Spicer had gotten ahead of him. Then, as he drew a little closer, he saw that it wasn't Spicer. In fact, it wasn't any hide wagon that he knew about.

Indians didn't use wagons, so that left them out. But if it wasn't a hide wagon, who did it belong to, and what were they doing way out here, all alone?

Hank urged his horse into a gallop. It took about three minutes to catch up with the wagon, and when he did catch up, he was surprised to see that it was being driven by a woman.

"Hold up!" he called. "Miss, hold up!"

The woman stopped the wagon, then looked toward him.

"Oh, thank God," she said. "Am I glad to see you."

"I know you," Hank said. "It's Miss Stewart, isn't it? Rachel Stewart?"

Rachel brushed her hair back. "Yes."

"What are you doing out here all alone, Miss Stewart?"

"I am heading for Adobe Walls," Rachel said. "At least, I hope I am."

"Alone?"

"Yes. Well, I wasn't alone when I started. Mr. Garrison Wade was bringing me."

"Wade? Works for Bob Wright?"

"Yes, that's the one."

"Where is he? Surely he wouldn't leave you out here all by yourself. He's a pretty good man."

"He had no choice, I'm afraid," Rachel said. "He died, three days ago."

"Died? What happened?"

"I don't know exactly, but I think it may have had something to do with his heart. He had been complaining about his arm and chest hurting. Then, three days ago he suddenly grabbed his chest, let out a little moan, and fell back into the wagon. He was dead by the time I could get back there to look at him."

"Where is he now?"

"I passed a ranch house shortly after that, and the rancher helped me bury him. He also promised to send word back to Dodge City."

"That's a shame," Hank said. "I believe Wade has a wife back in Dodge."

"Yes, and two children, though both children are nearly grown by now."

"You still haven't answered my question," Hank said. "I know you said you are heading for Adobe Walls, but why? What is so important that you would risk being out here all alone?"

"I have run into a social problem," Rachel answered.

Hank frowned. "Don't tell me the new marshal is running all the whores out of town? When I turned the badge over to him, I told him that none of you were causing anyone any problems."

Despite her situation, Rachel laughed. "No, nothing as drastic as all that," she said. "My social problem is my own, though it is something that happens frequently to girls in my profession. I am pregnant."

"Oh."

"I wrote to Silky and asked if I could come stay with her until the baby is born. That's where I'm headed now."

"By coincidence, Miss Stewart, that's where I am going as well," Hank said. "I hope you will allow me to escort you there."

"Allow you to? Mr. Tyreen, I'm begging you to. You are the answer to my prayers," Rachel said.

Hank tied his horse onto the back of the wagon, then climbed onto the seat beside Rachel and clicked at the mule team.

"How much longer will it be, do you think?" Rachel asked.

"Oh, we should be there by nightfall," Hank replied.

"I'll be glad to get this trip over with."

"So, Miss Stewart . . . ," Hank started.

Rachel laughed. "Oh, for heaven's sake, Hank. That is your first name, isn't it? Hank?"

"Yes."

"Can't you call me Rachel? I gave up being called Miss Stewart when I first went on the line. And since you are no longer the law, I think we could be friends, don't you?"

"I can think of nothing I would like better," Hank said. "Because of our, uh, occupations over the past three months, I haven't been able to do any more than speak to you when we passed on the street. But I've often wondered what path your life took since that cold morning when we rescued you from Black Kettle."

"That's right, you did call that a rescue, didn't you?" Rachel said. Then, almost as soon as she said the words, she wished she could call them back. "I'm sorry," she apologized quickly, putting her hand on his arm. "It *was* a rescue, and I am grateful for it."

"That's all right. As I recall, the Seventh Cavalry was a little heavy-handed that morning."

"You ask what has happened to me since that morning," Rachel said. "What you really want to know is how I became a whore."

"You don't owe me any explanations, Rachel. I figure we're all responsible for our own lives, and I doubt that anyone's past has been spotless."

"No, please, Hank, I do want to talk. I think I've been wanting to talk to someone about it for a long time now, I've just never found anyone I particularly wanted to tell the story to. But I think I would like to tell you, if you would listen. And it looks like we are going to have plenty of time."

"All right," Hank said. He looked over at her and smiled, and for some reason, Rachel felt warm all over. "I've got my listening ears on," he said.

By now the band of warriors who were following Jumping Wolf numbered over three hundred. For the last two years Jumping Wolf and his renegades had been striking at isolated farms and ranches, wagons, stagecoaches, and hunting camps. The army had been trying to find him all this time, but they had not yet come after him with any force larger than company strength.

On two occasions Jumping Wolf's warriors and the army had clashed, and both times Jumping Wolf had won. As a result of those victories, and his ability to avoid capture, Jumping Wolf's reputation was growing. He was the scourge of southwestern Kansas. What he needed was one, great victory. Then he could make the declaration to his people that the massacre at Washita and the murder of Lame Bear and the others had been avenged. He would give up the war and return to the village, where, he was sure, he would be regarded as a greater chief than Spotted Tail himself.

Jumping Wolf had spent last night on the Cimarron River at the place where it was joined by Crooked Creek. During the night he went off by himself to construct a sweat lodge. When he returned the next morning he asked Iron Hand to call the others together so he could share with them what he had learned during his meditation.

"I have sought wisdom in the sweat lodge," Jumping Wolf said when the others had gathered. "I asked for knowledge, so that I might know what to do, and that knowledge has been given me. I asked for a special power, and it has been given me." Jumping Wolf held up a bugle. "When last we fought the Long Knives, the bugle soldier was killed, and we took this bugle from the field as a symbol of our victory. I know now that if we blow this bugle before each attack, it will produce medicine that is so strong that we cannot be harmed by the white man's bullets. We will use this powerful medicine to attack Meade.''

"Meade? What is Meade?'' Iron Hand asked.

"Meade is a white man's town,'' Jumping Wolf explained. "In numbers of men, women, and children, it is the same as was Black Kettle's village. We will attack it, kill the people who live there, and burn the buildings. When this is done and the town is destroyed, the spirits of all our dead who have ever been killed by the white man will be avenged.''

As Jumping Wolf outlined his plan, the others listened. They were excited at the prospect of taking this battle into the white man's very home. It would be a great victory, and songs about them would be sung around campfires for generations to come.

"But first, we must have more guns and bullets,'' Jumping Wolf said.

"Where will we get those?'' Iron Hand asked.

"That, too, came to me in my vision,'' Jumping Wolf said. "There is a place called Adobe Walls. At Adobe Walls we will find guns, bullets, knives, blankets, food, coffee, and whiskey.''

"Do soldiers guard this place?'' Iron Hand asked.

"No. Only one man and one woman. They will not be able to stop us from taking what we want.''

The warriors were excited, not only because of the impending battle, but because victory seemed so assured. They began painting their bodies for the war party.

"Meade,'' they said to each other. "Yes, let the whites speak the name of that town as we speak of Black Kettle's village at Washita.''

Twenty

"So he had been a bad boy," Hank said, laughing, as he turned the wagon through the gate and into the walled court-yard of Adobe Walls. Spicer was just behind them, and True was riding behind Spicer.

During the last several hours of riding side by side on the wagon, Rachel had told Hank everything that happened to her, from the time she was rescued after the battle at Washita to her experience with the school board in Chicago, the great fire, and the incident that had caused her to become a prostitute. She had concluded with her encounter with Lyman Tanner and his insistence that he be spanked.

"He had been a very bad boy," Rachel said. "And I punished him. Believe me, I punished him."

Hank was laughing so hard that tears came to his eyes and he had to wipe them. "I do believe that's the funniest damn story I've ever heard," he said.

"Thank you," Rachel said.

"It is, I'm serious."

"No," Rachel said. "I mean, thank you for not being judgmental."

"Rachel, for me to be judgmental would be like the pot calling the kettle black," Hank replied. At that moment the wagons were just rolling to a stop in front of the saloon. Hank halted the team, then set the brake with his foot. Bat

Masterson and several others came over to greet them.

"Glad to see you made it, Miss Stewart," Bat said. "Silky—that is, Mrs. Oldham—has been some worried about you. She said you were coming for a visit." Bat looked up at Hank. "Didn't know you were going to be bringing her in, though."

"I didn't start out to bring her. I found her out on the prairie," Hank said.

"Alone?"

"Garrison Wade was bringing her," Hank explained. "But he died on the trail."

"Damn, that's too bad," Bat said. "Wade was a good man."

"Rachel!" a woman's voice shouted, and Hank helped Rachel down so she could meet Silky halfway. The two women hugged in greeting, then, talking excitedly, went back into the Oldham house.

"Good news," Bat said as Hank began unhitching the team. "Emanuel Dubbs found the herd. He rolled in here with over a thousand hides, dried and ready to go."

"A thousand hides?"

"Yes. And even summer hides are bringing three dollars apiece at the rail head."

"Does he have the herd located? Does he know where it is now?"

"He says he can draw a map that will take us right to it."

"Good, good. How many are here?" Hank asked.

"There are about thirty of us," Bat answered. "Oh, before we go out after the herd, though, I think you should know. Plummer found the McCoy brothers up on Chicken Creek. Both of them had been scalped and mutilated. One of them had a heavy stake driven through his heart."

"Jumping Wolf," Hank said.

"Yeah, that's what we figured. Don't know who else it could be," Bat said. "When we go out, we'd probably be smart to keep an eye open. And we might want to stay together."

"That's probably a good idea," Hank agreed. "Where are you throwing down your sleeping roll?"

"In the saloon," Bat answered. "There are about seven of us in there, eighteen or so over in the store, and the rest are sleeping outside, somewhere. Of course, Carl and Silky are over at the house. I reckon Rachel will stay there with them. What about you?"

Hank pulled the top of his shirt away, as if allowing some air to circulate. "It's so damned hot and muggy, I think I'll just stay out here. I'll throw my roll out in the wagon."

Hank and Rachel had eaten supper on the trail, but Silky had baked an apple pie for the occasion of Rachel's arrival. She invited Hank over to have a piece of pie and coffee with Rachel and her and her husband before Hank turned in for the night. Hank accepted, with thanks. It had been a long time since he'd tasted homemade apple pie.

Hank was sound asleep in the wagon when, at three o'clock in the morning, the main support beam in the roof over the saloon snapped. The cracking sound was as loud as a gunshot, and it woke the entire compound. With startled shouts, everyone came running over to the saloon to see what happened.

"A support beam snapped. The damned roof is about to cave in on us," Bat answered.

"Carl, I told you that roof was sagging," Silky said.

"I know you did, darlin', but I just never got a chance to get around to it," Carl answered defensively.

"Well, what do you say we get it braced up now?" Hank suggested. "There are enough of us here, we should be able to get it done."

"What, you mean fix it now? At three o'clock in the morning?" one of the hunters asked in grumbling protest.

"We have to now, Billy," Bat said. "If we don't, the entire roof is going to cave in. Then it's going to be a hell of a lot harder to repair."

"I guess you're right," Billy said. "All right, let's get on it."

The men worked through the rest of the morning, finishing the roof just as dawn was breaking.

"Well, now that the roof isn't about to crash in on me, maybe I can get a little sleep," Bat said. He stretched and yawned. "What about you, Hank? You want to come in here? It'll get hot outside, once the sun comes up."

"Yeah, maybe I will," Hank replied. "Let me just get my bedroll from the wagon."

When Hank walked out to the wagon, he saw Rachel standing in the back door of the Oldham house. The residence was one of only three buildings inside the partially walled compound, and it was set farther back from the front gate than either the saloon or the store. Rachel smiled almost shyly and waved at him. He smiled and waved back, then climbed up into the wagon.

Hank was just about to bend down for his bedroll when he saw a large dark mass advancing slowly out of the gray dawn. For a moment he thought it was the buffalo herd, then he realized, with a start, that it was Indians.

At almost the same moment he saw the Indians, they suddenly fanned out and gave a large, single war whoop. Then they did something Hank had never seen Indians do. They began advancing in line abreast formation—a full-fledged cavalry charge. Their horses thundered across hard, dry earth, and he could hear the thin, high yells of the warriors.

"Indians!" Hank shouted at the top of his voice. He would have fired his gun into the air, but he was afraid that the time might come when he would regret wasting a bullet in such a way.

Straight at them the Indians came, their horses leaping, gliding over obstacles, feathered war bonnets flying in the breeze, the half-naked, painted bodies of the warriors shining with the ornaments of silver and brass, the sun behind them just sending out its first brilliant rays. Despite the peril of the situation, the Indian advance was one of the most magnificent sights Hank had ever seen.

He fired once into the mass, though he didn't take aim at

a specific Indian. His shot, as he'd hoped it would, aroused the rest of the camp.

Hank jumped down from the wagon and ran toward the saloon. The men inside had already closed it tight, reacting to Hank's warning shot. Bullets and arrows whistled and thudded all around him.

"Bat! Bat, let me in!" Hank shouted.

Bat jerked open the door, and Hank stepped inside. At that moment Billy Ogg, one of the hunters who had also been sleeping outside, ran up to the door and fell inside, totally winded from his run. An arrow had been shot through the shoulder of his shirt, though miraculously it had found cloth only. He was not hurt.

Hank smashed out the windowpane, then looked outside. At that precise moment one of the Indians had ridden all the way up to the saloon. He was carrying a lighted torch, no more than fifty feet away. Hank shot him, his bullet striking the Indian just under his left eye, killing him instantly.

The surprise attack caught the defenders in three separate buildings. Hank looked around the saloon and saw that there were nine, counting himself. The others were either in the store or over in the Oldham house.

Hank thought about the house. There were only three people in the house. If the Indians knew that, they could easily overrun it. That would not only mean the end of Rachel, Carl, and Silky, it would also put the Indians in a strong defensive position inside the compound. Hank kept the house under observation, and every time an Indian came close to it, he shot him down. As a result, the house was not seriously threatened.

From the corner of his eye, Hank saw two men step outside in front of the store, possibly to get a better shot at the charging Indians. The two men were True and Spicer.

"True! Spicer! No!" Hank shouted. "Get back inside!"

Hank saw a puff of dust fly up, then a gush of blood spurt from Spicer's shirt. Spicer went down, and True, realizing then that they had made a tactical error, dragged him back into the store. When True slammed the door behind him it was hit immediately with half a dozen arrows. The Indian who had shot Spicer held his rifle over his head and gave a victory shout. It was the Indian's last moment on earth, because Hank hit him in the chest with the heavy cartridge of the buffalo gun. The Indian was practically hurled from the back of his horse.

The Indians greatly outnumbered the defenders, but they weren't being very smart. They were riding all the way up to the walls of the buildings, then leaning over and trying to shoot through the windows, or dismounting and running up to try to dig the chinking out from between the logs. As such, they made very easy targets, and the defenders, all of whom were buffalo hunters and excellent shots, were cutting them down like a scythe through wheat.

Finally the Indians withdrew, dragging their dead and wounded back with them. After what had been a thunderous roar of gunfire for nearly half an hour, there was absolute silence.

"How many of you fellas have ever fought Indians before?" Billy Ogg asked.

More than half the men answered in the affirmative.

"Any of you ever seen Indians do this before? Come chargin' right up to the walls like that?"

"I've never seen it," Bat said. No one else had, either.

"I hope they keep on fighting like that," Hank said.

"Yeah, many more attacks like the one we just had, and we'll cut 'em down like buffalo."

"You said only a man and woman would be here. There are many here," one of the Indians protested to Jumping Wolf.

"Where is the medicine?" Iron Hand asked. He pointed to the dead and dying. "Do you see that the medicine does not work?"

"The bugle," Jumping Wolf said. "No one played the bugle."

The Indians looked at each other, then smiled and nodded.

That was true. Only the bugle could make the medicine work . . . and no one had played it.

"I will play the bugle," Kicking Horse said, and he raised the bugle to his lips and blew. To his surprise, nothing came from the horn except a rush of air.

Kicking Horse looked at it as if it were broken. Another Indian tried to blow it, and he, too, failed.

"Maybe the horn will work only for the Long Knives," Iron Hand suggested.

"No. You must hold your lips like this," said one of the youngest of the group. This was Rabbit Chaser, and he raised the bugle to his lips and blew. A long, screeching note erupted from the horn.

"Ayiee! Now we have the medicine!" Jumping Wolf said.

The Indians gathered for a second attack. Jumping Wolf looked at Rabbit Chaser. Rabbit Chaser blew the bugle.

"What the hell was that?" Oldham asked. During the lull, Carl Oldham, Silky, and Rachel had moved from the house into the saloon.

"It's a bugle! The army's coming!" someone said.

"I spent twelve years in the army and I listened to lots of bugle calls," one of the hunters said. "I never heard anything that sounded like that."

"Here they come!" someone said.

The Indians came again, three abreast this time, galloping through the dust, shouting and whooping their war cries. Again they charged all the way up to the buildings. The Indians fired from horseback, shooting arrows and bullets at the cracks between the logs. They hurled lances toward the open windows. Two of them jumped down from their horses and tried to force the door open by hitting against it with the butts of their rifles.

Once again the buffalo hunters took very careful aim, making every shot count. Several Indian horses went down, and the riderless horses whirled and retreated, leaving their riders dead or dying on the ground behind them.

At first it seemed to the defenders that the Indians weren't accomplishing anything. But during the second lull in fighting, Hank could see that two of the hunters were lying dead out in the middle of the compound, caught by the Indians in their first rush. In addition, nearly all of the hunters' supplies were outside in the buffalo wagons. Many of the wagons were out of the line of fire of the defenders, so the Indians were able to steal the wagons. They carried away extra guns and ammunition, blankets, and food. The horses of the stockade had also been run away, or killed, and several of them now lay dead. One of the dead horses, Hank saw, was his own.

"Hey, boys, how are you all fixed for ammunition?" someone asked.

"I've got no more'n six bullets left," one of the defenders answered.

"I've only got two."

"We need to divide up what we've got."

"There's a lot over at the store," Oldham said.

"Figured there would be," Bat replied. "It's my guess that's what these heathens are really after." He laughed. "Only I don't think they were counting on us being here."

One of the others laughed as well. "I'll bet we surprised those fellas," he said.

"One of us is going to have to go over to the store and get some ammunition."

"I'll go," Hank said.

"I'll go with you," Billy Ogg offered.

"Bat, we'll need you and some of you others to start shooting as soon as we get out the door," Hank said.

"We'll do it," Bat said.

Hank looked at Ogg. "You ready?"

"Ready as I'll ever be," Ogg answered.

Hank nodded, then the door to the saloon was thrown open and the two men sprinted across the open courtyard toward the store.

The Indians, seeing the two men running across the open yard, began shooting. The Indians had been taken by sur-

prise, and the two men were halfway between the two buildings before the first shot was fired. Bullets smashed all
around them, kicking dust up at their feet and sending wood
chips and chinking material into their faces. Both reached
the store and dived inside without a scratch.

"How is it over there?" True asked. "Any killed?"

"No," Hank said. "How's Spicer?"

True shook his head sadly. "He was kilt right out."

"Damn."

"Hank, there ain't no need of the two of us goin' back,
is there?" Ogg asked. "I mean, I'll go back with you if you
think I should."

"No," Hank said. "No sense in both of us gettin' shot
at. You stay here."

"Thanks," Ogg said. "Tell the fellas over there that . . .
well, just tell 'em to shoot straight."

Hank filled two sacks with ammunition. Then, with a nod
toward True, who jerked the door open for him, he ran back,
crouching as low as he could, zigzagging across the dusty
courtyard, puffs of smoke and clods of dirt rising around
him once again. And, as before, he wasn't hit.

Throughout the rest of the day the Indians attacked several more times. But they prefaced each attack with the un-
godly screeching bugle, and that alerted the buffalo hunters
to be ready. The bugle calls served the buffalo hunters well,
because it allowed them to rest in between attacks.

"If we can just hold on until dark, I think they'll go
away," Bat said. "Indians don't like to fight in the dark."

Hank remembered the fight at Becker Island. The Indians
hadn't attacked during the night, that was true. But they
hadn't left, either. Instead they'd circled the island, burning
their fires and singing and drumming all night long.

And that was exactly what the Indians did on this night.
From every window in the building, all the way around, the
defenders could see campfires. They could also hear the
drums and singing.

"How long can we last?" Rachel asked, and Hank was

surprised to see that she had come up to stand right beside him.

"We can hold out as long as we need to," Hank answered. "We've got well water. We've got plenty of food and plenty of ammunition. And these walls are so thick that their bullets can't get in except through the windows and cracks."

"Hank, if anything happens, if it looks like we won't be able to hold them off . . . please don't let me fall into Jumping Wolf's hands."

"I don't think it will come to that," Hank said. "Anyway, what if it did? You were a captive of the Indians before and you survived."

"Before, I had Running Deer, Black Kettle, and even Stone Eagle to protect me from Jumping Wolf. This time I would have no one."

"Did Jumping Wolf . . ." Hank didn't finish the question.

"No," Rachel answered. "But only because I had my protectors. He is an incredibly evil man."

The long night hours stretched on. At about three in the morning, Hank was gently shaken awake by Rachel. He was surprised to see that she had put her blanket down beside his.

"Bat said it's your turn to stand guard," Rachel said.

Hank sat up and stretched. "Thanks for waking me. I'll see you in the morning."

"I'm going to stay awake with you, if you don't mind."

"You ought to get some sleep."

"I've been sleeping," Rachel said.

Hank smiled at her. "All right. Sure, you can stay with me. I'd enjoy the company."

Hank walked over to the window where Bat was standing. "Anything happening?"

"They finally quit their caterwauling about an hour ago," Bat answered. "If they had anything to drink, they're probably all passed-out drunk by now. But just in case, better wake us all at first light."

"Will do," Hank agreed.

He looked out across the open ground toward the ridge where the Indians were. Though the fires had mostly burned down, he could still see faint glowings here and there. There was also enough of a moon that he didn't think they could sneak up during the night, even if they wanted to.

"Here," Rachel said, handing him a cup of hot coffee.

"Thanks."

"Hank, have you ever been married?"

"No."

"Almost?"

Hank took a swallow of his coffee. "I was engaged once," he said. "But that was before the war. She married somebody else."

"I'm sorry."

"That's all right," Hank said easily. "When I came back from the war, *I* was somebody else."

"Do you ever think about getting married?"

"Sure, I've thought about it," Hank admitted. "When you spend a lot of time alone, you think a lot." He smiled. "I'll bet you didn't know that I've designed a house."

"You have a house?"

"Well, not yet, but I'm going to build one. This is my last hunt," he said. "I've got a little money put away, and I plan to start my own ranch. Of course, the house is going to have to come later. First comes the barn, then a seed bull, some heifers, and a few cow ponies. I figure ten years from now I'll be such a respectable rancher that no one would ever dare suggest that I was once a Confederate cavalryman, an outlaw, an Indian scout, a buffalo hunter, a gambler, or any of the other things I've been."

"Do you think you will ever be respectable enough that your wife could be a former whore, and no one would question it?" Rachel asked.

"What?"

"Hank, I need a home for this baby. A respectable home. And I can't provide one by myself."

Hank stared at Rachel for a long moment. "Rachel, are you . . . are you asking me to marry you?"

"I guess I am," she said. "I know this isn't the way it's supposed to be done. But then, I don't seem to do anything the way it is supposed to be done."

Hank laughed softly. "By God," he said. "By God, I'll do it."

"You're sure now, I wouldn't want to—"

"Woman?"

"What?"

"I said I'll do it. And I'll do it because I want to do it. After all we've been through, I don't know as anyone else would have either one of us."

Shortly after dawn, when everyone was awake and eating a good breakfast of bacon and griddle cakes, Hank announced that during the night he and Rachel had gotten engaged.

"Damn, that must've been one hell of a guard you two stood together," Bat teased, and the others laughed, then all hastened to offer their congratulations.

"How long of an engagement do you two intend to have?" Silky asked.

"How long? I don't know," Hank said. "Until we get out of here and can get married, I reckon."

"You don't even have to wait that long, if you don't want to," Silky said.

"What do you mean?"

"Carl is a justice of the peace," Silky explained. "He can issue you the license and marry you right here."

"You can?" Hank asked.

"I sure can," Oldham said. "Right now, if you want to."

Hank looked over at Rachel and saw a peculiar expression in her face.

"Oh, Hank, I don't know," she said hesitantly.

"What is it, Rachel? Are you afraid that I *won't* go through with it? Or are you afraid that I *will* go through with it?"

"A little of both, I guess," Rachel admitted.

Hank held out his arm. "Then it's time to fish or cut bait.

I'm asking you now, properly, in front of these witnesses, to be my wife.''

Rachel paused but a second longer, then a smile softened her face and she came to him. Arm in arm, they turned to face Justice of the Peace Carl Oldham.

"I'll be needin' a Bible," Carl said.

Hank thought of the Bible he had salvaged from his family farm back in Mississippi. It was in his bag outside in the wagon. He held up his hand. "I'll get one."

With the Indians some distance away, Hank was able to stroll almost leisurely out to the wagon. He took out not only his Bible, but his binoculars, and before he went back in, he took a long look at the Indians up on the hill.

Most of the Indians seemed to be milling around. Only one was mounted, and he was elaborately painted and festooned in a long, flowing war bonnet. Although Hank had known about Jumping Wolf for a long time, he had never actually seen him. He wondered if this Indian was Jumping Wolf.

Before he started back into the saloon, the door over at the store opened.

"Everyone make it through the night all right?" True called to him.

"We did indeed, Mr. True, we did indeed," Hank said. "Oh, by the way, before we begin our exchange with the Indians today, I wonder if you and the others might like to step into the saloon for a few minutes."

"Sure," True said. "Are we having a meeting?"

"No," Hank said. "A wedding."

Fifteen minutes later, as everyone lined up to kiss the bride, Hank wandered over to the window and, using his binoculars, once again located the Indian he had spotted earlier. Then, after putting down the binoculars, he took two of the fifty-caliber shells out of the ammunition bag and separated the bullets from the cartridge. These were manufactured shells, and when he looked down into the cartridge, he saw that it held no more than 90 grains of powder. Using the other cartridge, he started filling the first one. He poured in at least 125 grains of powder, which was 15 more grains than he normally used.

Bat Masterson came over as he was working. "You should hear Silky and Rachel making plans over there," Bat said with a chuckle. "They've already got that house you've been talking about decorated, and you haven't even built it yet. What are you doing?"

"I'm loading a shell."

"I can see that. Why? In case you noticed, those are Indians out there, not buffalo."

"Would you know Jumping Wolf by sight?" Hank asked, not responding directly to Bat's comment.

"No. Truth to tell, I don't think I would."

"Neither would I. But if that fancy-dressed son of a bitch sitting on that horse back up on that hill is Jumping Wolf, I'm going to kill him."

"You mean next time he comes down?"

"No. I mean now."

"Now?" Bat said. He laughed. "What do you mean, now? He's a thousand yards away if he's a foot."

"Light that candle, then hand it to me, will you, Bat?" Hank asked.

Shaking his head, Bat lit the candle. Hank tapped the bullet back into the cartridge, then used the dripping wax to help seal it.

"Mrs. Tyreen," Hank called.

Rachel was busily engaged in conversation with Silky and didn't hear Hank call.

"Mrs. Tyreen," Hank said again.

Rachel laughed, then put her hand to her mouth. "Why, that's me," she said. "I almost didn't recognize my own name." She walked over to see what Hank wanted. Hank handed her his binoculars.

"Take a look at that man on horseback. The one with all the feathers," Hank said. "Tell me if you recognize him."

Rachel did as Hank asked, then she gasped and jerked

down the binoculars. "It's him," she said. "Jumping Wolf."

Hank smiled. "Good."

"What do you mean, good?"

"I'm going to kill the son of a bitch," Hank said. "Maybe we can get this business over with."

By now several others had come to the window as well. Bat had told them what Hank had in mind.

"You really think you can hit him from here?" Jim Hanrahan asked.

"Yep," Hank replied easily.

"Is anybody here a betting man?" Hanrahan asked.

"Why do you ask?" Bat said.

"Because I'm betting two to one that he doesn't make the shot."

"How much can you cover?" Rachel asked.

"Well now, how much do you want to bet, Mrs. Tyreen?"

"I'll bet one thousand dollars," Rachel said.

Hank looked up in surprise. "Rachel, what are you doing?"

"Do you think you can make the shot?" Rachel asked.

"Yes."

Rachel smiled. "Well, I've got that much money with me. Let's say it's a show of the faith I have in my new husband."

Hanrahan shook his head. "I don't think I can cover that much. It's a pity, too, 'cause I don't think there's any way I can lose."

"What about your land?" Silky asked. "You have two thousand acres right next door, don't you? How about putting that up?"

"Oh, Silky, we could be neighbors," Rachel said.

Hanrahan laughed. "All right, I'll put up the two thousand acres against your one thousand dollars, if you'd like. But don't you two ladies go inviting each other over for quilting bees. Like I told you, there's no way Hank Tyreen is going to make that shot."

Hank picked up the rifle then and rested the barrel on the windowsill. He aimed, then lowered the rifle and adjusted his sights, picked it up, aimed again, then lowered it for another adjustment.

No one in the saloon said a word.

Hank aimed a third time. Then the rifle roared and bucked against his shoulder.

Bat had been looking at Jumping Wolf through Hank's binoculars.

"Missed!" Bat called.

Hanrahan chuckled. "Well, you can't—"

"Wait!" Bat shouted. "I'll be a son of a bitch! You got him!"

Iron Hand was standing next to Jumping Wolf when he heard an angry buzz, then a loud pop. Half the top of Jumping Wolf's head was blown away, and the chief tumbled backward from his horse.

"Jumping Wolf?" Iron Hand called.

The Indians were disoriented. Not only had the medicine not made them bulletproof, but it had seemed to have just the opposite effect. For surely no ordinary rifle could kill from this far away.

"What manner of men are these who can kill every time they pull the trigger?" Young Calf asked Iron Hand.

"And from so far away? Their medicine is strong," another said. "Surely, if we stay here longer, we will all be killed."

"Iron Hand, what shall we do now?" Young Calf asked.

"We will leave this place of death," Iron Hand said.

"And shall we attack Meade?"

"No," Iron Hand said. "We must go where we can find our center."

Epilogue

The sign that stretched across Belle Meade Street read "Meade, Kansas, Celebrates Our Nation's Independence Day, July 4th, 1904."

Willis Joshua Bailey, Republican governor of the state of Kansas, had been speaking for forty-five minutes. The Meade County Band, in their brand-new red-and-black uniforms, were sweating profusely under the sun. Several hundred people were sitting on folding chairs in front of the bandstand, Belle Meade Street having been closed for the ceremony.

Hank pulled his watch from his pocket, flipped open the cover, and looked at it pointedly.

"Grandma, Grandpa is looking at his watch again," Sara Sue said.

"Shh, I know, dear," Rachel replied. "He is trying to remind the governor that he has been talking too long. Let's just ignore him, shall we? That's what the governor seems to be doing."

Hank frowned, but when Rachel smiled at him, he reached over to take her hand in his. They had been married for thirty years, and damned if he didn't believe she was as pretty now as she was the first day he ever saw her.

Hank didn't like events like this. But as Rachel said, being the largest and most successful rancher in Meade County did carry certain responsibilities. People expected him to attend civic events such as this. In addition, one of Hank's sons was a state representative, another a high-ranking official with the railroad, and his daughter was married to a young rancher whose own spread was nearly as large as Hank's. That made them very close to a family dynasty in this part of Kansas.

"And now," Governor Bailey said, "as I bring my speech to a conclusion on this glorious day of celebration, it is my great privilege and high honor to recognize one of our favorite sons. You know him as a rancher and businessman. His family knows him as a husband and father. But the entire state of Kansas knows him as a man who, thirty years ago, used his unerring eye and trained trigger finger to make what is still called 'the Shot.' With that shot, later established by official survey as four thousand six hundred and fourteen feet . . . just six hundred and sixty-six feet short of a mile, Hank Tyreen broke the Indian siege of Adobe Walls. That not only freed the people who were trapped at Adobe Walls, it single-handedly turned back what we now know was a plan to burn and pillage this beautiful community whose hospitality we are enjoying today.

"Ladies and gentlemen, as governor of this beautiful state, I know how difficult it is to get our legislators to agree on anything. But what I hold in my hand"—the governor lifted a rolled scroll—"is a legislative declaration of honor, unanimously approved by both the House and the Senate of the state of Kansas. Mr. Tyreen, would you please step forward to receive your honor?"

Hank had not known about this, and when he looked over at Rachel in surprise, he realized that she had known. There were tears of pride in her eyes and a smile of triumph on her lips. She knew she would have never gotten him to come into town today if he had known about the award.

Self-consciously Hank walked up to the podium to accept the scroll from the governor as the crowd showed their approval by its warm applause. He started back down, but the crowd began to yell.

"Speech! Speech!"

"You don't want me to say anything," Hank demurred.

"Sure we do! Anything to keep another politician from getting up there," another shouted, and that remark was greeted with a great deal of laughter.

"Mr. Tyreen, it is customary for the recipient of such an award to say a few words," Governor Bailey said.

Hank nodded, then cleared his throat. He held up the scroll and looked at it.

"I accept this award with humility, and with thanks," he began. "But I accept it not for myself. I accept it for people like Fred Becker, Ed Masterson, Wild Bill Hickok, Black Kettle, Running Deer, Garrison Wade, Silky Sommers, and Ben Spicer. These people are all dead now, but don't think for one minute that they are no longer with us. They are a part of the land, the sky, and the rivers and streams and will be with us as long as those elements endure. They are our history, our corporate soul. They are, as the Indians say, a part of our circle."

When Hank stepped down from the platform, he didn't return to his seat but started instead toward his carriage.

"Dad, no," Tom called after him. "We have a reception planned. We want you to be with your friends."

Rachel put her hand on her son's shoulder. There were tears in her eyes. "Didn't you understand what your father just said, Tom? He *is* with his friends."

TERRY C. JOHNSTON

THE PLAINSMEN

THE BOLD WESTERN SERIES FROM
ST. MARTIN'S PAPERBACKS

COLLECT THE ENTIRE SERIES!

SIOUX DAWN
92732-0 _____$5.99 U.S. _____$7.99 CAN.

RED CLOUD'S REVENGE
92733-9 _____$5.99 U.S. _____$6.99 CAN.

THE STALKERS
92963-3 _____$5.99 U.S. _____$7.99 CAN.

BLACK SUN
92465-8 _____$5.99 U.S. _____$6.99 CAN.

DEVIL'S BACKBONE
92574-3 _____$5.99 U.S. _____$6.99 CAN.

SHADOW RIDERS
92597-2 _____$5.99 U.S. _____$6.99 CAN.

DYING THUNDER
92834-3 _____$5.99 U.S. _____$6.99 CAN.

BLOOD SONG
92921-8 _____$5.99 U.S. _____$7.99 CAN.

ASHES OF HEAVEN
96511-7 _____$6.50 U.S. _____$8.50 CAN.